LIVING IN A DARK HOUSE

A Novel

Renee Verite

Living in a Dark House is a work of fiction. Any resemblance to people and incidents are the workings of the author's active imagination from years of interactions with the public as a student, restaurant professional, journalist, and teacher.

ISBN: 978-0-578-20776-6

This book is dedicated to friends and family, dead and alive, who helped me to write in the light.

CHAPTER ONE

The small block building, across the alley from the dark house where I lived, was in full production making body bags for American soldiers returning home from Vietnam. That white powder remnant of the created carriers of corpses, looking akin to, but definitely not baby powder with its indescribably foul smell as it floated through the air, landed on cars and our bicycles, and attempted to cover things like the truth. This gritty white talc, coupled with the black soot from the rubber factories making tires, kept food on our neighbors' tables, so we didn't really mind or complain. We were a working class town; we understood hard work and breathing it in; we sucked it up.

Richard Nixon had announced his resignation as president of the United States on that scorching August day in 1974 when Jim Dandy arrived. Jim Dandy was a demon, and he was my father. He strategically positioned himself and stood in the middle of the painted white wooden bleachers, directly parallel to me in my pee-wee cheerleading uniform on the fifty-yard line at a football field called Parsons Field in Akron, Ohio. When I saw him, I was ready to perform a half-time cheer on dry and crunchy brown grass. He was a pendulum, swaying back and forth, ready to topple me, a small and fragile heap of dominoes.

Of course, Jim Dandy was immune to the moms who were sporting platinum blonde hairdos and modelling Daisy Duke cut-offs, when he began to move his right pointer finger from his belt to me, belt to me, over and over; this simplistic movement of his one finger continued for about thirty minutes and carried the weight of the world as he focused on the attack. Legs spread like Clint Eastwood in a cowboy movie, even with his well-advertised club foot, he stared intently at his prey, not even aware of the people who wondered, by the looks on their faces, exactly what it was that he was accomplishing.

My best friend Kathie, who stood next to me also in a red and white pleated skirt, first noticed his performance—excitedly for me. "Hey, Del," she whispered, her voice rising. "Jim Dandy is here! He must have come to watch the half-time cheer!"

After all the cheerleading at pee-wee football games that other parents sat through and endured, it would be the first time that Jim Dandy managed to make an appearance, and that was a good thing. Jim Dandy, with his shaggy beard and his club foot, this life-long obsession, would never be associated with the word "cheer."

"Yea," I replied as my heart began pounding loudly in my chest as blood began to pulsate through my ears. My shaky knees began to buckle under my heaving chest. I tried to understand the commands from the coach, but the words were in slow motion. "Kathie, after the game, will you r-r-race me back to my car? Just start running, as fast as you can; I need you to do this for me, okay?"

My mind often wandered to current events. Before Jim Dandy's arrival, I was thinking how history was being made and that the very next day our country would have a new president. His name, Gerald Rudolph Ford, was whirring through my mind and sounded strange to my ear. President Ford, the word "president" before his name would soon sound normal and would become a familiar after a while. Just that quickly, however, I had to drop that impractical thinking about a president a world away and become decisive and think, think, strategize, and come up with a plan, because here and now, just a few yards away lurched a demon ready to attack. I needed to redirect the developing scene. Jim Dandy was going to beat me no doubt. I was planning because I wanted some control over the place, so I could avoid the spectacle in front of my classmates, in the middle of a football field.

The other parents were still sipping coffee from Thermos cups in slow motion, nudging each other, and wondering about the unfamiliar man with the cowboy stance. I knew what was about to happen through repetition and conditioning, but nobody else did. If Kathie would run with me, it would appear like we were having an innocent race to our family's Chevy Caprice in the parking lot, and only those who happened to walk nearby would witness my beating, not the whole football team in the middle of the field. "When the ref blows the whistle, will you run with me to my car?" I asked Kathie.

"It's by the concession stand," I whispered sideways to Kathie. She did run beside me, a best friend for the ages. I wished we could have kept running forever, four peaceful yellow ponytails swinging back and forth. I allowed her to win, then I urged her to go back to the coach. I huddled inside the backseat of the unlocked car, waiting for the crunching of gravel under his work boots.

Inside that melting Chevrolet, I could hear other parents talking about football plays with their sons. I could smell hot dogs and popcorn as players squeezed between cars wearing their cleats, holding their sweaty shoulder pads. As time was whirling by in my head, I still remember my father's piercing blue gray eyes and that full head of silver hair on his forehead, as he opened the long car door in slow motion. He removed his belt like a gunslinger. This was one of his many perfected skills that led to utter control and, in turn, the reflected fear for our lives. "Do you know what you did?" he asked.

"No, I don't know! I'm sorry! Don't hit me here! Please!"

"Don't know, huh?

"I really don't know," I pushed the seat forward with my feet.

"Well, we'll see if we can learn ya," he twanged, slinging his weapon like a snake.

"I r-r-really don't know. T-t-tell me! I'm sorry! All these people, please!"

Parents were walking by, talking by, and gawking by, as the swishing continued mostly across my legs. I could still hear a discussion a few cars away about President Nixon's resignation, but it soon became a blur as doors were slammed, goodbyes were yelled across the thick and muggy air, and cars chugged away. Soon, hurry up, everyone please be gone. Not one person uttered a word, as people noticed, I am sure.

He continued making a masterpiece of red stripes until he got tired and bored; eventually the proclamation would come: I fed our dog Mickey a piece of bologna before I left for the game, and the rind was still on the kitchen floor—testimony to my sin. Actually, I had only given him the rind which he must have rejected, but there was no way to explain.

This was my life.

My name is Delanie Dane; my days and nights were filled with the terror of uncertainty of when, where, and why the belt would lick my arms and legs, and I would be forced to repeat some inane statement about how I had failed to live up to his standards, and why everything was a waste of money, why women were useless, why education is stupid, and why everyone and everything was wrong except him.

This time, I had to say, "I won't play Elton John records," over and over until he got tired of this little game in which he would always win.

One by one, as cars disappeared down the road, the scars multiplied, the bars went up around my heart. He had won again. I was shaking and crying in the backseat, wondering if Kathie and her dad Andy had seen the spectacle. I was wondering if my coach or Jeff Farnsworth had witnessed it; he was the quarterback who sat next to me in my fourth grade classroom.

Meanwhile, on the AM radio, Seals and Crofts were telling the "Hummingbird" not to fly away, but I wanted to fly away with them—or with anyone who would take me. Details about the "peaceful transition of power" of the presidency was described on the radio. These words, about an organized place where people lived decently and comfortably in White Houses, began to soothe me as we wheeled back to our little, safe neighborhood, where polluted and gritty air floated down, where everyone was living life centered around lawnmowers, baby strollers, bicycles, and Big Wheels.

I spent that afternoon in my bedroom, listening to more radio news about President Gerald R. Ford and avoiding music that might upset Jim Dandy, making sure to avoid Kathie, my across-the-street neighbor, my confidant, and my best friend in the whole wide world. The aftermath of these Jim Dandy scenes was the most difficult because explanations were confusing and humiliating. Do I explain or just pretend that nothing happened? If I could avoid her the rest of that day, maybe it didn't really happen, and the event would pass unspoken; we would have President Gerald Ford, and Kathie and I would just proceed to some fun adventure that we had created in our tiny corner of the world outside.

But when I was inside, I was living in a dark house.

CHAPTER TWO

Three weeks later, when the crispness turned into falling leaves, and my daily walks commenced to Thomas Edison Elementary School with Kathie, things had normalized. Kathie never said a word. That day had never occurred. I think I had imagined the whole thing. It also appeared that even if it did happen, it wasn't as bad as I remembered it. Jim Dandy had changed, and everything was going to be just fine.

My teacher that year was Mrs. Jackson, and her son Michael was fighting in Vietnam. I didn't really understand Vietnam, but I knew that some people didn't want the war. There were protests all around the country, including nearby Kent State University, and almost every song on the radio echoed those feelings. Mrs. Jefferson, a heavyset woman who wore bright red lipstick, called me to her desk and praised my coloring skills like I was Leonardo da Vinci. "Such a beautiful picture, Delanie dear," she said calmly. "You certainly look lovely today."

I loved the way that word lovely rolled off her tongue, so natural, so intelligent, so soothing. I wanted to sound like her someday. I wanted to be a nice and nurturing guide who illuminated the way out of darkness for kids. Lovely, lovely, I like that word, I thought. "M-m-my mom made my dress," I told Mrs. Jefferson, proud of Mom's ingenuity and ability to stretch a dime.

"Well, she certainly has an eye for detail," she whispered, adjusting the large pearls around her neck. "I just love the lace trim."

Certainly, certainly, I like that word too, I thought.

I jotted the *lovely* and *certainly* words in a small tablet that I kept in my desk. My plan was to build my vocabulary, so I could sound smart too. I loved language and the way that one word could change the meaning of a sentence. I loved how that word lovely demonstrated that Mrs. Jefferson was a genteel lady, who wore perfume, dined with her husband at restaurants, or shopped in a department store for a new purse. I wanted to be like her someday.

Jeff Farnsworth and I usually borrowed each other's supplies; I had the Crayola sixty-four-pack with the sharpener, and he only had a forty-eight-pack. I was proud of my sixty-four-pack, a yearly indulgence in school shopping thanks to my Grandma Delanie, my maternal grandmother. Jeff kidded me about my precise coloring and my blending of periwinkle and seafoam green into a hopeful sky, and I smirked at his monochromatic coloring which was sloppy and outside the lines.

After school, Kathie waited for me outside the fourth-grade door, being in third grade and one year younger. We walked home together every night as a ritual. We would unload the cares of our elementary school days to each other and on that particular day, I told her what Mrs. Jefferson had said about my dress. "I can't wait to tell Mom because she was proud when somebody noticed her sewing," I told Kathie.

I burst through the back door, where Mom was telling my four-year-old brother Justin that he could only ride his bike three houses up the street, while she was peeling potatoes on the kitchen countertop. "Mom, Mom! Mrs. Jefferson said that my 'dress certainly is lovely'— just like that. Lovely. Doesn't that sound so smart?"

Jim Dandy shadowed the doorway and interjected himself into our conversation. "What did she say?"

"She said, she said, that my dress—that Mom made—it's l-lovely! She said that Mom 'has an eye for detail' because of the lace trim."

"Lovely?" he repeated in a mocking way. He possessed that often unknown Appalachian hatred for Northern "Yankee" learning and education.

"Yes, she said that it's l-l-lovely."

"Where ya come off talkin' like some hoity-toity teacher? Pay these bitches to talk like they're the Queen of England?"

I didn't know how to answer the question, but he demanded a response.

"Now, Dandy, that's how kids learn new words..." Mom offered, sensing tension.

"You bettered get outta here," he yelled, that gleam in his eyes. "Not gonna take no more of that, ya hear? Don't need no God-damned lovely dresses around here!"

Mom said that I could skip dinner at the table, so she brought me a peanut butter sandwich which I ate on Kathie's back porch. I worried about Mom that night, but I stayed there with Kathie, at least physically. It was still only September, so we were allowed to stay outside to enjoy the last warm nights outside. I still remember her yellow ponytails and her hot pink shirt as she stooped a Matchbox car on the sidewalk. She was kind of humming to herself while I talked and talked about my plans and dreams. These cool evenings with Kathie on her back porch, with seafoam green and periwinkle light still painting the sky, brought peace and security to me.

Being at her house, with her dad Andy whistling and smiling out the window at us, rank among my fondest childhood memories.

CHAPTER THREE

The times were tough, according to Jim Dandy, and electrical wiring jobs were hard to come by.

Most of my classmates expressed sadness because they never saw their dads; they worked day and night in the Akron rubber factories. That wasn't the case with me. I saw Jim Dandy Dane all the time. He was always home, and I was sad that he was there. We got used to the scenario when Jim Dandy kept losing job after job as a highly-skilled, high demand electrician. We knew when things were going to be bad. We would hear Mom crying, and the screams indicated that we needed to keep away from the dark house. When the street lights came on, we reluctantly had to go home. I usually had four-year-old Justin in tow, but Jimmy, the brother who was seven, always had to be found somewhere, and I was usually the one to retrieve him. He would often be on his bike, riding far away to the next street, ignoring Mom's calls for him, and pretending to be Evel Knievel. If it were Jim Dandy's voice calling him, Jimmy was home in a flash.

Jim Dandy was unpredictable and his tantrums never made any sense. He had a brilliant mind in his areas of math, wiring, and growing things, but like a rerun TV show, I knew that when his rusty old truck came rattling down the street earlier than expected, trouble was brewing. I began to understand when to stay away and avoid Jim Dandy if I possibly could. Jimmy wasn't so keen sometimes. Jimmy, the one with a strong will, would continue with his prodding questions, while Mom and I could sense a growing maelstrom. Mom would do everything she could to make a perfect meal for Jim Dandy out of cheap and bland grocery items like ready-made and packaged hamburger patties, hot dogs, or macaroni and cheese. Jim Dandy did not allow us to cook with spices. Spices weren't allowed in the house even though Mom loved spaghetti, chili, and favorite recipes from Grandma Delanie that contained these ingredients. "Ken grow 'em better than those money-grabbing companies," he said. Once Jim Dandy arrived home and found a can of tomatoes on the table which he promptly threw at the living room wall, leaving a huge dent, because the tomatoes contained garlic and basil.

Once a week, Mom pulled roast beef pot roast out of the oven, carrots and potatoes wrapped around the soft brown meat tied with string, this was a special meal, and placed it on the table as soon as the door of his truck slammed closed. From Kathie's front porch, I watched him walk up the little sidewalk and into the little gray house. I knew I had to hurry back to the dark house. Inside, he would plop down in front of the TV onto the filthy chair that used to be green. "Bring me a plate," he'd say, and Mom would spoon gravy over his meat in the kitchen and run it to him, like he was a king on the throne.

"Don't want no gravy on the meat! Want it in a boat!" he would yell. "How many times do I hafta tell you?" We didn't have a gravy boat, so his wish for a boat—whatever that was—was not possible. In fact, we had exactly enough dishes for all of us to eat together. After each meal, Mom would wash the five plates, five forks, five spoons, and five cups and stack them in the cabinet.

We ate in silence. I could hear the food in my mouth as my jaws went up and down before I swallowed it. Jimmy, being unaware of Jim Dandy's foreboding presence, often broke the silence and asked for more food—before Jim Dandy got seconds – and Mom would glance at Jimmy, the whites of her blues eyes set on alarm.

"I want more meat," Jimmy would demand.

"Jimmy, wait a few minutes and then you can have more," Mom would tell him evenly, again moving her eyes toward Jim Dandy.

"Jimmy, just wait," I would say, touching his hand gently, trying to give him a hint.

"But I want more!" He pushed my hand away.

Mom and I would take deep breaths. We knew Jim Dandy was very sensitive about his club foot, and whenever someone mentioned the word *foot*, he would break loose. "I'm hungry!" Jimmy would say again, with urgency. Then he'd throw a spoon or a fork on the floor and once, it touched Jim Dandy's club foot. That was the beginning of a Jim Dandy performance. The belt came out, the screaming began, and the scene transpired until we were all in tears.

The words that we had to repeat, uttered during the beatings, never matched the offense. "I won't throw my spoon," would at least be logical, but the words were something weird and unrelated to the incident like, "I won't leave my bike outside anymore."

Throughout childhood, Jimmy would get the worst of the beatings because of his persistence. He was often in the bathtub when Jim Dandy's attacks occurred. I was fortunate enough to avoid this beating style once I got to a certain age, being a girl. Justin, the youngest, learned to negotiate, and he was the smartest of the four when Jim Dandy was in the equation. Justin knew how to be charming and totally agree to any insanity that Jim Dandy put out there, making me often wonder if Justin actually believed the words he had to utter.

When the beating was over, we could pretend that our lives were peaceful because two people were usually not beaten in one day nor was one person ever beaten twice in that same day; it was an unwritten rule. Sometimes, after Jim Dandy had left welts on our bodies, the next day he'd bring home a surprise or play hide and seek with all the neighborhood kids. Once he installed a tire swing on the giant oak tree, so we could swing over the garage. Once he brought home a candy bar for each of us. He would take us swimming at the Portage Lakes and pretend to be Shamu the Killer Whale and do tricks for us. "Got a club foot, but ken swim like a God-damned shark," he'd say. Yep.

Once, he brought home patio furniture from a house where he had done some wiring. The people weren't home, he said, and they had money to buy more so they wouldn't care. One early spring day, he brought home a packet of radish seeds, and we planted them in the small area between two garages, just enough space for the sun to invigorate the seedlings. Before Jim Dandy and I had cultivated them, I had never seen or eaten a round, red radish but I learned to love the clean, white insides of our home-grown vegetables, the first bite marring the barn red exterior of the little ball with a mouse-like tail.

Jim Dandy loved to plant flowers and vegetables as seedlings in trays in the basement and then transplant the delicate little green buds outside in the spring. God had created balance in Jim Dandy's love of watching things grow.

CHAPTER FOUR

Eclipse Avenue was a colorful place; my neighborhood was a little village inside the city; it boasted stories of even rougher days when Pretty Boy Floyd ran through these parts, shot at the police, and hid inside the now vacant gray and dilapidated sundries building next Joey Cole's house. The body bag building was once used to manufacture fine horseless carriages owned by rubber baron grandfathers. The vacated millinery, boarded up butcher store, and deserted shoe repair shop –shoes still on the shelves— gave the neighborhood a leftover Old West, small town feel, even though Akron annexed our neighborhood into the city some forty years earlier. Some of the people, still thinking they lived in the olden days of the village, knew the lore and the families going back generations and still addressed their mail as Cardinal City, Ohio.

My next door neighbor Joe retold his dad's stories of the famous 1939 sit-down rubber strike at Goodyear. Joe, who was a chemist at Goodyear, told how the heavily armed police waited outside the factory gates anticipating trouble, but no shots were fired, and then settled peacefully. Andy detailed the clank of the cable cars as they passed up and down the boulevard; the trolley cars long gone, but the tracks still led to the big city department stores. Both Joe and Andy told stories of glamorous women, wearing fur coats and pump high heel shoes, taking the trolleys to eat lunch at the Garden Room in downtown Akron. Joe's wife, Rosie, said her dad worked with a younger and skinnier Clark Gable who once made tires at Goodrich. He was known to the world as Rhett Butler of *Gone with the Wind* and uttered the first "damn" in a movie. He rode all the way from Akron to Hollywood on those Goodrich tires. Rosie said her dad remembered Clark Gable reciting Shakespeare while the other guys quietly ate their lunches from metal lunch pails. "Those rough and tumble factory workers," she recalled, "thought he was a little strange, with his outstretched arms asking, 'shall a rose by another name smell as sweet?' My dad used to retell it with my name, 'rosie' instead of 'rose,' to make me laugh."

Thomas Edison, after his marriage in Akron, lit up the universe about two miles away —as the crow flies —from the dark house on Eclipse. Harvey Firestone lived here too, and he helped create those factories that employed hundreds of men, and women too, during World War II. His company and Goodyear Tire and Rubber made tires that traveled all over the world. A hundred years before all of this, abolitionist John Brown walked these streets and lectured on the evils of slavery, before he was hanged for treason, fighting for the just cause. Sojourner Truth was here; union founders, inventors, spiritual searchers, rock stars, movie stars, and sportsmen also made footprints in the dirt and soot of this town. Some of the remaining characters from those olden days, or their children and grandchildren, still populated the neighborhood beer joints like Lucky Corner and Carl's Cove where they lined up, filled in, blended in, and they conveniently forgot, as they drank another beer, that the legacy their fathers and grandfathers had created was an important part of the past.

They weren't aware that a new day was pulsating onward, so they were left behind, inside and outside these establishments, grabbing bottles instead of golden rings. These various characters would stumble and fall, yell inside from the outside, yell outside from the inside, and yell at each other, and for them, it would all turn into a blur. I often watched them from a vacant city lot and wondered who they were and why they had lost their way.

But we, just starting on life's journey, overflowed onto that vacant city lot where spindly and tall white Queen Anne's lace and periwinkle wild chicory flowers exemplified freedom. Our vantage point was adjacent to the shameful body bag factory, also lurking there, doing the dirty work, behind the dark house. A tire swing, being Akron of course, hung from a huge oak tree and carried us away in the hot air balloon or airplane of our imaginations. In this magical place, bee stings and mosquito bites were counted, butts and cans were kicked, and baseballs were ruled out or rolled in as dusty city bus fumes perfumed the blazing heat. But it was in summer that I realized that those simple times would soon dissipate like the gas shortages of the 1970s; challenges would arise, and I –and my generation— would have to face the pollution and ugliness that was created—whether it was our fault or not. I was heading for adolescence, although that word wasn't in my word journal, but changes were coming as we looked forward to celebrating our country's Bicentennial the next year. I could sense it in my growing curiosity about the world far and near, the resetting of the political landscape with President Ford's administration, and the changes in my own body and neighborhood.

I inherited my love for the outdoors and getting my hands dirty from Jim Dandy. I was not a little dainty flower of a girl. I kicked cans. I rolled down hills. I played hard. I came home with skinned knees and stubbed toes. Even though I hated Jim Dandy completely, I had a few of his traits, and I had no choice but to accept them in myself. I had his blue gray eyes. I had the freckles, and I had pieces of his mind: that part scared me. We shared a curiosity for understanding how things worked, how they fit into place, especially history and politics, but he was not interested in reading about these things. Reading for me, however, opened the world. Mom, on the other hand, could read and write, but she had little interest in learning about anything old or new. Her mind was already full of worry; nothing else could be squeezed in there.

Grandma Delanie also loved the outdoors, so on the other hand, maybe I got it from her. She had a flower garden and was always outside poking around in her snowball bushes or her hens and chicks whenever we would stop by for a visit. Grandma Delanie called it her "outdoor world," which I thought was a little more genteel way to describe it. I noticed patterns in the way people spoke and Jim Dandy's spoken words always lacked grammatical correctness. He used double negatives. His subjects and verbs did not match. Often, he spoke in fragments that struggled for completeness of thought.

I also learned early, just from observation, that Grandma Delanie's outdoor world provided freedom and liberation from the dark house. If I were not seen or heard, I couldn't be in Jim Dandy's crosshairs. In the outdoor world, even the air seemed to move with more spirit, more vibrancy, and I wanted to breathe in every ounce of emancipated oxygen that I could, when I could. That spring, as I was finishing the fourth grade, Grandma Delanie gave Mom some lilies of the valley and snapdragon seeds which we planted around the house, and with Jim Dandy's vegetables, from the outside, it appeared to be a place of light, but we knew the darkness.

Kathie wasn't allowed to cross the street and play at the dark house, so I would often go to her house, and those were happy times. Mom claimed that Andy "was overprotective," but I always wondered what he knew about Jim Dandy. Andy, a thinner man than Jim Dandy with wide brown eyes, stayed home due to an injury at the Firestone Rubber Factory. Kathie's life was a complete contrast to mine. She was an only child; her mom died when she was just two, so she had no memories of her mom. If your mother dies young, I guess it is a blessing when you don't remember her.

"Hey, Del!" she would yell over to me. "Can you come over?" Even though I had to ask Mom if I could cross the street, she always agreed that it was okay. If the weather was nice, Kathie and I played outside, because the houses were so small, that most parents didn't want kids underfoot.

"My dad made us grilled cheeses.... Come on over!" Kathie called from across the street.

"Does your dad ever make boy cheeses?" I remember asking her once. I didn't get the joke, but Andy laughed and laughed when he heard my question. "I gotta write that down," he said.

Andy participated in our wonderment of the world. He took time to teach us games like hopscotch and checkers. He'd set up Kathie's little table and chairs in the backyard under the huge old maple tree, and we'd eat our sandwiches like we were at an elegant restaurant while Andy listened on his transistor radio to the Cleveland Indians play baseball.

Kathie got one of those blue plastic swimming pools that contain about one foot of water, and we were so happy just to splash around and cool off. We played and played, jumping in and out, shivering off the wetness in the sun, until Jimmy tried to pole vault into it with a shovel, cracking the whole side of the pool. Water gushed out, and the pool was ruined. I felt terrible about the damage, but Andy never said a word to get Jimmy in trouble. We had run through Joe's lawn sprinkler instead.

One day, while searching for grand daddy long legs in Kathie's garage, we found the most unusual caterpillar we had ever seen in our short lives. It was as large as a hot dog bun, green, and had pink, yellow, and blue dots protruding in ridges along its back. Beautiful in a strange kind of way, we were originally scared that it was an alien and began telling all the neighbors about the interesting creature, showing them as we pulled it around the neighborhood in Kathie's Western Flyer wagon.

But Joe, the chemist who was my next-door neighbor, with his checkered shirt, black and silver crew cut hair, and black-framed eyeglasses, brought over his encyclopedia of insects to classify the being. He took one look at the alien in its egg carton casket, and declared the thing to be a cecropia moth. "No, don't bury that guy. He will turn into a beautiful butterfly one day this summer, and he will fly away," he said, pointing out the encyclopedia drawing. He and Rosie had a complete library in their house, and we kids always asked them questions for which they would always find answers. Before Joe's scientific research, we assumed the cecropia moth was dead, so we had a funeral service for it. Several neighbors, the big kids and even some adults, did make a visit and swore on their lives they had never seen such a strange display of nature.

Other summer activities included riding our bikes to visit lonely dogs tied out at doghouses in the sun, coloring on discarded tin foil from gum wrappers with my semi-melted sixty-four Crayolas left over from the school year, or going on rock expeditions in neighbors' driveways. A good expedition would yield a chalky stone, and we could draw on the city sidewalk or play hopscotch. We nearly destroyed Mrs. Nerz's garden playing "hamburger shop" when we mixed up a batch of mud and spread it between two round hydrangea leaf hamburger buns. Broken, uniform sized, small sticks were served up as a side of French fries. We finally had to give up hamburger shop when Andy told us we needed to find a new bun supplier because the hydrangea leaves were looking pretty scarce.

It was glorious to wake up and see that Jim Dandy's rusted old truck was gone doing setting up electrical complexities, and it was just the three of us with Mom. We'd watch cartoons; she'd make us cereal and milk, and by nine o'clock, we were outside for the day. I treasured these numbered days, for fall would come; school would start; the weather would get cold again, and of course things would change. The rickety old truck would amble down the street, Jim Dandy would walk in, take off his dirt-crusted pants (and belt), and sit in his underwear and eat supper Mom had prepared with only his taste buds in mind. We kids, at least I, tried to be quiet and keep any controversy at bay. When it was dark, we'd all be inside in the small house, no room to spread out and play, and we would watch Jim Dandy's smelly and sweat-drenched body become one with the television. Jimmy would oftentimes disrupt the tranquility with questions about bikes or footballs or pets that he wanted. Justin, with his wide brown eyes—the only brown-eyed person in our family— was too young to really want anything. He just slurped his Campbell's chicken noodle soup quietly, while I took it all in, trying to read and, in turn, smooth Jim Dandy's mood.

Summer evenings included prolific lightning bugs at night, neon against the black backdrop stillness of Joe and Rosie's patio. They blinked off and on and floated around and were housed in mayonnaise jars while all the adults sipped beer or Pepsi, told stories, and laughed. The fluorescent creatures, makers of light, seemed in wonderment to exist for our entertainment. My parents were never among those on the patio because they didn't socialize. Nobody entered or exited the dark house—except us. Mom never told him about drinking coffee with Rosie or Andy. Jim Dandy wanted to control our lives. He wanted her especially to be isolated. Jim Dandy held out his proud proclamations about his status as the best electrical contractor on earth. "I'm the best electrical contractor on the planet," for that matter. "Nobody's good enough for me," he would brag. But the laughter of the other people—safe people on that patio —would lull me to sleep at night, a promise that someday I could laugh, an open window to their murmurings with the smell of rhubarb from their garden and their citronella candles as my tonic. To Justin, in his little bed next to the window, and Jimmy in a sleeping bag on the floor, I would retell them stories that I had read in books from the Thomas Edison Elementary School library.

I'd anticipate the occasional night when Jim Dandy would bring home an orange or even a bag of Swenson's hamburgers. If an orange arrived, I'd sit on Jim Dandy's lap while he peeled it with his rusty pocket knife. I took the peel tendrils and scraped the pith with my teeth, proving my frugality and winning praise from Jim Dandy. He would then take the leftover peel, and burn it in his ashtray along with smoldering cigarette butts. The smell of burning orange peel was a sign of peace, an unspoken message that physical exhaustion trumped his mental instability.

Solemn summers balanced harsh winters as payment for Jim Dandy's sad lot in life.

CHAPTER FIVE

Barbie Country Campers and the accompanying dune buggies with trailers were the big push for Christmas 1975. The orange, fuchsia, and yellow contraptions were all the rage. Girls, at least Kathie and I, had been creatively using shoe or Kleenex boxes for Barbie cars until some toy manufacturer, Mattel, finally realized our quest for independence and decided that girls in America needed cars for their Barbies. This was a generation of girls who dreamed they could have it all: a life of travel, love, education, and adventure. Finally, toy manufacturers had caught on that Mary Tyler Moore and the Bionic Woman were not mere anomalies. Women could go to college, have careers as well as families, and they could make decisions for themselves. For example, would they even marry Ken and would they drive a camper or a dune buggy? Cars were symbolic of driving forward. Kathie and I, around ten years old, dreamed into the J C Penney catalogue and envisioned our Barbies driving up and down our city sidewalks, miniature versions of ourselves, happy, independent, and successful. With falling snow and jingling bells, Andy took us in his giant Oldsmobile Delta 88 to a store called O'Neil's in downtown Akron to see Santa Claus and the diminutive Barbie cars in real life. They had that great new toy smell, and it made us want them all the more. Each purchase included necessary accessories like plastic Barbie sleeping bags and fold out camping chairs.

Along with this orange and fuchsia plastic dreamscape, we were anticipating the last day of school before Christmas break. That day fell on a Friday and the Rankin /Bass animated production of "Santa Claus is Comin' to Town" was on TV. My aunt had just recommended Jim Dandy to do some electrical contracting work on a friend's business in Youngstown, and Jim Dandy would have to stay overnight. We were thankful to my aunt because we needed money, Christmas was coming, and it was a blessing from God that the stars had lined up in such a way that Jim Dandy was gone on this special day.

Mom was also so thrilled; I could see it in her eyes. First, because Jim Dandy might keep this job, and "he would be making the big bucks." Second and secretly, "he would be gone a couple nights a week," and we could relax and not worry about his attacks. That morning when I got up for school, Mom whispered to me that we would celebrate the last day of school. We could order a pizza and watch the Santa Claus movie because Jim Dandy would be gone. "Kathie could come over," she said, "and spend the night, and we could decorate the Christmas tree after the show." I was so excited. "Del, you have to take the wagon to Ed's market, return empty pop bottles, and with that money, pick up the pizza and a cold carton of Pepsi, okay?"

"Sure," I said. "I can do that."

Mom, Jimmy, and Justin were lined up on the couch when I arrived with the pizza. Kathie and I sat on the floor near the coffee table. Each had a glass of cold Pepsi and a plate for pizza, when Burl Ives the snowman started narrating about Christmas town and the North Pole snow storm. It felt so cozy and warm as Justin and even Jimmy sat there and behaved. We opened the pizza box and pepperoni smell permeated the room, blanketing the stale stank of Jim Dandy's sweat, his chewing tobacco, and cigarettes. Just then, we heard a strange sound clattering from our front lawn. It was not a miniature sleigh and eight tiny reindeer. It was Jim Dandy. His rattling truck door slammed.

The once happy music of Christmas town turned into a slow-motion garble, like the recording was melting and disintegrating on the turntable in some warm climate faraway California studio. His arrival signaled not only more misery, but was doubled with the fact that he had apparently lost another job.

Our plates, still awaiting the greasy and chewy pizza, never held one slice. Jim Dandy opened the door, surveyed the scene, grabbed the opened box of Rizzi's pizza from the coffee table, and winged it into the front yard like it was a Frisbee. Pizza was everywhere. "Got pizza without me, huh? That'll learn y'all," he said as I turned to see Kathie react.

I remember trying to laugh nervously. She shot a glance at me, then at Justin, and then looked for an escape hatch. I began to spin out into the universe, and then I ricocheted back down to earth as I tried to think of a way to save the day, to save face, to protect my best friend from what was going to transpire. He wouldn't dare hit her, would he?

"How'd you get money?"

Mom stammered about the returned pop bottles.

"I don't get any?" he yelled.

The events seemed to overlap and in the confusion, my mind was processing as best as it could.

"Get me some food!" He strode to the TV set, changed the channel, took off his pants and belt, and lit a cigarette all in one movement. "Want some pizza!" he screamed. "Where's my pizza?" I thought about picking the pizza slices up off the ground in the snow. He plopped into that dirty tar-covered chair in his underwear. He stunk, of course, and he announced loudly and in general, "Boxin's on."

I protested the channel change, thinking that maybe Mom would take my side. "Please, Dad, let us watch our show! It's our favorite Christmas show, and it only comes on once a year. Kathie's here...."

"I'm the bread winner. Ain't watchin' no stupid made-up bunch of crap," he said. I did hear "Get her home!"

Despite the risks and my ignorant stubbornness, I persisted in begging for the show. Like a serpent waiting to be charmed, his belt was lassoed up and was put to duty all over my body. I bore the belt, thrashing, thrashing, as my thin nightgown rode up around my underwear while the purple stripes started appearing on my legs, arms, and trunk.

Kathie was gone at some point during this time. I couldn't spare her from this demonstration like I did back in the cheerleading uniform, and I was unsure of when she left and how. I hated what he did. Hate, a word I was told not to use at Sunday school, was not strong enough to describe the feelings that were exploding in my heart and mind. Hate, a burden I would carry for many more years, was etched there in my memories of the possible joys and the Jim Dandy-created tortures of Christmases past.

Back in my room that night, shaking, sobbing, and embarrassed, worried again about my best friend Kathie, my little beagle Mickey curled up beside me and tried to lick my feet. I looked out the window and saw snow mounting up on the rooftops of the small houses that were built during the Great Depression with 1970s added detached garages. The Marathon gas station down the street was now selling Christmas trees in an area behind the building lit with a strand of Christmas lights; the two beer joints within my view were decorated with red and green tinsel for festivities near a deserted grocery store built in the 1920s; I dreamed of getting away. I thought of Santa arriving with his sleigh on these rooftops, creating parallel lines and footprints from flying reindeer. It could happen, I used to think. Anything could happen if you believed in it.

The snowflakes kept twirling down as I looked out that window that night. My view of the world: Snow was silently making a new landscape, creating a peaceful wonderland, covering up the hurt and scars that would otherwise linger there. The snow instilled a quiet that rarely came to a city block in Akron, Ohio, in 1975. From my second story bedroom window, I could see things far and near. I watched the older next-door neighbors, Joe and Rosie, the people with the insect library in their house, dressed in festive clothes. They were holding a tray of food and laughing as they made their way to their GMC Pacer. They were living, like people do, and feeling free. They were enjoying life, I suppose. They didn't know that just a few feet away, from the dark tower, I was watching, wishing that I could be part of their vigor, basked in their laughter and light. They inspired me.

Snow, with all its beauty and ability to cover up the dirt, always takes me back to Christmases past and cherished memories with Kathie and Grandma Delanie. I knew I had to move forward and put these memories behind me.

When Santa did deliver that new Barbie camper on Christmas Day, I called Kathie with the news. "Our Barbies can go camping together," I said joyously. Kathie announced that she also got the camper and was excitedly putting the stickers on the orange gem at that very moment. I heard Jim Dandy yelling in the other room and knew that I needed to get off the phone right away. He screamed at Mom that all the toys cost too much money, so I decided to put Barbie into the driver's seat and head upstairs. Before Barbie could get away, he walked over to my play scene and smashed the orange and fuchsia vehicle to smithereens with his crusted work boot.

I tried to glue it back together, but it kept falling apart.

CHAPTER SIX

Jimmy Carter was running for president of the United States. Jim Dandy supported him because Carter was a conservative Southern Baptist and because, according to Jim Dandy, he "wanted to help the working man." I supported Carter because he just seemed like an honest man. That same summer, in the midst of the economic challenges of the gas crisis, we could barely afford gas for the Chevy, Jim Dandy came home with another announcement that would change our lives: The Marathon gas station a few blocks away needed people to work the counter and handle those long gas lines. "Linda, you might be able to siphon some gas into the Chevy," he said, "or maybe not." His plot was thickening, and he laughed maniacally. With Justin starting kindergarten and Jimmy in third grade, I was old enough to babysit, and Mom was in support of getting a job.

She rejected his idea about siphoning gas, but she jumped at the chance. "I always wanted to have a career of my own," Mom proclaimed to Grandma Delanie on the phone that night, "and I can maybe work my way up to a manager or something."

Mom started the training before the presidential election and was well into her working career when Carter won the presidency in 1976. He was a Southerner, spoke with the same buttery drawl as Jim Dandy, and Jim Dandy finally felt included and vindicated of his Mississippi heritage. "Well, Mom, this way I know we will have food in the winter when Dandy can't work," Mom told Grandma Delanie that same night.

I could hear Grandma Delanie's loud voice reply, hilariously, through the phone, from across the room, "Well, why can't he work in the winter? Why can't the lazy numbskull find electrical work inside?" I remember laughing in my head—God forbid he would hear me—but Grandma Delanie always spoke the truth so bluntly.

"Mom, you know I've always wanted to be a teacher and have a career. This way, I can be working when the kids are at school or sleeping; I won't siphon gas, but maybe I can bring home stale bread and donuts."

"Why would you siphon gas?" I heard Grandma Delanie ask, aware that Mom repeated Jim Dandy's rejected idea without thinking.

"Oh, with gas prices and all," she said. Her response didn't really address Grandma Delanie's question about Jim Dandy's laziness, but it was a fact that Jim Dandy was not going to hold a job—any job—and Mom was finally understanding of that truth. We needed to come to that realization.

The incentive of bread and donuts sealed the deal and by that fall, when I was finishing my last year in elementary school, Mom got hired at the Marathon gas station two blocks away. I could see the little station lit up at night from my bedroom window and feel that she was still close-by even when she was working. Thank God for her job because that was a rough year. Jim Dandy's plans to open his own electrical contracting business didn't work out, and because he got fired for his performance from another electrical contracting job, he couldn't collect unemployment. "No jobs out there!" he used to scream. "Maybe Carter will get me a job," he repeated throughout the rest of the 1970s. I laughed in my mind at the phone ringing and President Carter asking for Jim Dandy. "I know you didn't apply, but I have a job for you, Jim Dandy," President Carter would be magically saying. On the other hand, thank God for Mom because those stale donuts and loaves of bread from Marathon fed us. I knew that if she worked, we had food, so I did dishes, laundry, and made sure Jimmy and Justin did their homework and had had their baths when she got home.

The job wasn't without lessons. She once learned the hard way not to cash her check and leave the money around because Jim Dandy found it and used every penny to buy a hunting knife. We had no grocery money. To make ends meet, my aunt's neighbor gave us four quarts of green beans that his wife had canned, and my uncle dropped off a few pounds of hamburger and a carton of milk. Luckily, we already had ketchup and mustard.

Grandma Delanie never knew about these things, and I was forbidden to tell her. She would have had a "conniption." Grandma Delanie, trying to remain dignified, disliked Jim Dandy already, everybody knew that; she hated his name; she hated his lack of work, and spending our grocery money on a knife would not put a point on his scoreboard. She always lamented that he "was taking it out on us because he is brilliant, but he can't keep a job." She often told me, "I can't stand that Mississippi hillbilly. Your mother could've done so much better." I knew this to be true. Mom was pretty, even though she wore over-sized glasses, and she had gorgeous curly red hair and dimples. She was kind, funny, and too good to be stuck with Jim Dandy.

To alleviate stress and soften his meanness, I tried to find little trinkets on my way to and from school to bestow upon him as gifts. This often did the trick for a day. Once I found one of those stretchy pull-cord tie-up things, discarded on the side of the road and it was good as new; he loved it. "This is worth a lot of money," he proclaimed proudly to me. "Come in handy when I need to tie something to the car."

Trinkets or not, his mind started to deteriorate more rapidly when he couldn't get outside during the winter months. I tried to encourage him often and talk about math, his favorite subject, and I really did need his help with long division. It made him feel good that his method of casting out nines worked, and I got all the answers right on the test. I even showed my teacher who was impressed with this tactic.

Even with our math talks, free bread and cupcakes, and Jimmy Carter as president, the darkness of the winter months enveloped Jim Dandy; he hated cold weather, it fueled his mental depravity, and brought more darkness. He screamed about the pardoning of Patty Hearst on television and that began his hatred for Jimmy Carter, who hadn't, at least to this point, changed Jim Dandy's life. "I'd fry her!" he screamed at the television.

Jim Dandy got meaner and slept at weird times. He could often be found watering the snow with the garden hose "to bring spring faster." One year, he planted our dead Christmas tree to see if he could "get it to start." He played a chess game by himself. He would make one move, wait about fifteen minutes, and then move as another player. I never understood. He would be up at night, walking around the house in the dark, and when we would get up for school, he would be passed out on the floor with the TV blaring beside him, empty Coke bottles and cigarettes smoldering in the ashtray beside his aching hands.

These times were unpredictable. He walked heavily when his club foot was bothering him, and if you heard the pounding steps you knew he was coming. He tried to sneak around in the dark house, but I knew the thumping and Jimmy, Justin, and I would pretend to be asleep, even if we weren't, so he wouldn't bother us. But sometimes, he'd come into our room, yank one of us by the foot, pull us out from under the covers and start with his belt. We never knew when, why, or for how long. The questions would go on like the cheerleading/bologna event. The correct answer that he wanted was never there.

Trying to comprehend his thinking patterns was one of the greatest mysteries of the world.

CHAPTER SEVEN

Living in a dark house, I had learned how to build a fence around my heart.

He had taken his new hunting knife to some of the records that I bought with my own money or got as gifts from Grandma Delanie. Side B of *Elton John's Greatest Hits* was completely destroyed. "His songs make no sense," he screamed coming into my room. "What is a 'Rocket Man'? It's about a guy on drugs," he screamed, grabbing the album off my Mickey Mouse record player. He took out his pocket knife and dug a wedge across the entire side of the album. I kept the destroyed Elton John vinyl, and Side A still worked, so I could still listen to "Your Song" on real low when he wasn't home. I couldn't let Kathie borrow it; I had to keep making up excuses why not, because I didn't want to explain what had happened to Side B. "Rocket Man," I later learned, was about the astronauts landing on the moon, and the loneliness they must have felt up there by themselves in space.

I understood the feelings of Rocket Man. It would be lonely up there. If he would have arrived in the flesh, even Rocket Man couldn't help down here with Jim Dandy, and the pounds that kept thickening me and the need to build a bigger wall around my bumbling self. I was starting seventh grade at an inner city junior high school; I had gained twenty-five pounds that summer from all the cupcakes and bread, and developed these things called hips. Oh, how I hated hips! I even hated the sound of that word! Most of my clothes from sixth grade wouldn't go over these lumps at the tops of my short legs, and I had to wear Mom's jeans to school. At five feet three, I was curvy, short, and in a growing spurt that went horizontally and not vertically. It was an embarrassing and depressing time in my life.

As if the dark house weren't enough, Jeff Farnsworth, my old grade school buddy who shared my Crayola sixty-fours, took it upon himself to make me the butt—excuse the pun—of his jokes at junior high school. Not a day went by that Jeff didn't have a comment about my, well, you know, or about the fact that I was the fattest girl in the seventh grade. My heart was broken and I hated myself.

While the Bee Gees were "Stayin' Alive" on the radio, I was barely. Images of skinny girls in disco dresses, floating along the dance floor, were everywhere. Then there was me. I would never float anywhere. I was grounded in more ways than one, so I tried to escape my life with music, books, my neighborhood, my lady Kathie, my beagle Mickey, and my brothers. The junior high school library became my refuge, and I traveled quite a bit to Victorian England where I met my friends the Bronte sisters and Charles Dickens. I read *Gone with the Wind* in three days and then was able, at Kathie's house, to watch the two-day television event. I wondered if Clark Gable had remembered Rosie's dad from his Goodrich days and dreamed of wearing the dresses of Scarlett O'Hara.

But I never floated away or left the plantation. Tomorrow was another day in Akron, Ohio. I stayed firmly on the ground, farm-fed but city-bred it appeared, so I steadfastly decided that next summer a regimented exercise program and a strict one-thousand-calorie diet would get me to where I wanted to be: twenty-five pounds thinner. With Jim Dandy still doing his thing with the belt, at least I had some control of what went into my mouth and what didn't, and I could try to regain some confidence. I began running around the block several times a night, jumping rope for about an hour every day, and I convinced Mom to buy canned green beans, spinach, and carrots. If I only had a few cans of vegetables a day, along with cottage cheese and no bread or cupcakes, I could drop some weight. That summer, I was successful and my hips disappeared. I could have easily fit back into my old Super Denims from grade school, but they were too short!

Fortunately, that summer I had earned enough money babysitting that I didn't have to wear the Super Denims. I was able to shop like the other girls at the coolest store called County Seat at Rolling Hills Mall. I bought a pair of straight-leg Levi's jeans, a pair of white painter's pants, and crew neck sweaters in teal, burgundy, and navy blue. Grandma Delanie bought me a pair of cool boots and several pairs of Avon earrings to start school, and I was finally proud to be in my own body. Knowing lots of people and doing a good job, I had established myself an in-demand babysitter. This kept me safely away from Jim Dandy, and the money was flooding in. I was getting a life for myself, and I was satisfied with my prospects for the future. I had Kathie and Andy, who stood with me through everything, a neighborhood where firmly I belonged, pretty good grades at the inner city junior high school, growing popularity, respect among my friends and teachers, and a body that reflected back thin enough in the mirror. Things were on an even keel.

But that was about to change.

CHAPTER EIGHT

"Movin' to the country," Jim Dandy proclaimed when this movie star named Ronald Reagan was running for president of the United States. Maybe, finally, Ronald Reagan could change Jim Dandy's life. It was the summer before my freshman year in high school, and many of my Akron friends' parents had just heard the news that Firestone Rubber Company would be closing six plants. Jim Dandy was shoveling roast beef in his mouth, sitting on that gray chair that used to be green. "Well, haha for them. Supposed to be so great," he said. "Know hard times like I got, but nobody can handle me. I'm the best electrical contractor in the world." I thought this was a pretty cruel way to look at it, but I kept my mouth shut.

"Why are we moving, Dandy?" Mom asked.

"That snickety gym teacher of Del's told me how to raise my own kid, so now we gotta get away from here. I told 'im what I thought! Runnin' aroun' in gym shorts like he owns the place...I work for a livin'."

We don't have to leave Eclipse Avenue, I thought. What about Kathie, Andy, and my neighbors Joe and Rosie with the insect encyclopedia? What about the field with Queen Anne's lace? What about finding rocks and playing kick-the-can? What about doing cartwheels on the devil strip? What about my life here? What about all the money I was making as a babysitter?

"It's yer fault," he charged, "going into that gym class, sluttin' around with shorts on, openin' your big mouth about fallin' off yer bike." He was referring to questioning by Mr. Townsend privately in his office for the bruises and welts that prompted a terse phone call to Jim Dandy.

"You don't want to move either, Mom?" I asked, as Mom walked to the front door and gazed at Kathie's house. She was sobbing noiselessly.

"Found a fixer-upper. Ken pay cash for it. Sell this place, and that teacher of yers won't find us," he proclaimed. "You and the boys ken move us," he ordered, "while I'm at work. I'll take the Chevy and leave my truck, and you can have us all moved by the time I get home."

Along with leaving Eclipse Avenue where my world originated, I would be turning fifteen in a few months, and I had already started churning out a plan to get out of the dark house someday, some way. Changes were ahead anyway, I thought, and at least the move would be something new. Maybe my life would take another direction. I couldn't bear to think about leaving my people, Kathie, Andy, Joe, and Rosie, and this place that was my home. I told myself that Kathie and I would talk every day, and she said it again and again. We would stay the best friends that we are now. We just knew it.

Christopher Cross could "Ride Like the Wind," and I had no choice but to join him. Jimmy holding onto the sofa; Justin holding a lamp in each hand, and I sitting on the sofa cushions, we rode in the back of Jim Dandy's beat up truck, held on to our stuff on the highway as Mom drove to the falling-down 150-year-old

Victorian house in nearby suburban Western Star. The gray house was two story with a large fireplace and high ceilings. It even had a few remaining crystal chandeliers. It had four bedrooms, a bathroom on each floor, a large dining room, and a large veranda that went the entire length of the house. I felt like Scarlett O'Hara moving into Tara. It was built on a high embankment on a state route with busy traffic passing by. Although it needed paint in all the rooms because the previous owners seemed to like bright, obnoxious colors, it was much more spacious than our house on Eclipse Avenue. The electrical work couldn't accommodate modern appliances such as hair dryers or curling irons anywhere except the kitchen, and Jim Dandy began working on it, but there were trade-offs: Jimmy and Justin shared a huge bedroom, I had my own bedroom, as did my parents. His talent in electricity came through, and we had light switches on almost every wall. Like people set free from prison, we finally had the spaciousness of six acres to run and walk in the surrounding woods.

Our new neighbor, Elton Jenkins, who was about my age and the only Elton I've ever known in real life other than Elton John, arrived when we were moving in and grabbed a few things and helped us before Jim Dandy got there. Elton told the four of us tales that the house was part of the Underground Railroad, and the previous occupants claimed that it was haunted. The wealthy man who built the house published a children's magazine in the mid-1800s and supposedly a chest of money was mysteriously buried on the property, Elton said, as he placed a cardboard box labeled "kitchen" on the counter. Once we were settled, he promised, he would show Jimmy, Justin, and me "the Indian fountain," part of a deserted Chippewa encampment near the creek, about a mile away. Maybe this was part of the adventure of my new life, I thought.

New people and adventures, it appeared, were ahead of me. Elton, I learned that day as we walked to the Indian fountain, was an only child with much older parents, and it was apparent because he was somewhat of a demanding baby. He was a little peculiar and particular, but his tales of the house were interesting, and he seemed harmless. In appearance, he was heavyset, yet very tuned in to fashion, and didn't seem to have many friends of his own. "I'm thrilled to have new neighbors," he told us as we were walking. "You are the first kids in the neighborhood in many years. It's kinda lonely here," he said, "on the main street." I noticed that other guys, in particular, avoided Elton. He was more like talking to a girl than a guy. He noticed things like make up, hair, and clothes, which seemed a little out of the ordinary for the guys on Eclipse Avenue. "Del, that eye shadow is definitely not your color," he said to me one day when we were walking. "You need a pair of those new Calvin Klein jeans. Everyone is wearing them." These comments were often biting but true, and sometimes I would lash out about my lack of money to buy his suggested fashions because my babysitting jobs were left behind in Akron. He was a little strange that was for sure, but he was there, and he was interesting to talk to, and he gave me the low-down about all the kids at Western Star High School. He gave feedback, and he was a good listener, which was my favorite characteristic about Elton Jenkins.

To make some money for the Calvin Klein jeans, I landed a babysitting job for a distant cousin who lived near Western Star because his wife decided to go back to work. I would often get the kids to nap, and I would watch the TV news as the presidential election drew closer. I really had this feeling that Reagan was going to win. He was a slick talker with slicked-back black hair that looked like plastic; he was an actor after all; he was convincing that he knew what he was talking about, and it was about time for a Republican to be back in the White House. This meant bad times for the working man, Jim Dandy had reported, and jobs, of course, would once again be hard to come by.

These cousins lived close enough to Akron that I could talk to Kathie as a local phone call when I wasn't catching the TV news. I needed a real wage-earning job, I told her one day over the phone, babysitting wasn't regular enough, and she told me that King Arthur's Round Table, at our old stomping ground at Rolling Hills Mall, was hiring. I told her how I had applied to every business within walking distance of our new old house in Western Star, but had no prospects. "You could easily get hired over all those burnouts who were working at King Arthur's Round Table," she said. "If you get a job there, I can stop in and see you."

I told Mom my situation, and she drove me directly to King Arthur's Round Table after my babysitting day was over. I confidently walked into the English medieval castle-themed restaurant, and I asked to speak to a manager. "I need a job," I stuttered breathlessly to the man who approached me, a short Italian fellow with a black receding hairline. "I would like to work here," I finally got the words out.

"Well, we just hired a bunch of kids from the vocational program," he informed me. "You missed the job fair."

"I will work real hard," I continued. "I'm an honor student."

"Keep your eye on the newspaper," he said. "We do major hirings about twice a year."

Then I did something that I hadn't planned on doing. Kathie's words had encouraged me, but this part just happened. In that moment, something, a force, took over my body. I got down on my knees, cupped my hands together, looked up, and begged him for a job. "My father just lost his job again, and I need the money. I will work for free on a trial basis," I urged. "I am begging you to give me a chance." I just kept begging, not letting him interrupt me. He waved his arms around, feeling helpless, and shook his head back and forth, then up and down.

Just then, another manager approached the scene that was transpiring. "Who is this? What is going on here? This girl is making a scene," interrupted the newly arrived tall manager with a pitted face.

"This is our newest employee," announced that Italian fellow, putting a hand on my shoulder. I would soon learn that this man was Mr. Al Camparti, one of my angels. "Follow me into the office, and I'll get you a uniform. Call next week on Wednesday for the schedule. And you'll need to fill out this application."

When I called, I had two days on the next schedule, for pay, I might add.

Jimmy had just bought a used moped from Elton Jenkins' cousin. He had saved his birthday money and helped another neighbor bale hay to buy the thing. I told him that if he would make the ten-minute drive and take me to work in the warm weather, I would keep his tank full. Although he wasn't street legal, we took back roads and traveled only a short distance on a major thoroughfare to get to King Arthur's Round Table.

It wasn't glamorous— and lots of small things had to add up— but it was my first step toward independence on the long journey out of the dark house.

CHAPTER NINE

That slick-haired, plastic Ronald Reagan won the presidency in 1980, so things were getting buttoned up. In fashion, Polo shirts with preppy collars were standing at attention; in music, the punk rockers, with their rebel lyrics, were upsetting parents everywhere and putting safety pins through their ear lobes; and Nancy Reagan was getting ready to roll out "Just Say No" as the simple solution to illegal drugs. With Carter's policies still in place for a while, we qualified for free school lunches from the government, but Mom wouldn't allow the embarrassment. I understood her philosophy and pride, but it didn't feed us. Most of the time when I arrived at work, I had eaten crackers from the school salad bar or a stray apple or banana from someone's lunch.

My routine was to ride the Western Star school bus as far as it would go toward the mall and then walk the rest of the way, carrying my books and uniform, singing the lyrics to Devo's "Whip It" or some other popular song while trying to tame the rumbling in my stomach. When I saw the Parthenon mall perched atop that blacktop paved parking lot, rising from the weeds in the working class neighborhoods surrounding it, I contemplated my future: Someday, I prayed to the Universe, things would be different without Jim Dandy in my life.

In spite of his mathematical and electrical contracting genius, Jim Dandy was illiterate and proud of it. He told anyone who would listen about his inability to read, yet he claimed to read the Bible, one of his many contradictory statements. He argued with anyone about subjects that he knew nothing about, citing the Bible as his textbook which he only knew from hearing fantastical stories at Sunday school as a child. Jim Dandy got into an argument with Joe, the neighbor on Eclipse Avenue, because he overheard Joe tell Kathie and me that we are descendants of apes and according to science, life is "survival of the fittest." Jim Dandy strutted over to the devil strip where we were talking, asked Joe to show him that fact in the Bible, and drew back his fist to swing a punch toward Joe. Joe dodged it, laughed, and said, "Jim Dandy, that kind of reaction could get you in trouble someday. The kids were asking where we came from. I was telling them about Charles Darwin. Have you heard of him?"

Jim Dandy screamed back, "Believe the God-damned Bible, you pencil pushing sissy, not someone saying I'm a ape. I got a damned club foot!" I thought the damning of the Bible by God himself was a hilarious study in paradox, but I didn't dare utter a word. I just kept the laugh inside.

Because of these uncountable embarrassments from Jim Dandy, I liked being new to Western Star High School. Nobody really knew about Jim Dandy. These Western Star dads passed through my serving line at the Round Table daily, so I knew his competition. They took their daughters school shopping at The Limited and the County Seat and then treated them to dinner. It didn't really faze me too much. I waited on them with my usual smile and praise of their new outfits. I would rather earn my own money, talk to Mr. Camparti, and do things for myself than spend one extra second with Jim Dandy, so working was a way to stay safe and unbothered. Mr. Camparti was a good substitute for a father. He saved leftover baked potatoes and broiled fish from the afternoon lunch rush for me. He demonstrated work ethic. His advice shaped who I became. "I have a degree in languages from Akron U," he recounted to me one night as we were closing. "I really don't use the languages that often, but I use my education every day of my life," he proclaimed as was preparing to teach me how to balance the cash drawer. "Get a college degree. You'll never regret it."

Since Jim Dandy had everyone believing that "the country was in a depression" and "he was the best electrical contractor in the world" --these were his favorite sayings during most of the 1980s — I worked diligently to keep my job. Mr. Camparti was impressed with my famous "potion" of hot water and lemon juice to clean the serving line to a high sparkle. Every night, I restocked the dinner rolls, the glassware, and the straws, wearing my "Hi My Name is Delanie" badge with pride. I closed with Mr. Camparti just about every night and we often talked about current events and music. One night, we were talking about President Ronald Reagan's chances for recovery from the gunshot by John Hinkley. "That Hinkley is delusional," Mr. Camparti was saying as he walked past me with a broom and dustpan. "He claimed that Jodie Foster told him to shoot President Reagan."

"I know; he is crazy," I said. As I began to count the cash in the drawer, a man sauntered in, wearing a vaguely familiar ski mask, and only his mud-colored, squinty eyes were visible out of the eye holes. The hair on my arms stood straight up. I instinctively scanned the dining room for Mr. Camparti. That quickly, before I could really do anything else, a gun was against my temple. I pushed the drawer closed.

"M-O-N-Y," read a note he tossed onto my sparkling serving line.

I pressed the secret manager call button on the side of the counter and heard it ring into the dining room where Mr. Camparti was describing closing procedures to a new busboy. "I will be right there, Delanie," he loudly shouted over his shoulder.

Again, the gunman pressed the gun harder into my temple and the gun clicked. "Hand me the cash! Now!" he yelled, finally, trying, it seemed, to disguise his voice.

I put my code in and opened the drawer. I started pulling out George Washingtons.

"Big stuff only!" he mumbled, muffled through the ski mask.

Just then, Mr. Camparti appeared from the dining room. "What's going on here?" he said, trying to chuckle.

"MONEY!" yelled the gunman. "Now!" as he pointed his gun toward Mr. Camparti.

"You won't get away with this!" Mr. Camparti yelled. "You should think this over and leave now while you can."

"Now!" Ski Mask ordered.

Mr. Camparti shouldered me aside, and he told me to go into the dining room.

"No!" Ski Mask yelled. "She stays!"

Mr. Camparti started taking out the fives. "Here," he handed Ski Mask a stack of five-dollar bills.

"Move," Ski Mask ushered me with the gun. "Move! Don't leave." Then he turned to Mr. Camparti and shouted, "Big stuff only!"

Mr. Camparti clicked open the slat where the twenties were kept. He handed Ski Mask three twenties.

"Big stuff!" yelled Ski Mask, gun still pointed at Mr. Camparti. "Fifties!"

Mr. Camparti raised the drawer where two fifties were nestled. "Here," he said. "I don't have any more cash. Take this and leave us alone."

"In the back—you two," ordered Ski Mask, waving the gun toward the backroom. "In the back!" Jeff the dishwasher had just left through the metal backdoor to take trash to the Dumpster behind the restaurant.

"Wait twenty minutes," Ski Mask warned. "A man in the parking lot is watching the clock. Twenty minutes or we will come back."

Mr. Camparti nodded his head toward the back. "Do what he says, Delanie," he said calmly. Jeff was coming back as Ski Mask was about to leave through that same door.

"You, kid," Ski Mask snapped. "Get over there with the other two. Listen to my orders, doya hear me?"

Jeff didn't say a word; he was dumbstruck. He joined us in the corner where we all agreed we would wait to call the police. Mr. Camparti reasoned, "We're alive; let's do as he says." After Ski Mask ran through the back door of the restaurant, the new bus boy, who had managed to stay low key in the dining room, came to check on us in the back.

The back door is only left unlocked when someone is taking out trash or when orders are being delivered. While we were waiting to call the police, Jim Dandy barreled in the back door, yelling my name.

"I'm so glad you're here," I called to Jim Dandy, maybe happy to see him for the second time in my life. "We just got robbed! It was so scary!"

"Yes, Mr. Dane," Mr. Camparti said, regaining his composure. "Delanie will need to stay, if possible, to make a statement to the police. We can call them in about ten minutes."

"She is coming home with me right now," ordered Jim Dandy. "I have things to do. I have electrical work to do. I'm an electrical contractor. I don't have ten minutes to wait around."

It was strange, I thought. Usually my ride home was Jimmy on his moped. Jim Dandy picked me up this one time and the place got robbed. It was uncanny.

CHAPTER TEN

Two fifties, three twenties, a few fives, and a stack of ones—over one hundred eighty dollars—were taken that night from the cash drawer. Whoever took the money understood the layout of the restaurant; they knew the storage room was in the back; they knew about the back-exit door. They also knew that only one manager and a couple of teenagers worked alone after closing.

Then there was the noted accomplice, who watched as Ski Mask escaped.

That particular ski mask, black with red snowflakes on it, the object plain and simple, kept haunting me. That night I didn't sleep; I knew the stupid thing was familiar, but I couldn't pinpoint exactly where I had seen it. Finally, when I arrived at school the next day, I saw Jimmy's best friend Tom at his locker, and suddenly I remembered that Tom had left the same black and red ski mask on the workbench in our garage a few weeks earlier.

Interestingly enough, Jim Dandy had asked me about that back-exit door of King Arthur's about a week before the robbery. "Does that door always lock?" I thought it unusual, but then again, Jim Dandy asked questions about electrical things all the time. Things always look clearer in retrospect.

"We prop it open at night when we are taking out trash," I remember telling him.

"Well, could someone get in there?" I remember him asking.

"Yea," I said, "but we don't have much trouble." Jim Dandy was often interested in weird mechanical things like doors, wiring, or engines, so I didn't think about the conversation again until the robbery when it became pertinent.

I kept replaying this conversation in my head because I had to give a statement to the police after school the next day. I worried because the ski mask appeared to be the same one left in our garage—which had disappeared. Was the ski mask still in the garage where I had seen it last? I also thought about Jim Dandy's questions about the door. Was he concerned about our safety?

I was paid for the hour I spent with the Rolling Hills police, and then Jimmy buzzed to get me on his moped. We rode home to the hum of the motor, and I didn't explain to him why I was there only an hour, and he didn't ask. I asked him nonchalantly about the ski mask when we arrived home. "Did you ever return that ski mask to Tom?"

"Why?" he asked.

I hurried for a dumb explanation. "Well, I saw Tom today..." I tried to come up with filler. "It's cold and I thought he might need it."

"Tom wanted me to bring it to him," Jimmy said innocently. "It was on the workbench, but I couldn't find it. Have you seen it?"

Oh, yes, I have seen it, I thought.

"No," I said, and kept my mouth shut about it. Jimmy, a guy of few words anyway, left me off at the dark house, and zoomed away.

My heart pounding, I took a detour through the garage, and I verified Jimmy's story that the ski mask was indeed gone. When I came into the kitchen, thrown askew on the round oak table was a new bb gun and some extra bbs that were loose and rolling onto the floor. Tucked underneath the gun, along with some cigarette rolling papers, was a receipt for one hundred seventy-seven dollars, a cash sale.

Where would Jim Dandy get one hundred seventy-seven dollars in the dead of winter without electrical contracting work? We had no groceries. Ironically, we had to stop using our electricity; our heat was shut off until Mom got paid in a few days. We slept in our coats and put the milk outside to keep it from spoiling. I shoved the receipt back under the gun and decided to take a walk out by that Indian fountain, where I could think aloud and pray. Half of me didn't want to know the truth: the other half was afraid that I might blurt out my suspicions to either Jim Dandy, Jimmy, or the police. I needed to be out of the dark house, so I could think, unanchored, without fear.

As I approached the Indian fountain, my thoughts became clearer. It came down to one question: Could Jim Dandy stage a robbery against his own daughter? Yes, he could in my mind, but the actual robber, a man with brown eyes, wasn't Jim Dandy. Jim Dandy has bluish gray eyes. Could Jim Dandy have instigated someone else to put a gun to his daughter's head, so he would have some spending money? Again, yes in my mind that scenario could play out, and as scary as it was, I realized that Jim Dandy was probably involved, at least in the planning. Jim Dandy did whatever he wanted. He was Jim Dandy.

I kept trying to deny the possibility, pushing the thought to the back of my mind, but the truth seemed to get clearer, closer, and bigger. My intuition kept telling me that Jim Dandy was involved. He was the getaway watch man. He was there that night, bounding through the back door, after the robbery. I would have believed any story about Jim Dandy. Jim Dandy, in my mind young mind, would do anything, sacrifice anyone, and hurt anybody to get what he wanted. Like a child without limitations, he wanted a new bb gun.

That red and black ski mask, even though a small circumstantial clue, was a key, and I knew it. Jim Dandy actually being there and his earlier questions about the door added to my suspicion. The gun purchase made it a mathematical certainty, at least in my paranoid mind.

I had discovered even scarier Jim Dandy traits, and instinctively, for self-protection, I had to feign ignorance and silently, in my mind, I decided I would cover for him.

Only one question remained: Who was the gunman?

CHAPTER ELEVEN

Guns were everywhere.

President Reagan, I had learned, would recover, but his body guard, a man named James Brady, would be paralyzed, probably for life. Then there was the gun at King Arthur's and Jim Dandy's new bb gun which he used pathetically to shoot any animal on our property, including harmless squirrels, rabbits, birds, or neighbor's dogs or cats.

I was back out in the woods with my dog Mickey, walking toward the Indian fountain, when I understood Robert Frost's line that "Nature's first green was gold." The ground was swelling, and life was trying to come back to the earth. Yellow buds were trying to burst forth. I was telling Mickey about the essay we were reading in Mrs. Tetley's sophomore English class, called *Walden* by Henry David Thoreau, about living alone in the woods—it sounded very peaceful—when I saw a human figure in the distance. From another era, a white-haired and mustachio'ed man, dressed in a white suit, puffed on a pipe, and he sure looked like Mark Twain.

"Hey, Delanie," he broadcasted, coming closer, waving this corn cob pipe my way, creating a little circle of smoke in the air around his head, like that picture of Santa Claus at Grandma Delanie's house.

His white suit showed up very clearly as the March sun intensified. "Are you reading any of my books in literature class yet?"

"Well ...." I couldn't talk. It seemed that I was in a trance. I reached for Mickey to make sure he was real. Mickey was there, solid, undaunted, sniffing the air, staring straight ahead. Animals, they say, can sense things we cannot. He kind of growled, but then he stopped as if the man were familiar or friendly to him. Mickey squirmed so I put him down. He muzzled my leg in a protective manner.

"Well, Huckleberry Finn escaped on the raft down the Mississippi River, of course?"

"Yes," I stammered.

"He found an unlikely friend in Jim. Jim helped him. Jim, the escaped slave, was a kind and supportive friend."

"Uh," I still couldn't talk.

"You have a way of finding friends. These friends will help you too."

"Yes?" I said with a rising in my voice.

"Have you a plan to escape? How are you keeping your head together with that crazy fellow who does everything he can to hurt you and to embarrass you—and even break the law, steal from his own daughter, for his selfish and cruel wants?"

His question was loaded. "Mark Twain?" I asked, feeling the hair raise on my arms.

"Yes, it is me," he said. "I have come with a message."

"A message?" I picked up Mickey again and drew him close to my body. I kissed his brown, furry head.

"This is your vision," he reported mysteriously. "You brought me here."

"I did?" I asked, stunned at the power of my own mind.

"Yes, but I am here to tell you that you will be fine," he revealed.

"Can I ask you a question?" I uttered, getting some nerve and thoughts together.

"You can ask whatever you want...."

"Here it is: How do I begin to write? And then, how do I write so that the reader can see my life and can understand my ideas without sounding like I'm a know-it-all, or that I'm preaching because I really don't know it all? I'm a humble girl."

"I didn't know it all either. I just knew a little piece of what I saw. But you gotta write," he said confidently. "You just gotta sit down and write. Keep your goals in mind, but let the words flow out. Because, if I understand your situation, these words need to come out. Your heart needs to bleed a little. Your story needs to be told."

"You're right. These words—my story—my heart—they are all covered up. They are exploding in my head—all the time. I'm in Mrs. Tetley's class, she's my English teacher, and I just want to write my story. I knew that back when I was five years old, and I know it now."

"Escape through reading," he proclaimed. "It is safe, and you will see progress in its returns."

"Escape. Yes, I'm doing that right now with Mickey."

"Yes, you need the outdoor world," he said. "But read. Keep reading and writing."

I wasn't sure if I was speaking or thinking, but this was the gist: Writers help me to escape. Thank God for them. They are there for anyone who needs to escape their own backyards. Laura Ingalls Wilder, Mary Higgins Clark, Charles Dickens, and Shakespeare, and that poet, Edna St. Vincent Millay? Just sitting on the shelf, waiting, getting dusty.

"You, my dear, need to write your heart out! That beating heart of yours is buried under cinder blocks," he said.

"Cinder blocks," I know I said those words aloud.

"Lift the cinder blocks," he said. "Lift them up."

My thoughts continued swirling like this: I want to travel, Mr. Twain, and I want to be free. I want to meet lots of people, from all over the world, not just those who look like me and believe like me, but different people.

"I know that," he said. "You will meet those people. But your father is trying to keep you from living that life. Don't let him, do you hear me? Don't let him keep you under cinder blocks!"

I can't not have those things. They are as natural to me as breathing. I must find a way to get them full time so that I am not punished for being me, and for using big words, and for learning and for exploring, I thought.

"Keep searching and searching, dear girl, and you will find a way out. And write!"

He turned away from me and began to walk through the creek, toward the Indian fountain. I tried to hold onto him as long as I could when he turned back to me and yelled, cupping his hands around his mouth, "Write: Let it be your raft!"

Then he walked toward the trees and faded into the forest.

CHAPTER TWELVE

I kept that vision of Mark Twain recorded in my head and buried in my heart. I never told anyone, not even Elton who had recounted similarly strange things happening at the Indian fountain including visits from ghosts bringing messages. This scenario was so unbelievable that even he—with his creative, artistic outlook and beliefs in the supernatural—might think that I had completely lost my mind. Elton had always supported me so fervently whenever I needed to talk, so I tried to reciprocate by standing by him whenever bullies at school called him names.

"I am so glad you moved in, Del," he once told me as we were walking to the Indian fountain. "You are the best friend that I have ever had." My heart broke for him, so I tried to live up to his words and spend time with him whenever I could.

He could be annoying sometimes when he acted a little too smarty pants or asked questions about Jim Dandy, but I realized that I should be patient with him. I also realized that Jim Dandy's personality wasn't my fault, although when in high school, a parents' reputation becomes your own sometimes. Being the next door neighbor, he did get glimpses of the dysfunctional dynamic. With an air of superiority, like he was chosen to be privy to my secret dysfunctional world, he would say things like, "Is Jim Dandy in one of those moods again?"

I would brush it off with something like, "Oh, he's okay. He just gets a little grouchy sometimes." Elton would persist with a comment like, "It's more than just grouchiness, Del. He is a mean person." I knew he was right, but it is difficult when someone comments on your parent and defending them—to save your own face—is difficult.

To his credit, Elton never disclosed what he saw or sensed at the dark house to anyone at school. For that, I appreciated him, even though Jim Dandy got into a yelling match with his much-older disabled father over Elton's dog walking on our property, and the police came out. Miraculously, like Jim Dandy can magically do, the police left without filing a report.

Elton became invested so soon into our lives with Jim Dandy, and got swept up into our problems, and it was overwhelming, I'm sure. He witnessed Jim Dandy in his usual form; I didn't want to be pitied or the source of someone's worry, so I kept up my happy act with the fence secured around my heart, even with Elton. Even though it was a house made out of Popsicle sticks, it was my life and I wanted to control the appearance.

Elton was a great friend at home, but it was in my junior year at Western Star High School and I needed female friends with whom I could pretend to enjoy high school. Jessica and Alana were equally in the misfit club like Elton and me. Jessica's mother had died the same day that Sandra Day O'Connor took the oath as justice as the first woman of the Supreme Court of the United States. I remember seeing her hand on that Bible on that very same day; I cheered her on and felt this wave of newness coming in for women. When I later learned of the timing coincidence with Jessica's mom, I felt guilt that I was celebrating a woman rising star while Jessica's star was being shot down.

Because her mom had died, Jessica lived with her affluent, well-groomed, elegant maternal grandparents who owned a company that manufactured plastic shipping containers. They were, as I saw it, wealthy. Both her grandma and her grandpa drove brand new Cadillacs, and they ate out every weekend at top restaurants. Jessica had inherited her mom's new Camaro, she wore Chanel perfume, and purchased all new clothes at either Higbee's or The Limited. Everyone thought Jessica was spoiled, so she kept to herself. I decided that junior year that I was coming in with a blazing saddle, unconcerned about her reputation, and I decided that we had at least an interest in clothes and fashion in common. I figured out that she lacked confidence, and the other girls thought she was stuck up. Her parents had divorced when she was in kindergarten, and her father had remarried a stereotypical Southern Belle in Tennessee and had two sons. Though he visited only a couple times a year, he threw money at Jessica to make up for his absence. Money was coming from all directions in her life. Her mom had a corporate, jet-set lifestyle and traveled all the time before she died. Jessica's center of gravity was, and always had been, her grandparents. But I soon witnessed, money, with all its privileges and power, didn't buy happiness or security.

My other friend, Alana, was the only black girl in our white-bred, suburban high school. Her father, who was a few inches shorter than her mother, was a doctor. Her parents were the opposite of mine and Jessica's: they hovered and worried about Alana assimilating into suburbia. I related to Jessica and Alana because they had aspirations to get somewhere in life, and although my life with Jim Dandy was far from ideal, I understood how to get where I wanted to go, and they did as well. This set us apart from some of the girls who set their sights on getting a guy, getting married, getting pregnant, thus finding the quickest route out of working or studying.

In addition to Alana, Jessica, and Elton, I had my own life about thirty hours a week at King Arthur's Round Table, and with my job, I could assimilate into a well-to-do suburban girl appearance, even though it was as fake as that orange suntan lotion out of a tube, but it meant something. We tried to go to Pizza Hut or Chi Chi's once a month or so.

To preserve all of this and to escape Jim Dandy, although I did enjoy my friends, I was a good employee and Mr. Camparti gave me all the hours I needed because I worked hard and the customers, it appeared, also liked my smile and jokes as I always refreshed their coffee cups, brought extra ketchup, and set up the highchairs for babies without being asked. I worked tirelessly to keep that job, even though the robbery case wasn't closed, and Jim Dandy's name kept swirling around like the dirt from the stockroom floor. He had found a way to bring embarrassment to my new life in Western Star and would continue to do so, it appeared, wherever he went.

In Mrs. Tetley's class we were studying the Salem witch trials, and I teared up when innocent and intelligent Rebecca Nurse was hanged. It affected me profoundly, and the Arthur Miller play opened my mind to the judgmental thinking of Jim Dandy's Mega Church of the Salvation. He didn't' attend, but he dictated our attendance every Sunday. I remembered Sunday school teachers making me feel ashamed because my hand-me-down dress made me "look like a hussy."

"Some girls in this room are encouraging lust by the boys," the teacher proclaimed, looking down at my exposed shoulders. I was ten years old, and *seductive* was tallied into my word journal. Another time, the minister made a surprise visit— I call it an attack— to our house on Eclipse Avenue and discovered Kathie and me listening to music on my Mickey Mouse record player while we were doing homework on the porch. The minister proclaimed to Jim Dandy that "Mr. Fleetwood Mac was a Satan worshipper," not even realizing that Fleetwood Mac was not a person but a group of people. I quickly came up with an excuse that I wasn't feeling well, and told Kathie she needed to take Andy's *Rumours* back home. I didn't want it to end up like *Elton John's Greatest Hits*.

The Mega Church of the Salvation was originally built for the hard scramble rubber workers and their need for fundamental beliefs that they find a home in heaven in the afterlife. Gleaning some sense of peace and spirituality despite the strict interpretation of the Bible, it was at least a place of sanctity. Jim Dandy, with this rigidity and righteousness that was taken dangerously too far, held himself out to the world as "born again" and snubbed his nose at anyone who didn't attend The Mega Church of the Salvation. He called it "the only real church in the world." Some people were fooled by his piousness; other people, like Grandma Delanie and Andy I suppose, saw right through him. "I can read him like a book, although he himself does not read books," I remember her often saying. "He's a lazy man, even though he is supposed to be a genius, who picks on people and animals who are smaller and less powerful than him." How she knew this, without my being allowed to speak about it, I will never know.

That summer, like someone was watching over me, I was allowed to attend church with Grandma Delanie. It would prove to be one of the greatest blessings of my life, and you will soon understand why.

She'd pick me up in her sparkling new blue boat Mercury Marquis, and then when I got my driver's license, I would drive us to the Victory Chapel. It was a small, wooden, peeling white paint church with a New England steeple. The people there demonstrated spirituality and, I felt, really connected with God. Sometimes, in the enveloping of the dark house, I wasn't always sure if my prayers were heard because Jim Dandy was still there, but I continued to broadcast them to the Universe just in case. I always made sure to thank God for the special people in my life, making sure to omit Jim Dandy's name on my list. I wasn't thankful for him in any way, and I always made that clear to God.

About this time in my spiritual journey, Jim Dandy was becoming proficient in a new torture technique: he would enter our rooms in the middle of the night, yank us out of bed by one foot, and start beating us in the dark, asking us why we had committed some foggy crime, while sleep and darkness confounded our confusion.

"Why'd ya do it?" Vague questions, in the dark, while the victim was asleep, were his attack plan.

"What did I do?" we would ask, heart pounding us awake, terrified.

"Left on the garage light! Probably cost fifty cents," he screamed.

On one particular night when I was the victim, I was blinking my eyes into focus, but still not seeing in the darkness. "I'm sorry!" I bellowed. "I was asleep! You scared me!" My eyes— when they could finally focus— revealed the devil himself, spoken of so often in the Mega Church of the Salvation, incarnate with his pitchfork belt hissing back and forth and fire consuming his black soul.

I kept blinking to make the image disappear. "Tell me not buying that shirt for school. Looky here and say it." Again: unrelated things, changing topics, in the middle of sleep, in darkness. Fire surrounded his soul. The words made no sense. There was no context for this intrusion into peaceful sleep. What was I supposed to say and why? He was there, hovering, and this session would continue until I repeated whatever nonsensical words—however unrelated and incoherent—until he got bored and felt like he had gained power.

"I won't buy the t-shirt! I won't buy the t-shirt!"

"Do you know why you can't buy the t-shirt?" he'd say, still thrashing the belt.

"No. Why? Tell me!"

"Don't have no money for no stinkin' t-shirt. I have a club foot! Hear me?"

"Yes! Yes! I won't buy the t-shirt. I won't buy the t-shirt! I won't buy the t-shirt!" I screamed it louder each time I repeated it. I wanted to call him Satan.

"Yes or no? You said 'yes.' Do you mean 'no'? Bettered not see you in no t-shirt!" he roared.

"No, then. No. I mean 'no!'"

"Are you telling me 'no'?" The game would continue until I was utterly confused.

He would leave sometimes. Sometimes Mom would beg to make him stop and she'd cry. Sometimes she would pile on. Sometimes, from mere exhaustion, she'd sleep through it.

It was darkness.

He had nothing to accomplish the next day. He did not have to go to work, he had lost another electrical contract, but he had the power to interrupt our sleep— our peaceful sleep— our escape from this living hell that he had created and beat the victim of his choice for no reason. He got away with irrational behavior and nobody ever called him on the carpet for it. The police never came. He never went to jail. He never felt guilt. He never apologized. His life was one entitlement after another.

I think the incident was spawned when he heard me on the phone with Alana, talking about the t-shirts we were getting for French Club. I don't know if he knew anything about Alana, because race was another sore subject. In my opinion, he was a sick racist. At least this time he didn't start beating me while I was on the phone with her. That had happened before while talking to a friend about an algebra test—he disagreed with the formula we were using— and trying to get off the phone with dignity while you are being beaten can be quite a challenge.

He would sleep all day—any time that he wanted to sleep. He sat there and wallowed in his own stink, eating all the food that we had in the house, watching one TV show after another, yanking us out of our beds at night by the foot, and beating us for absolutely no reason.

He could do that. It was power.

I heard the foot stomping back: a double whammy was very rare. I lay there quietly and waited to see what would happen next. The thumps came into my room. "You're taking drugs," he screamed at me. "I know you are taking drugs!"

This statement made no sense at all. Drugs make you lazy, right? They make you a loser, like, like, him. But I had to keep my mouth shut. What is the right response to this inane statement? If I disagreed, he might get out the belt again. If I agreed, the same could happen. I was damned either way. So I uttered nothing and allowed my poor heart to pound while the blood coursed through my ears.

"You are taking drugs!" he barked.

"No, I am not taking drugs," I finally responded. "I'm not taking drugs. I am an honor student. I work thirty hours a week. I take care of Jimmy and Justin. I am not taking drugs!"

I wanted to tell him how much I hated him. I wanted to tell him that I would never say a prayer to thank God for him. I wanted to tell him that drugs make people losers, like him, but I knew better. I didn't say another word. I waited for his cue. I remained silent.

"You bettered stay away from that nigger," he whispered. Oh, so that is what this is about...I didn't know what to say. I didn't know if I should agree, disagree, lie, or pretend: I was at a loss. "Do you hear me? Bettered stay away from that nigger." I hated it when he used the word *better* as a verb. I hated the word *nigger* even more. He didn't have much of a vocabulary, and he couldn't read, but his book of fear tactics was always open.

"Yes, I heard you. Okay," I finally uttered humbly. "Okay. Please, I need to sleep. I have a big test tomorrow and I have to work. Please, let me sleep."

Amazingly, he left and I felt this strange sick love for him because he didn't attack again. This was sick love and I knew it was sick, but as justification, I dreamed, in my now twisted mind, that he fell down the steps, hit his head on the hard floor, and he died instantly. There was his twisted leg and that damned club foot sticking out like the Wicked Witch's foot in *The Wizard of Oz*. In this dream, I got out of bed and danced, circled around his dead body with Jimmy, Justin, Ronald Reagan wearing a King Arthur's Round Table apron, and Mom, while listening to Fleetwood Mac's *Rumours*; I was wearing that "hussy" sundress when I was lifted to the sky, seeing the green grass and feeling the warmth of sun as I lifted up and saw him shrink into a ball of clay.

That next morning in real life, I woke up feeling nauseated and sore. I had black and blue marks all over my arms and legs proving that the attack was real. Even though it was May, I wore long sleeves to hide the marks on my arms, so another guidance counselor would not see them, like that gym teacher in Akron had seen, and we would have to move again. I wasn't really protecting him; I was protecting me. And we were happy in Western Star.

Alana, not having a clue about the darkness, was waiting for me when I got off the bus that morning. "Why the long sleeved-shirt?" she asked, always interested in fashion and clothes.

"I was just freezing this morning," I lied, looking away from her quizzical eyes.

"It's like eighty-five degrees," she joked. "We don't have air conditioning in the school," she said plainly. "Did you have air conditioning at your old school in Akron?"

"No," I said.

If you only knew, Alana, if you only knew, I thought. Why bring you into the dark house? You have your own issues to deal with –a world apart from mine—being the only black girl at our school, with over-protective parents who dote on you. Beautiful, smart, and so kind: This world ruins the sensitive and sensible.

"You're going to burn up," she reiterated.

Jessica joined us as we walked to our lockers. She had that pile of short black hair stacked on her head. The three of us, we helped each other feel less alone in the halls of that crowded suburban high school where secrets were so often buried under Jordache jeans, Frye boots, and Love's Baby Soft perfume. The popular kids, consumed with their own insignificant yet seemingly important presentation to the world, made loud conversations about all the things they did the night before. We were quietly there for each other, standing by the locker, talking about last night's French homework, making it appear and maybe believing that we, although scared and insecure, had something to offer the world.

"Have your dads started the college drill yet?" Alana asked both of us. She was not condescending. She was really her, living through the eyes of her parents, just like I was.

"Not yet," Jessica piped in, spraying more hairspray on that pile of hair. "I'm sure it will come. It is all about going to college and joining a sorority so I can meet a successful man. My dad is flying in from Tennessee tomorrow night, and he wants to take me shopping. I never like the same clothes that he does! It's such a pain!"

"Well, my dad is shopping colleges," Alana announced, rolling her head back and waving her hand across her face. "Grades, honor roll, the ladder of success, that's all I ever hear." I started floating high above them, where I was watching a movie of us, Western Star High School, circa 1981: we were trying to make our way in a confusing and competitive world. For that twinkling moment, suspended on dreams of what-could-be, and what would-be, we were safe and together and I was grateful for them.

I did try to relate, but I was truly there alone. Jessica wasn't arrogant either, as some other girls thought. She really did try, but they didn't see her struggles. This was a real problem for her. Her dad wanted to buy her the designer clothes, so she could meet a rich fraternity boy and find comfort in his job as an accountant. Alana's dad wanted her to go to Harvard, so she could become the first black female president of a major corporation or of the United States. Her problem was a racial one. Jim Dandy, on the other hand, awoke me in the middle of the night and beat me senseless about a t-shirt, my algebra formula, or some weird, delusional infiltration of his mind.

But Jessica and Alana were there for me. I thanked God for them. They were the light from the darkness; they kept me from sitting alone at those inane, never-ending pep assemblies or from eating lunch by the trash can in the lunchroom. They took my mind out of the dark house and welcomed me into the normalcy of their illuminated lives.

These things were so important in high school, and I was happy to pretend that my life was just like theirs, and we would all live happily ever after.

CHAPTER THIRTEEN

Wonderful, flowing, winding, winded, woeful, soulful words were becoming my life. My word journal, starting with lovely and certainly back in Mrs. Jefferson's class, had grown into stacks and stacks of handwritten journals, and I was taking Mark Twain's advice: I was writing. "Let it be your raft," he had proclaimed. It was my raft. It was my life-raft. I had read The Adventures of Huckleberry Finn that year in Mrs. Tetley's class, and I understood his metaphor. Huck and Jim used the raft to get away from *civilization* and I too needed "a raft" to get away from the dark house.

I found it amazing that someone had seen fit to collect all these ideas, written by diverse people from all different eras and places, and combine them into one book and call it an anthology. Of course, I would never admit my love for it to my classmates, but as cornball as it sounded, I got to experience all those places and meet all those people for free. This heavy book with graffiti in the margins about lost loves, made me thankful that I was born an American in 1964.

Similarly, just like the writings were preserved for us to read and discuss, I had so much to say about these things. I couldn't wait to get the words on paper, though I often struggled for direction, because that ragged tinge of anger often took over my thoughts. One day, I was just confounded with my sheer confusing thoughts for Jim Dandy, when I opened a journal at the Indian fountain and words to a story spilled out on the paper. They flowed like water, like Niagara Falls; without thinking, I jotted this title, *Living in a Dark House*, at the top of the page. I don't know where it came from, but I had opened a vein, like Mark Twain had promised, and I was becoming a writer.

Books, this book, and school were safe havens for me and many people before, I'm sure. In these things, I couldn't be hurt or humiliated. I could think what I wanted to think –and occasionally Mrs. Tetley thought that my thoughts were pretty thoughtful. She always asked for my ideas in our discussions, and she often praised my interpretations. She made me feel like I was worthy of her time. I could feel my blood come to my cheeks, and the hair on my arms stood up because I felt passionate about these ideas and stories. These signs had meaning; God, I felt, was giving me a nod to head in this direction.

Characters were engaging. I loved and hated them. I could meet them and then put them away when I needed to do something else. I could totally immerse myself into their worlds, understand or disagree with their reasoning, deal with their problems, and nobody was going to leap out of the page, pull off a belt, and start beating me into submission. Nobody in ink was going to force me to say something that I didn't believe or understand. I could make my own judgments. I was free on those pages, if only temporarily.

Like Eliza Doolittle, I longed to talk like Mrs. Tetley someday. My heart exploded in the need to someday stand up, talk without stuttering, and make people ponder. I longed to use words in my notebook. Someday, I thought, I want to be paid to be smart. I drifted away from the English classroom to words Jim Dandy often remarked to me, "Think someone gonna pay you good money to read stupid books?" I wished I could see the future. I wanted to get in his face, push him to the ground, and scream, "Of course someone will pay me to be smart one day—unlike you, you loser!"

So, one day, after worrying and worrying about my prospects for the future, I got up enough nerve and decided to talk to Mrs. Tetley about my dream of being a writer.

"Think practical—like teaching," she advised me. "You are a hard worker, Delanie. You could definitely teach. Teach English. Writing is a tough field to break into without a job to pay the bills. Get a teaching degree and try writing on the side."

When I got home from school that day, I decided to tell Justin my plan. "Don't tell anyone," I made him promise. "Don't tell anyone. It will never come true if people know." Jim Dandy would shoot it down and make fun of me: Words on paper were impractical. They didn't make money. My world wasn't soft, true, honest, pondering, or precise; my world was unpredictable, dirt, concrete, bricks, and belts.

"Del, you can do whatever you want," Justin said encouragingly. "I think you would be a good teacher, and Mrs. Tetley is right. You need a job while you are writing. Are you going to write this?"

"How did you know?" We laughed because he had read my mind.

"Mrs. Tetley said to write what you know. This is what I know," I professed.

"You have it figured out. But I don't know what I'm going to do," Justin said as he was slapping pasty government-issued peanut butter onto a slice of white bread for dinner. "I don't want to be like him that much I know."

We differed on a few dreams. I wanted the family I didn't have. As a male, Justin confessed that he was afraid of his inner unchecked demons. "Justin, you are over-thinking things," I said. "You are different than Jim Dandy. You are a gentle person."

In addition to being the only person in our family with brown eyes, Justin was different in other ways. He wasn't like Jim Dandy that I could see. He nurtures people. He loves music with his whole heart. He is more graceful in his movements. He is easy to talk to, and I guess that was the best characteristic of all.

"Thanks, Del, but I don't know yet," he said. "But I do worry about Jimmy. Do you know what happened to him at the football game the other night when you were working?"

"No. What happened?"

"Jim Dandy went to the football game. He screamed at a student working at the concession stand to get him more popcorn. The girl started crying, I think she is in your class, and the parents had to tell him they would call the police."

"Did he leave?"

"He finally did, Del. They were afraid of him. He kept saying he couldn't play football because of his damned club foot. I'm so sick of hearing about that foot!"

"Didn't somebody tell him to stop or yell at him?"

"I didn't want to be seen with him, but what could I do? I was there."

"Oh, my God, Justin! That's terrible!"

"Justin, isn't there a policeman who usually walks around? Why didn't he do anything? Who gets away with that?"

"Well, he gets away with it. He gets away with everything. Because nothing happened. Nothing ever happens."

"Did Jimmy play well?"

"Yea, he played, but not very well, and Jim Dandy beat the crap outta him when he got home. I hate him, Del."

"I do too. We need to talk to Jimmy."

"He's out on his moped. He has been very mean himself, Del. He is stressed. He catches frogs and throws bricks on them. I hate it when he does stuff like that."

"I know. I try to stop him, but he has this mean streak. How does Jim Dandy get away with this stuff, Justin? Why doesn't he ever pay the price for the things that he does?"

"I know. Why does Mom stay married to him? She's too good for him. We're all too good for this."

"We would all be better if he would just go away? You know?"
Go away meant die.

Thinking of my promise to Mark Twain, I wrote in my notebook that night: We were the battered tugboats, trying to cover up the holes and scratches as best as we could with smiles, jokes, jobs at fast food restaurants, and practiced grammatically correct language. The yachters, the rich kids with educated and kind parents, flaunt their beautiful crisp cruise ships—white and pristine, elegant on turquoise and tranquil seas—wearing perfectly matched clothing, purchased from prestigious little boutiques from the marina. Jimmy, Justin, and I, we would be the ones trying and scuffling along, clawing to stay afloat in ragged clothing, rowing with one oar, against rough waters, searching to find the lighthouse in the darkness.

CHAPTER FOURTEEN

Drowning in a sea of people in the auditorium at Western Star High School, it was National Honor Society induction day.

"I guess I'll be going up on the stage," laughed Jon Donovan, a cook at King Arthur's Round Table and my latest crush, as we bumped into each other in the crowd. His parents waved right on cue as Jon and I saw them in the stands. "They're so annoying," he said. "They were in a panic last night making sure that they had just the right clothes to wear. Now I know why."

"That must get on your nerves," I acquiesced, rolling my eyes, trying to act like I agreed, but secret jealousy filled my heart.

I realized that my old brown corduroy pants were too short for even my short legs, when I heard "Congratulations Delanie Dane," over the speaker. Then I heard my name again with a little urgency.

Being called alphabetically, only a few students were already on stage. I accepted my rose and pin, walked up the steps alone, and wished I could crawl under the curtain and hide. I kept my head up, pulled on the legs of my corduroys to make them as long as possible, I smiled shakily, feeling a thousand years old. I was a terrified girl thrust onto a stage where I didn't really belong. Some kids only had one parent there with them or three including a grandparent. I had the same feeling I get in those dreams when I arrive at school without any clothes. But just in time, Mrs. Tetley came up on the stage and stood beside me. She brought warmth and comfort, but still I was exposed to be a fraud; my life was now open for others to view as I rattled and shook on display like the Tin Man in *The Wizard of Oz*. I chuckled at my urge to yell "Oil can!" and run off the stage.

"Congratulations, Delanie," she said proudly, like she was supposed to be there, and she put her arm around my shoulder. "Aren't you surprised?"

I couldn't even muster a complete sentence to utter. "Yes," I managed to blink back tears. I was shaking so completely, I couldn't get my mouth to work. Then I tried to offer more, but only got out, "T-t-thank you for standing here with me."

"I know that some parents have conflicts in their schedules," she explained. "I think that was what we heard from your mother."

"Oh," I was swimming for more words to put out there, but I could muster nothing else. The number of words were an inaccurate measurement of the gratitude that I felt for her, but I couldn't express it at that occasion. The word *oh* would have to do for right now, as I tried to surface for oxygen.

After the ceremony, the new inductees were ushered to Jessica's grandparents' house where we swam luxuriously in wall-to-wall white foamy carpeting. We walked around softly, most of us had removed our shoes, and talked politely about "climbing the ladder of success" while her grandmother put out little snacky things that I learned were called hors d'oeuvres, a word we had learned in French class. Her grandpa, sophisticated in a navy blue suit jacket with gold buttons, mingled, arms outstretched to the parents, kids, and teachers.

"This is Delanie Dane," he offered to Jon's parents who then promptly acknowledged already knowing me. "She has been such a joy to our Jessica." I was? Well, his words made me feel happy and I should have felt included, but instead I felt like that proverbial fish out of water. I couldn't breathe the abundant and smokeless air. I was afraid that I might trip and spill the red punch on the white carpeting, it was so thick—the carpeting that is—and I was such a klutz. Or I might stutter. Or I might run into the furniture and knock over a vase. I refused the punch and went into the bathroom and chugged water out of the spigot in private. I drank the cold water thirstily and then viewed myself staring back from the mirror. What was I doing there? I prayed that nobody would ask about my missing parents. I prayed that I could sneak away and go to work where I belonged, without an inquest. I just wanted to leave.

The sun was shining through the big picture window in the front room, illuminating me, this awkward teenage girl, talking to friends about surface-y things, feeling so out of place, so alone in that room full of people. There was Alana, who kept finding me in the crowd, dark-skinned with her dark-skinned parents in that well-lit room, looking so regal and beautiful. I was pale in comparison, ghostly, and scared. Her parents, I knew from her stories, were community volunteers, and her mom made quilts for the hospital to comfort patients. I hadn't officially met them because we never really had the occasion so meeting them today was inevitable and necessary. I had bit off all my fingernails in the interim, worried that Jim Dandy would find out somehow, someway, that I had spoken to and was friends with black people. Could he show up with punch and drench the white carpeting? Would he dare peer through the big picture window? Could he find me here and beat me in front of the National Honor Society and their parents? I just needed to leave while everything was still as it was.

"Del," Alana called from the buffet line as she filled her plate with fruit. "Finally, you have got to meet my parents. They've heard so much about you. They knew you would be here."

Maybe it worked out okay that my parents—at least Jim Dandy —didn't make the reception. I could meet Alana's parents and have a nice introduction without worrying about what he would say or do. He could not find out where Jessica's grandparents lived, I told myself, but it haunted my every movement.

"Oh, I know. I was hoping that I would finally meet them." Then I said something really stupid. "I saw them over there. They are so attractive." Of course, I picked out her parents. They were the only black people there. Would Alana notice that I just assumed the black people were her parents? Was my stupidity racism? My head began to swim even more, but I tried, I tried to contain myself, to stay on dry land, to forgive myself because she hadn't noticed, and when we were introduced, we shook hands so warmly, and they began friendly inquiries into my life and plans, "So Del, what are your college plans?"

I didn't have an answer for them because I could not attend college. How would I pay for it?

"They are such dorks," Alana joked right in front of them—in front of them. She made a joke. She made fun of them in front of their faces. I was amazed. They just laughed. "My dad went out and bought a new suit! Can you believe what a dork he is?"

"We care," her mother interjected. "Is it so bad that we care? We don't want to be out of place, honey."

"I think you look fabulous," I said, reaching for words, feeling glad that words were produced at all, feeling so proud of them for Alana.

They were watching us talk, and they smiled at us, so proud that their daughter, a member of the National Honor Society in a group of all white people, was headed for a bright future. I always wished that I could have done more; I just didn't know what or how I could have known them more, considering my circumstances.

I wished I would have had the words to tell them how I felt. I wished I would have told them that I was proud to know them and Alana. I wished that I could have relaxed and enjoyed that golden time.

Jon and his parents were laying out the college choices to Jessica's grandparents. Parents who guided their children's lives and tried to lift up their children. They were there like lighthouses, beaming out flashes of brilliance into the darkness. Boys like Jon, they didn't choose girls like me, whose fathers beat them at night. We were hidden in the lower social order, cleaning up the mess, wearing long sleeves to cover up bruises, wiping down the counter.

But strangely enough, our worlds collided at King Arthur's Round Table, a place where he worked, not out of necessity but to understand "the working world," he had explained. With his educated parents and their high hopes for him, they would take one look at Jim Dandy, inhabiting and sustaining that dark house, see my eyes hiding something and my long sleeves on hot summer days, and they would usher Jon away from me. "Her father doesn't work," they would whisper. "The apple doesn't fall far from the tree."

I'd like to know what his life is like, I thought. I'd like to have just a chance with a boy of that caliber: a boy with upbringing, as Grandma Delanie called it, who was well-bred. I'd shoot an apple through that theory, but for now, I have my dreams, my books, my writing, my brothers, my friends Alana and Jessica, and of course, my job. I had quite enough, thank God, to take me away from that place of turmoil and unneeded strife, that dark house.

I looked at the golden clock above the mantel on the gorgeous yellow stone fireplace anchoring the room, and realized that I had to walk home and find Jimmy so he could take me to work. I tried to savor one more instant in that house with the white carpeting, with parents ushering and nurturing, and sunlight filtering in; I was safe from his voice, his smell, his belt. It became a picture to me; I was not part of it, but instead I was a spectator as I watched these nice people eat hors d'oeuvres, sip red punch, and chat about their children's bright futures, and I started to float away. I was floating through the roof and over the neighborhood when I realized that I could do this. I could do this: Someday, I thought, someday I'll have a house with lots of light and white carpeting.

Maybe I'll with even serve red punch but definitely, absolutely, for sure, no Jim Dandy and no punching.

I managed to leave the luncheon on foot out the kitchen door, pardoning myself with the excuse that I had an appointment nearby, and that I could easily walk there. After I turned down several offers for rides, I went through the park, and I allowed a reverie to elevate my spirit. I staged a scene in my mind where Jon came to my rescue, proclaimed his love for me, and we talked for hours about things that mattered to us because we were happy.

In this fantasy, he discovered that I am smart, and that I want to be successful, and that I am nothing like Jim Dandy. I became a teacher and a successful writer and we had a big, bright house although he laughs at me because I am a little cornball protective about love, writing, literature, and of course animals. "The apple does fall far from the tree," he said to me, and we laughed because I was so far away from that Jim Dandy. I shot that original apple off his head with my arrow. His parents accepted me, and they remarked how I was so good for Jon, so grounded in reality with feet firmly planted. I walked and talked among them, and they, in turn, accepted and loved me. I didn't stutter around them. I didn't trip on things. I didn't spill the red punch. We lived happily ever after.

"Oh, Lord," I uttered aloud, a little startled by my own voice breaking out of the reverie into real life realness of a park bench angled under a giant oak tree. "I'll never be able to be normal. I'll never get away from the dark house."

"Yes, you will!" a man shouted loudly to a woman about twenty feet away from me, seated on that park bench. He was standing in front of her, cuddling a white puppy.

They hadn't even noticed me.

"It will happen?" she was holding a book and was looking directly at him.

"Certainly, it will happen. Just give it time. It will happen. I promise!" he replied, unaware that my dream had coincided so well with their already-in-progress affirmation of something lovely.

I took it as a sign. I nodded to the heavens above as tears welled in my eyes, and I adjusted my thinking. Miracles can happen.

Kathie's kind, soft voice guided me as I continued the walk home. I could hear her saying goodbye to me last summer. We were standing in the middle of Eclipse Avenue. Wearing the banned from school Tom Petty & the Heartbreakers t-shirt, her hair was in golden curls around her face. My life had changed so much in that one year. Walking often brought her back to me because we accumulated so many miles walking to and from elementary school—every single day through sunshine, but also wind, rain, sleet, and snow. We had recorded songs from Andy's cassette recorder, danced disco at the skating rink, and exchanged homemade Christmas and birthday presents. Being across-the-street neighbors, I always felt so lucky that she existed—with Andy —and it proved to me that Somebody Somewhere had a plan because for those years, the dark house faded into the distance when Kathie and Andy were nearby. My path had changed that year, but together, we had created worlds fanciful.

We possessed so few material things, but we had a stockroom overstuffed with joy. We colored magenta and hot pink birthday cards with the leftover Crayola sixty-fours. We spread our Malibu Barbies on the lawn and made miniature pieces of furniture for our Barbies out of cereal boxes. We discovered and then bartered this sparkly pink rock that Joe identified as quartzite. We never surrendered to dismay or desiring of what we couldn't have. We were the richest people in the world in those golden pink summer days, and nothing, nothing—not even Jim Dandy—could darken our times together.

Not only did we see the exquisiteness of life around us, but we witnessed the progression of popular music on FM radio in the late 1970s with *Casey Kasem's Top 40 Hits*: The Eagles described how there was still room in some hotel in California while Stevie Nicks, just starting out with Fleetwood Mac, warned us to not to break "The Chain." Jackson Browne was talking about pretending. Linda Ronstadt opined about fishing boats, while Hall & Oates tried to put it back together, but the solitary toothbrush still hung there, and She was Gone. The cache of vinyl on Andy's turntable was always ready to spin: Barbra Streisand reminded us about "The Way We Were," Donna Summer described a "Last Dance," and Barry Manilow crooned about some girl named Mandy.

The aroma of Rizzi's Pizza, with those swimming pool pepperonis full of hot grease, always lingered and filled our olfactory senses in the humid summer air, and it mingled with gray plumes that were the fumes of the city buses, making regular stops at the beer joints across the field. In those last days of elementary school, all three colors of lilacs, deep violet, lavender, and white, with their innocent perfume, could be found in May on the way to and from Thomas Edison Elementary School. The nasty chemical—yet fastidious and organized—smell of fertilizer on Joe's lawn always signaled the beginning of summer: liberation from the routine of school. It meant playing outdoors all the long, light, eternal summer days with Kathie. Always lingering back there in my mind, balancing that quiet stillness of warm air, was that tap dance out onto the unknown dance floor of full-time life with Jim Dandy who may or may not be going to work the next day.

Akron, Ohio, was progressive in the 1970s with the Goodyear blimp hovering and humming overhead, casting a giant, friendly, and pungent shadow; the smell of rubber permeating the air; and that industrious soot settling on the cars parked along Eclipse Avenue. People were busy, and they didn't mind two little girls dancing through their yards or rolling down the embankment that sloped to the devil strip. We took expeditions to the falling down, vacated house with the unfortunate address of 1313. We cruised our bikes to the train tracks and counted railroad cars—waving to the man in the caboose. We scrounged food from our plates for lonely, skinny, flea-infested dogs tied out at doghouses. We stopped at the floral shop where Kathie's Sunday school teacher was making floral arrangements or wreaths for soldiers who had died—too young—in Vietnam. We bought five pieces of penny candy—with our nickels—out of the bin at Ed's Market, savoring Tootsie Rolls and Bazooka bubble gum.

Sometimes, on our backs on Mr. Swanson's hill, we looked up at the puffy clouds contrasting the royal blue sky and tried to make sense of our dreams from the night before or the days to come. Only Kathie knew of my dream to become a writer, and she steadfastly kept my secrets. We never spoke of the darkness, staying always in the light. Our relationship always had this trueness to it. We believed in each other. She encouraged me, and I encouraged her. We didn't compete for love, clothes, or popularity. We were on the same plane, all the time, every day. It was magic.

"We would stay close," we promised as I was putting a kitchen chair into the bed of the truck, so we could move to a new dark house in Western Star. "We will talk every day, and write. Things will never change."

As I was deep in this reverie from just last summer and how it proved to be untrue, reality struck as I arrived at the back door of the dark house, where I ran upstairs, changed into my uniform, and called for Jimmy to get his moped ready to take me to work.

It was peaceful for just one moment at the dark house.

CHAPTER FIFTEEN

"Picking up from work!" I heard Jim Dandy yelling into the phone receiver as I was descending the stairs, pulling my hair into a ponytail. He slammed it down. More details about the robbery were emerging, and Jim Dandy was still getting questioned.

"Doesn't listen! Picking up from work!" he hollered, this time addressing me.

"Yea, I'll tell him," I said.

"You'd bettered tell him," he screamed. "Make him know it! Little nobody ain't gettin' in my face."

I had heard from Jon that the other parents who were in the parking lot on the night of the robbery were questioned and were dismissed from suspicion—except for Jim Dandy. The interrogations kept pointing to him, he acted so suspicious, and I carried an uncomfortable feeling in my soul that everyone knew that he was involved somehow, but then again, stress makes people believe the unbelievable. I thought I could read the facial expressions on other employees. I could imagine their parents talking about Jim Dandy when they got home: Were they asking about the robbery to their sons and daughters? Was the subject of dinner time conversation? My mind was racing.

He was not like other parents and that was obvious, maybe because of his upbringing. My Mississippi grandparents weren't exactly cultivated people, and supposedly Grandpa Dane had abused my grandmother as well. That was what Jim Dandy always saw and came to believe, I guess, was normal life. When we traveled to Broken Wheel, Mississippi, for Grandpa Dane's funeral in 1975, Jim Dandy wanted to show us his "birth house." It was a deserted, one-room, ramshackle house, out in the middle of a farm field. "This is it," he opened the door of the Caprice. "... borned right here."

"You were born here?" Mom asked, making sure there was no tinge of judgment in her voice. It was fortunate that Grandma Delanie wouldn't ever see this house; it would have provided more ammunition for her statements about Jim Dandy.

"Right here the old lady and Dad raised Billy and Bobby," he revealed, describing his brothers—my uncles—noticeably omitting Aunt Lizzy, the oldest of his siblings. We got out of the car. "...Goin' in to see what's left," he stated.

We hiked toward the dilapidated shack; the smoldering sun beating down on the heavy air that smelled of upturned soil. The house was overgrown with weeds and tall tree branches meandered around the perimeter. The Indian red clay loam of Mississippi exposed itself here and there under scrubs of overgrown grass patches as the mosquitoes made a buffet of my exposed arms and legs. "...where Lizzy slept," he demonstrated, pointing to a falling down and rusted chicken coop behind the house. "...never could behave, so Dad made her stay there."

Mom and I were awestruck and embarrassed for him, but he didn't feel it. Justin just stared straight ahead. Even Jimmy—with his endless questions—was silent. I looked at Mom, our eyes wide, and she looked at me, but we didn't utter a word, out of fear, out of shock.

This was a darker house.

He opened the door, ushered us all in, as a mouse scurried across the floor. "I'm okay with mice," I told Mom, "but I can't handle snakes!" We laughed at the corny joke to cut the tension by a few feet.

"...wonder if we could get that old pie-safe in the car?" Jim Dandy directed, pointing to an ornately carved, oak pie-safe, lassoed in spider webs, just left standing by a window with dusty dishes still stacked inside. "Them there are gettin' pretty big bucks at auctions," he announced. "And that one there is a real one, not a copy. It's worth some bucks."

"It is beautiful," I intoned with honesty, hoping he wouldn't believe for a second we could take the thing in the Caprice. I changed the subject: "Did you have electricity here, Dad?" I asked.

"No electricity, no phones....where I was borned: Right there on the floor," he pointed to a spot near one of only three windows in the place where a huge black spot could have been blood stains. "The old lady never made the hospital. Some guy from the hospital came out....made a birth certificate. Never had a first name. Just started callin' me Jim Dandy. The old lady and Dad argued and argued and couldn't make on a name. They just started callin' me Jim Dandy 'cause a jim dandy being borned."

"You were a baby when Grandpa came to Ohio, right?"

"Came first in `44, after Uncle Bob told him about the rubber factories," he recalled. "Good payin' jobs—union jobs— and everybody wanted 'em. Dad...a strong man. Wanted strong mountain guys so they came here on horseback passin' out papers gettin' workers. Left the farm for the fact'ry. Had to make a livin'. Uncle Bob, he went first to Ohio. The old lady come the next year. Packed up us kids and left. Didn't even lock the door." I looked at the door that was ajar and wondered if she were the last person to touch that knob.

"She was still pretty young then, wasn't she?" I asked, wanting to verify the family mystery of the huge almost twenty-year age gap between my grandparents.

"...borned in '23," he said, calculating with his math brain. "Dad was borned in, uh, 19-5."

I never really doubted Aunt Lizzy's stories or her declaration that Grandma Dane was just a child when her 34-year-old husband took her away from her alcoholic daddy. Aunt Lizzy had always struck me as true blue. Jim Dandy always rolled out the worst of his small vocabulary when he talked about Lizzy; he seemed to especially hate women who told the painful truth. Aunt Lizzy recalled once how Grandpa Dane sharpened sticks from gum trees with his pocket knife making switches or whips, and he used them on anyone, Grandma included with little Bobby on her back, for not picking cotton fast enough. Lizzy recounted that she took care of all three of the brothers in the sun in the cotton fields every summer. Once even little Bobby, as a baby, came back with "red stripes across his back from the switch."

So, meanness can be inherited. Jim Dandy had a role model in Grandpa Dane. The apple didn't fall far from that tree, but I wanted to roll and roll away from that poisoned, worm-infested orchard.

Great Uncle Bob, clean, white-collared shirt tucked into his pressed khaki dress pants, once told Mom about Mississippi at a family picnic in his twangy Southern accent. "I don't believe in laying a hand on a woman," he said. "It's not that I don't love 'im," he said. "He's my brother's boy and all, but you must be a saint to live with 'im for all these years."

She didn't reply as I watched her; I was ready to look away if need be, but she just stared ahead. What could a woman say to such a hard-hitting, yet embarrassing truth? So, she told me later that night that she liked Uncle Bob, but she didn't know how to take him. "He's a Southern gentleman," Mom uttered, tears welling in her eyes. "But your dad, he's just like his old man—beats his wife with a switch. I wonder if he ever threatened to kill her?"

So, in that same way, sensing insecurity and fear, like my Grandpa Dane got young Grandma Dane twenty years his junior, Jim Dandy swooped down and grabbed my insecure, but beautiful mother—maybe by the neck like a hawk takes a baby duck—and her life was ruined. He had told her that she had to stay. He would keep us kids. She was afraid of that possibility like all women, I suppose. I had heard him say that.

Grandma Delanie couldn't stop the boulder from rolling down the hill. Grandpa Delanie couldn't stop it. They tried. I had seen pictures of Mom, tall and thin, an Irish beauty with cat glasses, red curly hair, and dimples, with that cute fashion sense that she tried to pass on to me, holding his hand in photos with terror in her eyes. My father was good looking, and he must have made her weak in the knees—at least for just a passing hour—one time, but threats change our abilities to think and reason.

This is what he knew: He ruled absolutely and without question. He never took a disagreement or the word *no*. He liked to be around people that he felt were lower than him. I guess it was good for his ego. It wasn't unusual for Jim Dandy to bring these lowly people—who knows where he met them— around the dark house. For some reason, this particular scene kept replaying in my mind, and my intuition told me that it was connected to the robbery: about a week before the robbery took place, I came home from school and saw this creepy guy, wearing all black with grease wiped all over his pant legs, watch as Jim Dandy patched a tire on his junky, rusted Chevy Nova. His name was Chuck Swartz, and he made my skin crawl. He was chewing tobacco and spitting the juice onto the garage floor as he proudly described killing a deer with a butcher knife.

"Hey, who is this cutie coming up the driveway?" I heard him say to Jim Dandy. Then he whistled that Wooo Hooo thing that creepy guys do.

"That's my daughter, Chuck, and you'd bettered not look at her like that," Jim Dandy warned.

I was actually proud of Jim Dandy for the third time since he had helped me with multiplication tables back in fourth grade.

That occurrence stood out in my memory for two reasons: first, Jim Dandy was actually looking out for me and second, Jim Dandy was fixing this guy's flat tire. Jim Dandy never did anything for anyone unless he was rewarded with some measurable material or money. Someone could be dying of thirst in a desert with him holding a five-gallon bucket of water, and he wouldn't take a step in the direction to help. Changing this creep's tire rang so strange to me. The world was out of joint.

The next night at work, Mr. Camparti told me that the license plates on Chuck Swartz's Chevy Nova matched those of the car that were peeling out of the King Arthur'sparking lot the night of the robbery. The car fled to Romig Road and then onto I-76 where it was apprehended, after a high-speed chase, by the Akron police.

"Hey, Del," Mr. Camparti called as I pushed my time card into the time clock. "Stop in my office," he said. My heart started pounding like it always does when I have to speak to authority figures.

"The police apprehended a guy named Chuck Swartz," Mr. Camparti reported.

I swallowed and closed my eyes and held them shut. It made perfect sense. It finally fit together. "When the police questioned him, he said that some guy with a weird name like Dandy Do or something told him how the door worked," he said.

"Jim Dandy told him?" I believed the story. It was the missing piece of the puzzle.

"Jim Dandy—is his real name—he's your father?"

"Unfortunately, he is," I managed to choke out.

"Why would your father—well, Del, the police are probably going to question him. Did you know about—no, you couldn't. He robbed you."

"Chuck Swartz is not my kind of person, Mr. Camparti. Don't think that I am like that," I said, swimming in confusion.

"How did the police link him to the robbery?" I was hoping for a last glimmer of hope that it was a mistake.

"Well, his car was spotted in the parking lot the night of the robbery. One of the parents saw this beat-up Nova, remembered the first digits of the license plates, and it fit the description of a car that was pulled over on the highway for speeding; the timeframe fit the time of the robbery. Do you think he would rob you, even though he knows you?"

That was the connection. Of course, it was Chuck Swartz. He was ticked about my lack of interest in his comments to me, and creeps like him think about vengeance.

It was like I had seen a ghost. I couldn't put a sentence together. Everything I tried to utter was a stutter and I was utterly, utterly—for the first time in a long time—completely wordless.

CHAPTER SIXTEEN

Parked in the driveway that afternoon, when I got off the school bus, was a City of Akron police cruiser. I had brought Jim Dandy an old, salt-stained, black ball cap that Nancy had found on a seat of the bus. She offered it to me as a joke, not thinking that I would take it. I knew Jim Dandy would love it. It was free, and it would hold his thick hair out of his eyes.

"Give me a math problem," I heard him say to the police officer as I was closing the back door. "Any math problem. Can work it out in my head."

"That's not why I'm here Mr. Dane," the officer emphasized, shaking his head back and forth.

"Can't read, and still own this house and everything in it," he bragged as I was walking into the living room. He was pointing around the room at all the tattered objects that Mom and I had somewhat successfully arranged to look like *Country Living* magazine. He conveniently pointed to Grandma Delanie's hand-me-down gold and yellow, French Provincial sofa, an antique vase recently purchased at Goodwill for a quarter, and that oak pie-safe miraculously toted through a wind storm tied to the roof of the Caprice all the way from Mississippi to Ohio.

"Look at that couch there. Paid for. See that pie-safe? Oak. Pretty good for a guy in the mental retard class at school," he told the officer who was obviously there for another purpose. "I'm not a retarded. Just can't read. Can figure any math problem you give me. At the vocational school, Hatcher said I was the best math genius ever. Got tested, and it said I was a genius."

"That is good, Mr. Dane," the officer blinked, obviously annoyed, holding a clipboard. "I was just wondering if you know a Mr. Charles Swartz?"

"Chuck Swartz?" Jim Dandy echoed. "Now he is a mental retard."

"Well, he said that you helped him with a tire? He said you told him to rob King Arthur's. Is that true?" the officer asked.

"Didn't tell 'im that," Jim Dandy used that voice that kept rising. "Didn't tell him that, didn't tell him that, didn't tell him that!" he repeated, standing up, pointing down with his finger, almost like he was disco dancing. I tried not to laugh, because the developing scene was not meant to be funny. I was audience and this was my life, but it was entertaining. His performance, while well-acted and believable to only him, was good and intimidating to an outsider.

I padded quietly to the archway between the dining room and the living room, where Jim Dandy stood, legs apart. "Hello," I said in a louder-than-usual voice. I was breaking the tension for the poor officer.

"Delanie?" the police officer asked, and he seemed to be relieved, turned around but still looked at the clipboard and not me.

"Yes," I agreed, knowing full well what I had stepped into.

"How do you typically get home from work, Delanie?"

"I get a ride from my parents. I don't have a car yet." I didn't mention Jimmy and the moped thing; I was afraid it would get

Jimmy pulled into the situation. After all, Jimmy wasn't street legal.

"That's right," Jim Dandy concluded. "Needed a ride home. There to pick her up. I'm an electrical contractor."

"Delanie," Jim Dandy whistled for me to stand beside him, and I obeyed. "Tell the pig the truth. Tell him that I always pick you up from work. Tell him I'm an electrical contractor—best in the world."

"You know Chuck Swartz lies all the time?" I told the officer.

"True. He has a rap sheet a mile long," he replied.

"Right. He tried to come around here and flirt with me," I said. "So, he was ticked off when I told him to get lost. My dad here, he supported me, and Chuck was ticked."

"Oh, so there is a possible motive," the officer said.

"Right," I replied. "He is a real creep."

Then I turned to Jim Dandy. "Do you think you need a lawyer? Did he read you the Miranda rights?" The police officer looked up from his clipboard. He needed to know that I wasn't a stupid girl, that I could read, and that at least I wasn't in the "mental retard class."

"Do you think I need a lawyer?" Jim Dandy was now turning on me. I was trying to help him—to basically help myself.

I felt sorry for the police officer, but I also understood the predicament that I was in. Jim Dandy was so mean and so ignorant of the world. He was so unaware of how stupid he looked—and how obvious the story unfolded. He had to be involved: the officer knew it; I knew it; Mr. Camparti knew it; the other parents knew it, but he thought that he had everyone buffaloed. But the law, the fact that he didn't have a lawyer present, could work in his favor.

"Delanie, you have a point. He might need a lawyer. This line of questioning could be out of hand without his lawyer present," the officer acknowledged.

Jim Dandy gloated—and I hoped he would remain silent—for he could ruin the whole thing with a stupid or mean comment. Jim Dandy looked vaguely handsome, like he could when he had a reason.

He opened his ignorant mouth and stupidity rolled out. "Chuck Swartz hangs around here sometimes when he needs stuff. He hangs around here because he has the hots for her," Jim Dandy finally uttered, pointing his thumb at me. The officer looked at me as if I were some kind of slutty, low life girl who would be interested in someone like Chuck Swartz.

"I'm not interested in Chuck, that scumball," I interjected, supporting my dignity. "That is where the problem started, Officer."

The officer looked at me, then looked down. "I know that," he voiced, in a serious tone. I wasn't sure if he was condescending or sympathetic to my plight.

"Okay, Mr. Dane, that will be all for tonight. Your daughter is right. You might want to hire a lawyer," the officer warned, knowing that he took his questioning too far. The smell of the officer's clean cologne lingered in the air, covering the stale stench of cigarettes and Jim Dandy's unbathed body. I wasn't sure how he would take my interjection about the lawyer, but in my opinion, I had saved him from further questions at least for that night.

I watched the officer get in his car and knew that as long as he was within earshot, Jim Dandy would behave. But after his departure, I couldn't predict what would happen next, so I started to go upstairs.

"Why'd you just stand there 'n' let him accuse me?" he questioned, his heavy footsteps coming toward me. He is so ignorant—or just so insecure—that he couldn't see that I had turned the whole thing around for him.

"I didn't' just stand there. I told him that you needed to have a lawyer present. He can't question you like that without your lawyer. I was protecting you," I emphasized.

"You don't need to protect me," he screamed.

"Well, I thought..." I said.

"I don't need you to think. Doya hear me? I don't care what you think—at all."

Then he directly contradicted himself. "Think I was in cahoots with Chuck? Do you?"

"I don't think so," I lied. "The policeman went away, s-s-so I think you are okay. I th-th-think he thinks you're innocent."

"Who doya think you are—judgin' me?" he asked rhetorically. "Stand there and judgin' me. I'm payin' the bills around here. I'm makin' it go."

"I know," I didn't dare to say what I really thought.

"Think you're smarter 'n' me with your lawyer talk? Do ya really still think someone gonna pay ya to read 'n' write? Well, you'd bettered think again."

I thought just that, but I didn't dare to say it aloud.

"Think you can throw some big words around at the police, and they go away?"

There was nothing else to say. I did throw big words around, and it did make the officer go away. I did just that, but Jim Dandy, in his pathetic ignorance, didn't understand what had just occurred. My words, and their power, worked like magic. Wonderful words, and I was learning how to use them!

"What do you want me to say? Do you want me to tell you that I think you are innocent? okay: I think you are innocent. Do you want me to tell you that the officer was wrong? okay: the officer was wrong. What do you want me to say? I'm, I'm confused."

"You'd bettered get outta here! Now." He shoved me toward the back door. "Get outta here!" He slapped my face and ended with "you slut! Go get Chuck Swartz!"

I did get out of there. I took a walk and ended up at the Indian fountain. I thought about all the times that my reading and writing had saved him. I thought about all the letters from the State Department of Employment that I had read and explained to him. I remembered all the certified letters that arrived in the mail— lawsuits –and how I tried to coax him into replying intelligently, then in my eighth-grade handwriting, carefully wrote and re- wrote letters, compiling information and responses to interrogations about how he lost this job, what vulgarity he communicated to an employee, why he spit on his boss' desk, why he decided to outrun the police car. I would handwrite a response; he would then sign his name where I would show him, but the signature bore out a distinguished illiterate script to any well-schooled reader.

I would stay up at night—going over his worries, helping him, and he would then say something like, "Really think all this school crap is going somewhere? Who do you think you are—some brain, some book writer? You are a bitch just like Liz."

As the Indian fountain approached, I kept walking and walking and talking to myself, talking to God, talking to the trees. Jim Dandy is so angry with himself, his own ignorance yet his brilliance, I thought, and he is so frustrated, that he doesn't know what to do. Here I am, in the middle of this mess— totally innocent—trying to figure out what to do to save face, to save my own life, not necessarily to save him, and to save my job. I told the Indian fountain just how I felt.

It understood.

In the whisperings of the water and the freshness of the tall blue-green pines, I once again saw Mark Twain. This time he didn't speak. The light was breaking through the clouds, beaming down on the earth, and I was given hope. The clouds in my head were gone; I was able to think clearly. I was on the right path. I was perfectly fine and would be fine, a voice whispered to me.

"All the beatings," I told the Indian fountain, "all the heartache, all the suffering, how I wish I could know it to be true, that I will be a teacher someday, that I can leave the dark house." I wanted to know it for sure that I could be somebody someday. But Jim Dandy wasn't worth any more tears that would come with his negative statements. At that time, with the darkness enveloping every day, and the days getting shorter and the nights getting longer, I dreamed that my life would amount to something. I prayed to God that I could get away. I dreamed that I could get away, but with all I had seen, I wouldn't have placed a bet on it.

It was too tough.

It was too tough to get a leg up, and I had to laugh at my choice of that expression because, of course, I thought of Jim Dandy's stupid club foot. It was too tough to stay out of trouble. I knew the odds were stacked against me.

"Education," I told the Indian fountain, "education is measured in understanding, comfort, and confidence. I may only be in high school, but I know that education creates illumination; something that he could never understand."

~

A few weeks later, Chuck Swartz was indicted in the robbery, according to a brief article in the Akron *Beacon Journal* that said, in part, that "an unknown accomplice monitored Swartz's movements from the parking lot at Rolling Hills Mall." The article went on to state that although the accomplice had not been found, the investigation would continue. Great, I thought, this can of worms gets to keep squirming around. Worms that eat red, rosy apples. This apple wants to fall far from that tree.

Mr. Camparti, Jeff the dishwasher, a parent who was leaving as Chuck arrived in the ski mask, and I had to testify to the grand jury about the intrusion that night. One of the great mysteries: Jim Dandy was not subpoenaed. He skated, it appeared, with the one-hundred-eighty dollars and a few interrogations from the police.

The discovery of yet one more evil within him flabbergasted me.

CHAPTER SEVENTEEN

As the Jim Dandy situation started to fade to the drama of other teenage hirings and firings at King Arthur's , Christmas was approaching. The mall was busy; everyone was buying Christmas presents; and I was excited that I had money to buy gifts for Alana and Jessica.

I was afraid that Mr. Camparti might decide that it was too risky to keep me as an employee at King Arthur's Round Table—knowing Jim Dandy and his propensity for trouble—so I worked extra hard, staying late, working off the clock—whatever I could do to show my value. At that same time, I kept trying to avoid face to face contact with Mr. Camparti for that reason. I needed to keep this job. Other than school, it was my life.

One night after closing, Jeff, Jon, Sarah, and I were decorating the store Christmas tree. We each got to select a piece of pie from the dessert case, and we hummed along to the Christmas Muzak songs like "Sleigh Ride" and "We Wish You a Merry Christmas."

Mr. Camparti was on the ladder, placing garlands around an artificial Christmas tree. I looked up to talk to him and at that moment, the angel, perched atop the tree, fell. I caught it like a bride's bouquet. "A good omen," he said, showing his shiny teeth.

"It sort of has a missing eye," I shook my head that I caught since athletic abilities were missing in my genetic code. "But I guess from far away, nobody will notice."

"Yea," he said with a wink back. "I think that's why my wife donated it."

"Guys," he announced to everyone. "You all have been good employees, and I would like to thank you with these," he said as he handed us each a heavy foil bag containing a frozen turkey. We all thanked him, finished the tree, and dispersed our separate ways to the parking lot and our waiting rides.

"Del, I need you to stay just an extra minute," he asked.

"This is it," I thought, "I'm getting fired."

My head was swirling with worry. Where else could I get a job where I could take the school bus, eat free food, find fast friends, and get enough hours to buy myself a life? Instead, he offered me a job as a manager trainee—just like that.

"This position will require great commitment on your part, Del. It would be forty hours a week, at least," Mr. Camparti declared. "But it would give you the necessary independence to start your own life, get an apartment maybe, buy a car."

What about college? I would be able to be free of the dark house and have enough money for college, but maybe not enough time to actually attend the classes and study for tests.

"Take your time and sleep on your decision," he advised. "We'd like to have you, Del, and when you finish high school, we could see what is next."

I loved Mr. Camparti and really, I loved King Arthur's , but I wanted to be a teacher, specifically an English teacher, and I wanted to be a writer, and maybe go to law school someday. Offers like these don't come every day to everyone, and I really did appreciate the fact that my employer saw me as a conscientious worker—especially because of Jim Dandy's most recent behavior. I was torn.

It was the day before Christmas break. Nancy stopped the bus at the usual last mile away from the mall. "I feel terrible leaving you off here in the snow," she said with the bell on her Santa hat jingling over the blonde hair hanging down.

"No problem, Nancy." I disguised my voice to sound like a rubber factory worker on his way in to work. "I know you can't take me all the way there. I can walk...." She laughed, seemingly getting my imitation of a tough guy going to work.

She handed me a candy cane from the Halloween bucket beside her seat. "Well, kid, have a Merry Christmas," she yelled with her hands cupped around her mouth as I started walking toward the mall. I waved to Mr. Camparti as I walked into the dining room, a few minutes late due to the snow, the candy cane still sticking out of my mouth. I heard him talking about the sale on Christmas lights at Sears, as Jeff, Sarah, Jon, and a new guy were filing in to punch the time clock.

I was walking out front, tying my apron, when I saw Jim Dandy, out of the corner of my eye, swaggering up the serving line, and things began to move in slow motion. Jim Dandy was holding something. Strange, I thought, he could make it here right after school, and I had to walk here in the snow. But more importantly: What was why is here and what is he holding?

"We don't have no pan for this thing," he screamed, as he pulled the thawed turkey out of the foil bag. "I said, 'We don't have no pan for this thing!'" He began swinging the turkey –by one leg —around his head and kept repeating this statement, "We don't have no pan for this thing." He loved to keep repeating sentences that he perceived to be important to his cause of misery.

Mr. Camparti ended his talk with the customer and approached the front of the store, trying to intercept Jim Dandy. "What is going on, Mr. Dane?" Mr. Camparti said with that chuckle that usually calms people. Jon, putting on his orange chef hat, began scraping the grill while peeking over his shoulder.

"Ain't got no pan for this thing, so that bitch has to go out and spend money so we can cook it," Jim Dandy explained as if the situation made sense. In his mind, it did. "Turkey ain't free, if you gotta buy a pan!"

Jon looked at me with confusion on his face. I understood Jim Dandy's crazed perception: even gifts were subject to ridicule. Forget the fact that he never gave a gift, nor did he ever think of anyone but himself, but the fact that the turkey had to be cooked, and we didn't own a suitable pan was Mr. Camparti's fault.

"I'm sorry, Mr. Dane," Mr. Camparti began, using my last name yet again. "I'm sorry about that, but you will have to leave."

Please don't use the last name again, I was thinking. Maybe nobody heard the name in all the excitement. Maybe the employees will think Jim Dandy is just some crazy maniac from the mall. At the same time, I was once again searching to find that hole where I could crawl and disappear —one that was big enough for me to fit in. Maybe I could stay there forever, and nobody would know that I had ever existed. Maybe the floor would fall through to the foundation of the building, and I could just fall through with it.

Why me? Why here and now? Why can't he just drop dead? The turkey pieces were splattering all over the ceiling, the stucco walls, and the medieval chandeliers, and he continued to swing –and waste—the pathetic, disintegrating bird, the only hope we had of a meal for Christmas.

We could have borrowed a pan from someone, I thought in disgust. We could have at least eaten the now wasted thing. God knows, we need food, but he finds a way to get to the mall so he can destroy a well-intentioned gift of food, and at the same time, destroy my dignity as well as any sliver he had left.

"Get the hell outta here!" Mr. Camparti yelled, pointing to the exit to the mall. "Get outta here before I call the police again!" This statement told me that he had had enough of Jim Dandy and when people start thinking like this, they make connections. "You can leave now before security gets here."

"Not afraid of some rent-a-cop," Jim Dandy yelled. "Some little twerp carrying a little pistol. I have guns and those ain't guns. Them are squirt guns!"

"You are a miserable person! You need help!" Mr. Camparti yelled back to Jim Dandy.

"She's comin' with me. You gonna have her leave with me?" he indicated me with that finger pointing in my direction.

"No, she's staying here," Mr. Camparti said courageously.

I began shaking uncontrollably. I felt myself fall to the ground even though the foundation of the building was indeed solid. I was the Hoover Dam, opened for the first time, as tears came out uncontrollably, uncontrollably. A customer came through the line, confused as to what was occurring.

I was spinning, spinning around, taking a ride around the Milky Way. My ears started ringing. Mr. Camparti stepped up in my place, to do the job that I couldn't do and took care of the customer. Jon ushered me to the backroom while the mall security guard arrived at the scene. The store continued to operate while Jim Dandy was still holding a turkey leg in one hand and a foil bag in the other. The rest of the pathetic bird had fallen to the floor. "Had to buy a pan!" he screamed again as mall security started ushering him toward the door.

"Al, what's going on here?" asked the guard over his shoulder. "I will be back to get a report."

"Don't tell me what to do, you rent-a-cop," Jim Dandy screamed, pointing at him.

"We need to leave, sir," I could hear him saying to Jim Dandy.

"Don't tell me what to do," Jim Dandy repeated. "Don't tell me!"

"One more word," the officer warned, "I will arrest you. Leave with me now!"

"Get that jackass outta here!" Mr. Camparti yelled.

"Don't use that kind of language," Jim Dandy yelled back as he was leaving. "I am a born again Christian, and I don't talk like that!"

In Mr. Camparti's office, drinking water, I was telling Sarah my life story; she patted my shoulder occasionally as she smoothed a lock of hair out of my face. Mascara was running down my face; my teeth were chattering; my soul was exposed; my heart was breaking: this job that I loved so much, and these people, who had been so kind, were not only spectators, but also entered, the darkness of the house with Jim Dandy.

The girl that I presented there that day: funny, bopping around and laughing, cleaning the counter with lemon juice, this was not her life. I was not that girl. I was not a well-dressed, smart girl from a good home. I was a poor, abused girl who tried so hard to appear normal, while living in a dark house. I was a piece of candy without a wrapper; I was unwrapped like that nightmare when I went to school naked. Nobody wanted a naked piece of Bazooka bubble gum or Tootsie Roll without the wrapper. Who keeps a candy cane without the plastic wrapping? It's exposed and dirty. It gets thrown away without a second thought. Mr. Camparti salvaged that Christmas angel with one eye. Some things are salvageable, but I wasn't one of them. Who would ever want this girl who was now exposed? Who would ever want someone who was living in a dark house?

~

The next day, when I did manage to make it back to work, embarrassed yet determined to walk through those doors, Mr. Camparti and Mr. Hensley asked me to step into the office. This was it: I was going to be fired; I just knew it. Instead, Mr. Camparti said, "We will try to avoid a restraining order, I know that could be embarrassing, Delanie. Could you tell him to stay away from here? He just cannot be at King Arthur's Round Table or on the mall property—ever. I'm sorry, kid."

"Yea," I managed to utter. "I totally understand. He's a jerk and I'm sorry. I didn't mean to bring all of you into this craziness. I'm not like him."

"We don't think that you are anything like him," Mr. Hensley said. "We really feel for you."

"I hear people say that 'The apple doesn't fall far from the tree.' But I'm not like him. I'll get back to being myself again sometime. For now, I'm just going to be quiet and think."

Jon was flipping a steak on the grill when I came around to the serving line. He managed to say "hello" with his face to the side. I guess he couldn't make eye contact with me. Sarah did the same thing at school, although, thank God, she didn't utter a word about it. That five-minute incident summarized my life. I was a façade. People knew my story. About a half hour later, Mr. Camparti came up to me, patted me on the shoulder and said, "Well, kid, you're in a tough spot. We want to keep you, but he can't come in here anymore. You know that, don't you?" He was smiling with his big teeth. "You okay, kid?"

Jon Donovan related that the plans that we had for going out for pizza on Friday were cancelled because his car needed to get fixed. A kid from that kind of home doesn't go out for pizza with girls whose fathers swing and throw thawed, donated gift turkeys around restaurants. Girls like me, well, we— with our strong need to be loved—we get pregnant; we drop out of high school after failing all our classes, and we repeat the cycle of abuse.

We live in dark houses.

CHAPTER EIGHTEEN

I was standing on the precipice, believing the promotion was an immediate step toward my ticket out of the dark house. Like an explorer in a new frontier, I needed to reach out beyond my fears and take the management job, even though I knew that it wasn't where I needed to go. I would never go to college. But incessantly, in my mind, the tug toward teaching and writing—attempting to earn a college degree— just kept pulling me away from the management job; I knew my decision: with torment in my heart, I told Mr. Camparti that I could not accept the position. I had never been one to take the easy route. Mr. Camparti might have been a little hurt because he was trying to help and encourage me. He had basically forged this path to help get me out of the dark house and here I was, telling him "not interested," like some ungrateful brat.

"I really feel that I can't give it my all," I told Mr. Camparti. "I want to go to college. I feel if I stray off course, I'll never go."

"I understand, Del," he said as he was rubbing his bushy eyebrows, the shiny fillings in his back teeth catching the light.

"Mr. Camparti, please don't be offended. Don't think that I'm ungrateful. I appreciate the offer; I really do. "

"I understand, Del," Mr. Camparti replied. "This is a career move that would almost force you to put work above your education. It would be full-time and challenging. I respect your decision. I really do."

Jon Donovan had overheard our conversation. "Delanie, did Mr. Camparti offer you a management training position?"

"Yea, Jon, but I've decided that I really want to focus on going to college. A full-time position like this would take the focus off school and onto work. I want to go to college."

"That's commendable," he spoke formally. "You will be successful someday, Delanie."

"Thanks, Jon. That means a lot to me. I have to just keep trudging along."

"My parents mentioned that to me the other day, after our Honor Society luncheon."

"The trudging thing?"

"No," he chuckled. "The success thing."

"Yea, they said 'that girl really handles herself with dignity,'" he said. "I agree."

I knew where this was going: now we were going to talk about my parents' absence from the Honor Society induction. We were going to splash into talk about the robbery. We were going to talk turkey. The topic was ready to totter over the cliff. I decided to rescue the conversation, in its tracks, before it spilled into Jim Dandy. There was only so much I could attempt to do. I was just exhausted.

"I'm a different bird," I realized, after I opened my stupid mouth, the unconscious pun to the turkey incident. I just smiled and laughed at myself. I was hoping that Jon would not make the bird/turkey connection. He didn't—thank God—he wasn't a word person like me.

I had to fix this humiliating situation that Jim Dandy had created. I was usually against lying, but this called for a doozy. I would go home, bake a cake, steal the details about his war-induced stress from my Grandpa Delanie who really was in World War II—Jim Dandy would be Vietnam aged—and I would deliver this cake with a totally fabricated message from Jim Dandy. "My father said he is really sorry," I told everyone as I put the cake on a table by the time clock. "I'm sorry, King Arthur's employees," read a card that I placed beside the cake in Jimmy's handwriting.

At closing, as I was swiping the serving line with my lemon juice concoction, I told Sarah about Jim Dandy's depression and how much he suffered—and still suffers—really intending for Jon to overhear—from battlefield depression. "He relives the battlefield all the time," I lied. "It's heartbreaking." I wanted to puke at the lie, but I felt my acting was Academy Award caliber.

"I have heard of people who keep reliving the war," Sarah stated with compassion. "That's too bad."

"Yea, he was running from bullets, snipers, hidden in marshland vegetation," I knew this from US History class of Vietnam. I felt guilty: Poor Mrs. Jackson's son, Michael, who had lost his life in that war, went home in one of those horrible-smelling body bags produced in the factory on Eclipse Avenue. He was the brave one—taking orders, carrying bodies, falling down; Jim Dandy, stayed here with his club foot, getting Mom pregnant, and then he created the misery of war in the dark house where there was no need for such pain.

They bought the story except maybe Mr. Camparti. I think he knew what I was up to, but he didn't unravel the story. But he winked, agreed that Vietnam was a tough one, and walked past us so he could count stock in the stockroom.

The wink told me that he probably knew that Jim Dandy wasn't in the Vietnam War; Jim Dandy hadn't even served Stateside in any armed services. He had no military experience. He really had no work experience. But sometimes, when things are stacked against you, and your father is a crazy ass, you create lies to save face. You begin to tell lies all the time; and sometimes you start to sort of believe your own lies because it is easier than believing the truth of the situation. You cover their ass to protect yours. It's the unwritten rule of the abused.

Sorry, Grandpa Delanie, I thought, that I took your Battle of the Bulge stories, twisted them, wrapped the flag around the truth to cover for this demented wimp Jim Dandy who never served his country or anyone. But I need those stories now. I needed those words to recreate the life that I had before Jim Dandy almost destroyed it. I needed to continue my life after the wars that I have lived through. I needed to save face.

"Yes, the war sent him into a depression and he never really recovered," I told Sarah. "He has these flashbacks and remembers the shots being fired in that jungle."

Jon Donovan came over and started asking questions about his service, because his dad had also served as a captain in Vietnam. Lamely, I changed the subject as best as I could. I didn't want to get caught with more questions that I couldn't answer.

Somehow, being raised by a Vietnam War veteran must have made me more attractive because Jon waited with me that night until Mom arrived to take me home. We stood by the delivery door of the restaurant, looking out occasionally, drinking Diet Cokes and eating leftover French fries. "I don't want you to have to wait all alone," he said. "Anyway, I have study hall in the morning, and I can do my homework then."

The next day we worked together was a Friday, and he asked me to go out after work. Apparently, his car was fixed. After all of this and my hopes to finally be normal, I had a date with a normal guy. But in this instance, it was not Jim Dandy, but me who was an absolute moron. I was worried that Jim Dandy would show up at the restaurant; I was afraid I would choke, so I drank only water. I couldn't stop biting my nails for fear that I would hear Jim Dandy thump by and grab me by the arm or hair and pull me out of the booth. I couldn't eat any of my salad because I kept having visions of coughing and then vomiting. All my insecurities were sitting there beside me with the face of Jim Dandy. The ride back to the dark house was even worse because I was just as self-conscious. At work or at school, I could rattle off conversations about steaks or tests, but alone in a car with a boy, I was a bumbling idiot. I so was afraid I would stutter, so I limited my talking. I didn't know what to talk about. I tried, perhaps too hard, to think of clever things to say, but I kept second guessing myself, worried that I would come off too intellectual or too stupid. I was spinning around in my own head, twirling, and this time, ironically, I was destroying my own possibilities.

I kept checking my watch, hoping that time would speed up, so I could go home where I would be safe. When we finally pulled into the long driveway, a few of the giant trees on our property added shadow and dimension to the foreboding presence that lurked inside the dark house. I wondered what was going on in there? I realized I was a long way, a long way, from the sophistication that I so desperately wanted, longed for as a fashionable, articulate, educated, respectable writer or teacher.

The words of Robert Frost kept repeating in my head and reminded me: I had miles to go— miles and miles—before I could sleep.

CHAPTER NINETEEN

The piece of my story, how I came to be, began to connect.

I understood why she stayed married, the financial worries and fear, but I didn't understand how or why she married Jim Dandy in the first place. It would have been, to me, so simple: Run as far away as possible. Why didn't she?

She told me about the missing piece of the puzzle.

One autumn night in 1962, Thanksgiving dinner plans hovering in the air, her high school sweetheart Juan, with his dark curly hair, his green eyes, and his Hispanic accent, told her that he had to go to South Carolina. He would leave upon graduation in May, 1963; he had to take over his terminally ill uncle's cotton mill; he proclaimed his love for her, and promised that when he returned, they would get married. "Wait for me," he said. "Give me time to get the mill under control, and then we will get married." She was angry with Juan for leaving. She wanted to get engaged before he left, and she threw a temper tantrum and decided "to make Juan jealous" by going out with Jim Dandy Dane, the hoodlum who lived down the street from Juan and his family. "How could he leave me in Akron, waiting tables at Lujan's, when I loved him so much?" she asked me, reflecting on that night as we drove to the discount grocery store in Canton.

"Well, Mom, he said to just wait a little amount of time," I offered, thinking she was very impatient. The way she saw it, he was in a glamorous and sunny Atlantic seaside town, waves crashing in, saltwater winds blowing his dark curls, sun tanning his shoulders against the white of his dress shirt, while she was serving French fries and Cokes at a lunch counter.

"We didn't have sex," she said. "I wasn't that kind of girl, but I loved him, Del. I really loved him. He was a good guy."

"You should have waited for Juan, Mom," I said.

"It would have faded too," she said.

"What would have faded?" I asked.

"Love," she said. "You know, this love you hear about from your friends, it doesn't really exist," she told me. "Don't believe all that bullshit in movies," she said wistfully, as if trying to convince herself, nonchalantly flipping the AM radio in the Caprice. Once again, she contradicted herself so convincingly.

"Sipping wine on the beach: It is only in the movies," she lectured, with a tinge of doubt in her voice. She was gazing off into the distance, looking at her fantasy sunset. I was disillusioned for her. I believed in love. I wasn't going to let her story crush any hopes for my future. What about Juan? She said she loved Juan. Too many artists, authors, and songwriters wrote about love, interpreted it, sang about it. It just had to be real—like Princess Diana—maybe it was invincible and hard to capture, but it just had to be real. She should have waited for Juan. He sounded so romantic. She should have had a better plan.

Her story was intriguing to me: "I loved Juan," she told me on another night, as if she were telling chapter two, when we were driving back from the grocery store. This was becoming a regular time of revelations, so I always made time to go with her. "I never loved him. I never could love him and I never will," she declared. "He's mean; he's not getting better." When she said those words, I could still see a glimmer of the beauty that she was years ago—before the streams of tears, broken blood vessels, and empty promises filled her body. Those words freed her in a way and made her seem like a real person—full-spirited with actual blood flowing through her veins—not the current robot who accepted the unfair demands and mean dictates of his regime.

"I had my first drink the night that Juan left," she recounted, wheeling that big two-doored boat down our street. "Jim Dandy Dane was there, smoking a cigarette, wearing rolled-up jeans and white t-shirt like James Dean, checking me out, and I thought, 'What a great way to get back at Juan.' So I went out with Dandy and the next thing I knew, I was calling my sister for a ride home."

"He was a gorgeous man," she bragged of my father, her eyes distant, as if she were seeing him there again. I knew that women did find him attractive, but I couldn't stomach the idea of him in a romantic way. He was just such a disgusting human being. "The next month, I was late for my period," she whispered. "It was wrong of me."

"You got pregnant the first time?" I offered, to help her out, embarrassed myself, looking down at my torn cuticles.

"Yea. I was young and stupid," she said. "It was wrong. The Lord punished me for having sex and not being married. Not with you, of course, but my life. I've always thought that there was a reason for it all. I just didn't think."

It was starting to make sense. No woman, in her right mind, could fall in love with Jim Dandy. Aunt Lizzy told me that he once put out a cigarette on her arm and when Mom came to her, Lizzy warned her not to marry Jim Dandy. He was cruel in so many ways.

"Well, everyone's human, Mom. I don't think God punishes like that. It was just a human mistake."

"Well, it was a sin. I made a commitment, and I have to stand by it," she proclaimed. "But it was worth the trade off—getting you and Jimmy, that is."

"That makes me feel guilty, Mom. You had to sacrifice your life for me? Why couldn't you just have me and raise me on your own?"

"Because I'm not that kind of girl," she quickly replied, back to the robot.

She tried to get out of the car, but I asked another question. "Why didn't you divorce Jim Dandy and marry Juan when he got back?"

"Delanie, things aren't that simple when you get older. In the 60s, we didn't do that," she said. I still had a burning question about why she didn't include Justin when she talked about trade-offs.

We sat in the garage a few more minutes, and I persisted to maintain the awkward conversation. "We drove all night to West Virginia to get married. Grandma Delanie about killed me. She hated him from Day One," she announced.

"Excuse the pun," I joked.

"What?"

"A pun. You know, a play on words. *Dane*, his name, our name: Dane: 'Day One:' get it? Never mind, I was trying to make comic relief.... Sorry."

Literary topics always confused her, so I tried to get her back on topic. "I know Grandma Delanie never liked him. She has made that obvious."

"Never. She hated his guts. She always said that I could've done so much better. But that one night, my goals— you know I won all kinds of state typing and shorthand contests— my goals got further and further away. I could have had a good job."

I pictured a red helium balloon floating off into the sky. "I felt like I was in quicksand," she recounted. "And as everything was added: then Jimmy, Justin, houses, dogs, lost jobs. I just felt like I was in quicksand and I couldn't get out."

And she was.

Now it made sense: I remembered that summer when I lived with Grandma and Grandpa Delanie before we moved to Eclipse Avenue. I remembered that dark-haired man who took Mom and me out in a blue sports car that smelled like Old Spice cologne. I thought it was a TV show that I was confusing with real life, but it was real life. I remember this man holding me on a big swing at the park and showing me the elephants at the zoo. I remember feeling safe around him. So, I thought, it was money for the divorce attorney that Grandma Delanie always talked about. Now it made sense.

Mom took back Jim Dandy when he came to Grandma Delanie's house with flowers. Grandma Delanie didn't know about it, but I remember seeing it. I thought it was a bad dream, but it really did happen then. Mom said it was the right thing to do—to go back—but she was terrified. Not only did I experience his power and understand the fear he created, I saw the abuse, the unfair demands, the unbalanced responsibilities, and the unrealistic expectations that he put on her. In spite of all this, I don't think she ever cheated on him, but I saw the smashed doors, the broken hearts, the holed walls, her blood on the carpeting, mascara running down her tired face. I heard the crack of the belt on her too. I heard the disrespectful words and the disgusting filth, the vile, the uncaring attitude toward our home, our comfort, our relationships with other people and with each other. Being the oldest, I saw it all and remembered most of it.

Jim Dandy taught us to compete against each other to get things —anyway possible, everything was fair—because his pitiful situation was and is someone else's fault, and everyone owes him something. Mom was afraid for her life and in the process, she became entrenched in his sick microcosm. She became more and more isolated –the robot—as she tried to cover up the scars. Fear and paranoia and insecurity moved her world, so, in turn, these things moved ours as well.

The normalcy of our abnormal lives was so, well, normal, that Mom and Jimmy didn't even venture out of the maze to ponder other possibilities. But I did. Justin did. All the time. Maybe Juan would have been the dad that I wanted? I often thought about her dismal life and the trap she was in, and my mind wandered about other possibilities—for her and for all of us. All of the times that I wished Jim Dandy would die, it was not meanness, just a natural wishfulness of escape from captivity. I prayed about it because I knew it was twisted thinking. Maybe without Jim Dandy, Mom and Andy could have gotten married and all of our lives would be so different.

This isn't my life. This dark house is only temporary for me. I'm getting away someday, I thought, as I was forced to watch him verbally abuse a tired and timid female store clerk when we went to the hardware store to get a plunger. I tried to smile at her as her hands shook handing him the receipt. I'm getting away from this dark house. If I ever do anything in my life, I'm getting away from this dark house.

But for Mom, it was world without end, and my heart broke for her.

CHAPTER TWENTY

I could work and work to prove that I was worthy of an educated, well-groomed, kind boyfriend as long as he didn't have to meet Jim Dandy. I was beginning to wonder if Mom was getting just as crazy as Jim Dandy because she supported his illogical logic half the time. I tried to make appearance count at school and at King Arthur's , but Jim Dandy had pretty much destroyed my façade with the connection to the robbery and the turkey incident. Word traveled fast now at Western Star, and I was back to having the same swirling reputation of the pitiful girl with the crazy ass father. People spoke softly to me; they called me *honey* and *sweetheart*, sometimes even patting me on the head. I saw people's eyes watch Jim Dandy enter establishments because they never knew what kind of spectacle he was going to make. We had no money or prestige, so my realization fueled my desire for education even more.

I had noticed that some girls from my low social order, hungry for love or that feeling of just being wanted, often settled for whoever swaggered their way, taking the first dick in tight jeans to come along, just so they weren't lonely anymore, for that brief moment of acceptance and attention. These girls, I have heard them talk, thought the words *love* and *sex* were synonyms. I didn't want to blur the lines and make this kind of mistake. At the same time, however, I had a burning desire to go out, see and be seen with attractive young men, talk and flirt, discover if it were possible to find more in life than miserable dark houses and men like Jim Dandy. Maybe like Lady Diana Spencer, who had married on national television that summer, I, too, wanted to make the loneliness disappear, if only for a shining hour although I wouldn't be wearing a hand-beaded wedding dress with a six-foot train or a Ceylon blue sapphire diamond ring.

The family norm dictated that love was very conditional. If I didn't do exactly what Jim Dandy wanted—which was never—I, as a female, was not worthy of love—and that message was absorbed by the rest of the family, for his repercussions could be violent. The word *love* was never spoken in the dark house. I heard it used for the first time referring to me when Andy told Kathie and me, one night when we were being tucked into Kathie's twin bed, "Hey, love you guys!"

She laughed, embarrassed, and said, "Oh, he says that all the time." I wanted to tell her not to be embarrassed. I would love to have love. In the dark house, we practiced repeating Jim Dandy's dicta of fear and hatred. Love was foreign to us.

Jon was that kind of guy, and although I knew I wasn't in love, he was from a different background than mine. His parents were so supportive. They were there all the time. They were educated, well-dressed, well-spoken. Even though he had witnessed the robbery and the turkey incident, he was giving me a chance. After about a month of seeing each other—mostly going out for pizza after work where we talked about college majors, jobs, and jokes about other King Arthur's employees— Mom got uncomfortable with the fact that we never had that official, 1950s cornball meeting of them as parents. It made me look like a "floozy" she said, so he would have to come to the door, ring the bell, and make small talk. This meeting was a huge worry for me.

"I was pregnant when I was your age," she argued. Exactly, I thought, and I don't want to take your path.

"What if Jim Dandy decides to be a jerk?" I asked, addressing the elephant in the room.

"Don't worry. Jim Dandy's better. He don't act like that no more."

Right. But nonetheless, I was the dutiful daughter, and Mom's plea to cancel out my floozy appearance was convincing, so I informed Jon that he had to pick me up at the house.

It was mid-July; the fireworks had all been displayed; summer was past its culmination; the nights were getting longer again, but I decided to give the meeting a shot. It was a long shot, that was for sure, but it was the reality of my life. It came down from the powers that be, Jim Dandy declared, echoing Mom's floozy theory, that Jon would have to meet him, or I wouldn't be allowed to see him anymore. Mom believed, or convinced herself to believe, of this enormous change in Jim Dandy: She bought him a new shirt, insisted his finally cut his long beard again, and he did actually brush his teeth and put on deodorant. That was the story of her cyclical life with him: she believed his once a year appearance of normalcy and that was enough to convince that he had changed. I took it upon myself to make the dark house appear less dark: I cleaned all the windows, planted a few flowers in pots, and picked up all the daily candy papers and pop bottles that Jim Dandy had thrown by the backdoor and around his king chair. I put away his boots, bloody hunting knives, and dirt-crusted clothes piled at the entryway. I boiled cinnamon on the stove, so on Jon's first encounter, from the outside looking in, the dark house smelled like a home.

Jon, embarrassed, rang the doorbell, walked into the kitchen wearing a blue, short-sleeved Ralph Lauren blue Polo shirt, collar up, and Jimmy and Justin huddled together nervously and snickered about Jon's Ford which was not a Chevy. Jim Dandy was overly stiff at first, so I thought the meeting might pass without a scene, but Mom wouldn't sit still. While Jon and I sat nervously apart from each other on the couch in the living room, she moved around the room spraying wood polish on the end tables while I asked her to sit down and talk. She accidentally spilled the over-filled ashtray from Jim Dandy's king chair area and went to retrieve the vacuum cleaner. She then proceeded to run the vacuum, using the hose attachment under the couch we were sitting on. We tried to talk, but she kept walking past us. After I finally forced her to sit still for a few minutes—this was, after all, her idea—Jim Dandy got up, turned up the sound on the TV and a boxing match out-shouted our awkwardly attempted, stilted conversation.

"So, Jonny, are you a hunter?" Jim Dandy asked, peculiarly, off the starting gate when he sat down again. I tried to direct the conversation in the direction of food so as not to create controversy, but Jim Dandy ignored the topic and steered the topic back to controversy.

"No, sir, I don't have time to hunt, but I do play golf. Do you play any golf?" he asked, setting up a social divide.

"No. Stupid game: chasing a little white ball around," Jim Dandy resorted back to golf. "Stupid. No. Golf— it's a sissy game! Make that a faggots' game," he spouted out as Jimmy and Justin nervously chuckled from the other room. I could still see some pain in their eyes for me, maybe for Jon, for they would someday have to meet parents themselves. Jon repeated their nervous chuckle to break the tension in the room, which was about a mile thick.

"Well, okay," Jon said, running his fingers through his hair. "Do you like to barbeque on a grill?" he asked.

"No. Another stupid thing. Got a woman to cook," Jim Dandy said.

I chuckled too, trying to pretend the comment was a joke, but it wasn't a joke. This was true Jim Dandy—feeling so powerful— and in his glory. "Oh, Ji—Dad," I joked. "Now, don't be so hard on golf. It's really a great sport. Jon is very good. H-h-he might get a scholarship for g-g-golf." When I started the stuttering, it was my body was telling me that it was time to get out.

"Wait'll ya see my hunting knives," Jim Dandy pointed out, so proud of items used in killing vulnerable creatures. "Use 'em too!"

"Oh, yea," Jon muttered, at a loss for words.

"You goin' to college, huh? That's for wussies too. Gonna get out and get a job to support my daughter?" he asked as I gulped, shaking my head.

"Well, Dad, he is going to college in Indiana," I interjected, trying to save him. "But I don't need him to support me."

"But you want me to support you? I don't wanna support you either. This one is a slut. Don't know what you'd see in her. Used merchandise."

"He is joking," I said, holding back tears.

"Take her, she's yours," he said, fake laughing. "One less person I have to support," he continued, starting to stand up.

"My dad is a real jokester," I remitted. "Right, Mom? He is just joking, Jon. He knows we are a long way from that."

"Dandy," she said, trying to calm the situation. "Del and Jon have only been seeing each other for a few weeks."

"Well, only seein' each other –naked that is—a few hours when you got pregnant with Delly Belly here," he laughed, thinking he was witty, sitting back down and lighting a cigarette. He was so ignorant. At that, I wanted to crawl under the sofa, but I realized I couldn't fit. I realized that I couldn't fit anywhere. Jim Dandy's dark house was going to envelope my whole life.

Here I was playing, like some stupid fool, into his hands.

Jon said that he needed to get going because he had to be home before dark, which was a strange, manufactured excuse. He stood up and started walking backward toward the back door. I could see that Jon was starting to spin, around and around, like a top, something that I did all the time, filled with stress and confusion. I knew the feeling; the perspiration was gathering at his temples. What did I get into, I'm sure he thought, and I was to blame for bringing him into this situation. I followed him outside, and he shuffled his car keys from one hand to the other, looking away toward the woods, keeping distance between us. His body language was different than before he had met Jim Dandy. I wanted to run to the Indian fountain, jump in, and let it take me somewhere else: a new life where I could start over once more.

There was a long pause. My heart was pounding so loud that I think he heard it.

"Well, I'm glad you said that," he hesitated. "He's going to ruin everything for you, Del."

"I'm really sorry," I replied. "I didn't know he would act that way."

"He's crazy you know?" Jon said directly and bravely. "He is really mean. People don't act like him."

"Yes," I simply stated.

"He did those things at King Arthur's , and I wanted to believe you that he was scarred from Vietnam, but Del, he is just a very mean person. I feel sorry for you."

"Well, I'm okay, really," I replied.

"I was scared for a while that you were maybe pushing him into saying that because maybe you do want to get married."

"No," I was direct, trying to find more words. "He wasn't charged with the robbery," I offered.

"I know you feel like you have to stick up for him. You don't have a choice. I'm sorry. I want to finish college before I even think about marriage. I know you need to get away, but not like that."

"We're too young," I stammered. "I mean, I don't even feel..."

"Nothing against you, but we're too young. My parents..."

"Oh, I know," I interrupted, understanding what he was going to say, but feeling so alone. All of the distance that had been lessened in these past few months by our talks, our outings, and our laughter had just been dragged out for miles and miles again, pieces of my heart, torn off and thrown to the side of the road like the trash in Jim Dandy's truck. Now there was a huge chasm between Jon and me. I didn't want to talk about marriage, but Jim Dandy paraded it out there like it was the winning steer at the county fair. My heart was hurting and pounding in my chest so hard that I could once again hear the blood coursing through my ears. Tears were welling up in my eyes; I couldn't stop them.

He probably won't want to see me again, and I did nothing wrong. "I am not a weird, clingy girl who wants some man to take her away," I told Jon. I want to get away from that dark house on my own, first, by myself, I thought. Not that Jon would take me out of the dark house, but he could help me to understand life outside and we could have fun—something that I need more of in my life. But this fledgling relationship, it appeared, was destroyed, and the dark house was getting bigger and bigger as we pulled into the long driveway after driving around, going nowhere, circling the neighborhood for about thirty minutes. He abruptly put the car in park and my head bounced back on the seat. Dionne Warwick was asking him why he wanted to be so hurtful, a heartbreaker. I was thinking, Dionne, that I was being what he wanted me to be, but I couldn't shake Jim Dandy. Your question, about heartbreaks, it didn't matter, Dionne. I tried, but it was over. "Heartbreaker" continued to replay in my mind.

He didn't get out and open the door for me. He just deposited me there, and he said, "Bye. You can get out now."

"Will you call me?" I called after him, desperation in my voice, but he sped down the road, gravel flying as he peeled out. I thought of Princess Diana's long, white train and how I could wrap myself in it and disappear forever.

CHAPTER TWENTY-ONE

I had ordered my cap and gown the same day the high school guidance counselor called me in to her office one blooming day in May. I was being notified that I had received a full scholarship to Vanderbilt University in Knoxville, Tennessee—not too far from the World's Fair which had recently commenced.

"Del, this is a great opportunity," she proclaimed over her blue reading glasses.

Yes, I thought, a great opportunity for someone else. It was like winning a dream vacation, but you must get to Hawaii first.

"You and your parents will have to go and visit so you can get acclimated. This came in late, but it is an excellent opportunity. They have a great teacher education program. You will accept it?"

"I won't be able to accept it," I muttered, wanting to get out of that room, wanting to scream that I didn't have the life of other girls. "Thanks for the offer, but I won't be able to go," I said. I closed the door to her office, and I am sure she hated me, not understanding why I reacted that way, but I couldn't put it into words.

I buried the information in my head and never spoke about it again for many years.

Meanwhile, Jessica and Alana and the other seniors, including Jon Donovan, were talking about colleges, dormitories, and majors. They were planning graduation parties, buying their dorm sheets and bedding with their grad party money; they were just generally annoying. I was, once again, trying to calculate college tuition expenses while wiping down the serving line at King Arthur's Round Table. I probably should figure out a way to get to Vanderbilt, I knew it, but it was all so exhausting. How would I even get there? Where would I live? All these thoughts were swirling around in my head when Mr. Camparti told me to take a phone call in his office.

"Del! Come home!" I heard Mom's voice as it enunciated each of the three words into the phone receiver. Her voice was strange.

"Why? What is going on?" I dared to ask.

"Grandma Delanie had a heart attack," she was sobbing.

"She will be alright. God won't take her yet. She is too young!"

"Delanie, she is dead!" These four words rearranged my life. Forever. Like that, she was gone from my life.

Jimmy came to get me on the moped, and without headlights, we were humming down the roads in the dark as I shined a flashlight that he had brought with him. I knew that his moped thing was getting out of hand; it wasn't safe for him. I also I knew that I had to buy a car, if indeed I was going to college in the fall. As I had learned from Mom's experience, I needed a plan: the plan had to be created, and calculated, and then welded together on whatever I could fasten together maybe like dandelion seeds blowing in the wind. I could enroll at the University of Akron; I could drive there, and I could pay for it if I had some financial aid —God knew we were poor enough that I should qualify. I knew the University of Akron, a gritty, real world place, wasn't for babies —nobody really cared about me; I was, like everyone else, just a number—but it did offer real four-year degrees. These unfolding plans, shaped in the darkness of the hum of the moped motor, helped me to avoid thinking about Grandma Delanie, the only completely sane person in my world, the only person who had ever believed in me—wholly—and who had wanted the best for me. If I kept thinking about cars and college, I could avoid the reality that Grandma Delanie was dead, and the force that she was —full, vibrant, strong, and opinionated—had been extinguished. The past tense verb would now be correct.

She always was everything to me: From the major encouragement that she had given me to the minor advice about surviving in the competitive world: She shaped my life. From small nuances in life to pressing life decisions, she had been there. She had taught me to love turquoise jewelry when she brought earrings and rings from the Indian reservations in Arizona. She taught me the importance of wearing a stylish winter coat every winter. "Nobody really notices your clothes," she had recounted. "But your coat: everyone sees it every day." She believed in the polish of correct grammar and "carrying oneself with good posture." But most importantly, she believed in a spiritual God, not the God of the money-making, "man-made" mega church. We talked about these things, and more, every week on our trips to and from her church where her minister, Sister Rosetta Roop, led the congregation with flair, personality, and an unquenchable love for the Lord. "Go to college," she once told me. "It is your ticket out," I thought I heard her utter the words "dark house" at the end of the sentence, but I wouldn't swear to it.

Jimmy and I pushed through the back door, and there a disheveled Mom was huddled with a wide-eyed Justin and a trembling Mickey on the couch, as Jim Dandy stood over them holding an outstretched extension cord. "Good thing that old lady is dead," he said disrespectfully, as he began swinging that cord like a lasso. "Tried to run my life, and to tell ya the truth, I'm glad she's dead. Glad! Tired old bitch, whining about me gettin' a job. Won't have t' hear it no more."

Jimmy and I stood there and watched the pathetic group in their sobbing confusion. Now we joined Jim Dandy's twisted view of the universe and watch Mom's absolute swallowing of his misdirected anger. "Mom, what happened?"

"She's just dead," she said, lifting her hands up and then dropping them. Her simplified view of things.

"Yes, I know. What happened? How?"

"Grandpa was waxing the car. He kept hearing Polly barking and barking, so he went in to see what was going on. Mom was slumped over in a chair. She was gone."

"Oh, God," Jimmy said. Simple and to the point, the greatest person I had ever known was dead.

"He called a neighbor, and they called the ambulance, but she was gone when they got in the house."

"Is Grandpa okay?" I asked.

"Danny is with him now," she said.

"This was so sudden. I can't believe it," I said. I shook my head at the imbalance. Jim Dandy lowered the extension cord and shook his empty, twisted head. I thought I might see some screws fall out of it and roll on the floor, but no such luck. I could see the vacancy in there. He was on another planet—Pluto, the most distant and coldest—where he lived without a soul.

Love was a confusing, perplexing thing for him. "Sit around here and mope like a bunch of losers—losers!" he screamed. He threw the extension cord against the wall.

"Disrespectful little floozy, comin' in here to save the day. Good thing the old hag's gone. Not one person gives a damn about your smart mouth, doya hear?"

I decided to stay quiet, rather than add to the tense atmosphere.

"Who do you think you are? You're not one of us!" he asked.

Damn right I'm not, I thought.

"We're not college people, and we think you think you are better than us," Mom began, changing the subject, inappropriately taking his side. "We don't have the money for college. She was a witch to you, Dandy." I blinked to see if reality would come back. Who was the witch she spoke of?

"I came home from work because Grandma Delanie just died, and now we're talking about my college. I will pay for it myself," I uttered, realizing that I had also taken the conversation in a completely different direction.

"You will have to pay for it yourself," Mom proclaimed. "Mom always said you'd go to college. She said you'd be the first. Now she won't see you go to college." This statement took another 180-degree turn and now supported Grandma Delanie, the witch, who was so unfair to Jim Dandy. That was my mother though: she was like a ping pong ball bouncing back and forth—never really knowing or understanding which side she was on.

"Already high falutin'," Jim Dandy uttered with disgust. I just shook my head, disbelieving this conversation, in light of what had taken place, was indeed taking place.

"Delanie, who do you think you are? Too good for us? You can't go to college," Mom said.

Justin looked at me, shook his head, and blinked in confusion.

"Always fillin' yer head with more crap about college and the high life. Who do you think you are? Rockerfeller? I thought you was gettin' married. Where's that husband been? He left you on the doorstep, didn't he? Probably pregnant."

My returning home accomplished zero, so I went to my room and put a Mahalia Jackson album on the turntable. The song was reassuring to me that Grandma Delanie was on her "Way to Canaan Land." I looked up to the heavens and asked for her guidance. Just as the song ended, the phone rang, and it was Grandpa Delanie. He asked to talk to me. "Can you contact that lady minister your grandmother loved?"

"Sure, Grandpa," I said. This would be very interesting indeed—especially for Jim Dandy— because Sister Rosetta Roop was a black woman, a seriously powerful black woman who ran Victory Chapel with a loud "hallelujah" voice, an unquestioning faith in God, and an attitude that no man—or woman for that matter—was getting in her way to her spiritual fulfillment. She took slack from nobody, no way, no how. Jim Dandy and Sister Roop's encounter would be very interesting. She told me once that Jim Dandy is a coward because "no real man has to beat up on the women folk and on chil'runs." She still had some leftover

Southern dialect which I loved. Sister Rosetta Roop, like Mahalia herself, was a tower of faith. I did not know whether Grandma Delanie told Grandpa Delanie that Sister Roop was black, but it didn't matter much to him. If Grandma loved her, he loved her. The rest of the family knew nothing of our soul searching investigations at Victory Chapel. This was our very comfortable secret. She had to be made aware that Jim Dandy was a loaded gun, and that she could be the victim, and I was the one who had to tell her.

Like a compass finding its direction, she could handle it though; Sister Roop was of my soul, and she could handle Jim Dandy.

CHAPTER

TWENTY-TWO

"Lord God in Heaven," Sister Roop said when I called her that night, "that woman was a walking saint. My darlin' Delanie, I know that woman lived for you. You were her shining star. I would be blessed to do her funeral," she said. "We need a layin' on of hands," she said, "to heal the worl' and yo' po' soul of her loss. Stop over to my office and let's say a word together."

I could feel the warmth in her voice. I could smell the rose water hand lotion as she threw her hands in the air as her bouffant hairdo tilted to one side with the flowing angel sleeves on her blue dress billowing as she moved. She always wore blue and loved lace and frills on her clothes. "Becky is going home! The Lord wanted her up there. I know we still need her or want her here, Delanie, but the Lord has work for her Up There in Canaan Land!"

"Well, why would God take her away from me? I know that sounds selfish, but she was my light, Sister Roop?"

"She's not yours, chil'. She loved you more than I think anybody in the worl', but the Good Lord's callin' her home." Sister Roop squeezed my hand. She grabbed me and kissed my cheek with a body embrace that I don't think I will ever know again. I didn't know what to say to that because she was right. It felt good to have Sister Roop and to have had my grandmother who loved me unconditionally.

"Thank you, Sister Roop," I managed to utter when I got my breathe.

"You know what, Del? Becky'll be back. She gonna come back again in another life." Sister Roop explained that she believed in reincarnation. "She still got work to do."

"How will I know her?"

"You will know her when she comes back to you," she said. "She will find you. She'll find ya, chil'. Look for her in the things she loved. Music, art, animals. Look for her. She there."

"I will," I said, still not accepting God's decision to take my beloved grandmother.

"One more thing, Del. I gotta tell ya somethin' else," she said. "This will be my last funeral in Ohio. It was meant to be, praise God," she divulged. "I just got called to the True Church House of Prayer in Georgia. I'm goin' back to Savannah." Sister Roop had told me about growing up in Savannah and how she had left there to pursue her ministry in Ohio. She came with her brother who attended Cleveland State. The South, she said, was just starting to accept women ministers— especially black female ministers— and she had talked many times about going home to "her people." The opportunity had arisen, her brother was going back to work at a bank, and she was also "called to the Promised Land back in Savannah." To Grandma Delanie and me, she was "our people," but she couldn't be persuaded to stay. "My family needs me back in Savannah." She alluded to the difficult life that she left and needed to attend to in Georgia. Her heap in Georgia wasn't any easier than my heap in Ohio.

In my own state of shock and denial at the same time, Sister Roop helped me to make the transition to life without Grandma Delanie. She helped me to clear my head of the anger I had for God. She helped me to realize that even though Grandma Delanie was dead, my love for her was still alive, and it would remain alive as long as I lived. "In Ephesians, the Lord said, 'In anger, do not sin. Do not let the sun go down while you are still angry,' honeypie. This will give the devil a foothold," she said, reaching out her arms toward Heaven. "Anger is trouble," she said. "Don't answer the door."

"I try not to let the anger in," I said, "but it is just there. I hate it that He took my grandma. I hate the Lord for giving me Jim Dandy as a father. She was all I had, Sister Roop. Do you know what my father, Jim Dandy, is like?"

"Chil', I was raised on the streets. My mama picked cotton and we was sharecroppers. My daddy was gone. I never knew my daddy—maybe that was a good thing," she chuckled. "Daddies can be pains in the asses sometimes..." her voice trailed off and she laughed. "Amen to that!"

"I'm sorry. I guess it could be worse," I looked down, thinking about all the times that I had wished Jim Dandy would go away. Maybe her life was better without her father, but we don't know what didn't happen.

"Delanie, honeypie, you okay. Just gotta remind you, honey, that life is tough. You gotta get goin' 'cause it's not gonna get easier."

"I know," I said.

"Now, Becky, she was a lady who understood what is like to be somebody else. That's why I loved her so much. She saw that I was black. She saw my life, Delanie. You just like her, honey. Always remember her ways," Sister Roop said. "Don't forget what she taught you. You was lucky to have her."

"I can't live without her," I said.

"You will live without her. You don't have a choice, Sugarpie. The Lord won't give you more'n you can handle. Becky is still there. You can still talk to her. And she will be with you, down here, lookin' out for you. You gotta do it yo'self." We were comforted in a little kitchenette where people had brought cakes, cookies, and a huge coffee pot which brewed the smell of morning or needed caffeine to anyone whose nose directed them to the little room. Just outside the comforting hospitality, we heard Grandpa Delanie, all five feet six inches of him, with his black and silver military crew cut hair standing straight up on his head, scolding someone. "By God, I don't wanna see you disrespectin' Becky with anything about that lady minister. Or anything for that matter. And I God damn mean it! She loved that woman."

I peeked my head out of the room and I was correct. There was Grandpa Delanie shaking his finger at a stupid looking Jim Dandy. Jim Dandy was standing, looking dumbfounded and pathetic, wearing skin tight black dress pants with dirt crusted work boots, a white dress shirt, wrinkled and untucked, with a too-small putrid yellow tie, also crinkled, hanging down the front.

"Listen here, Munchkin," Jim Dandy initiated.

"I said 'not a word,'" Grandpa Delanie repeated, shaking his finger. "By God, I will call the police. I was in the Bulge, buddy."

Leave it to Grandpa Delanie, the guy who survived the infantry in the Battle of the Bulge, essentially a man of very few words, to tell Jim Dandy the what-for of funeral behavior. All the years that my Grandma Delanie had declared to me that Jim Dandy was a misogynist, a term I hadn't heard before that, Jim Dandy didn't make one peep of a noise in disrespect to Sister Roop, to the Mahalia Jackson album that crackled on the turntable during calling hours, or to anyone in attendance. I thought maybe Mom drugged him, because he was so out of his element. It was delightful to watch him toe the line and look stupid.

"Now to hear that, it was worth arriving early," Sister Roop chuckled from the hospitality room. "That little guy, your grandpa, he ain't takin' nonsense from that big stupid guy."

"I know...." I replied. "That stupid big guy is Jim Dandy."

"Your daddy?" she asked. "Becky had no good words to say about him. He's a coward of a man. I guess he don't like my black self. I know that for a fact. He will meet his someday; you mark my words, Delanie."

"I hope so," I said. "Thanks for all you have done. We love you!"

"Jim Dandy.... That's a stupid name," she laughed. "He makes my skin crawl."

"He is a pretty bad person," I said. "Very abusive."

"I want to know how this ends with that Jim Dandy out there," she tilted her head nonchalantly.

"Let me know where you are in Savannah," I said.

"I will, honeybunch. I will."

"You can still talk to her," she proclaimed, changing the subject, looking up to the Heavens.

"Do you really believe that?" I asked.

"I sure do, Honeypie. I speak to my Mama all the time. I know she hears me," Sister Roop coyly admitted.

"It's not like in real life," I acknowledged.

"No," she said, "but whenever you need her, just talk to her. You will feel her with you." She gave me another one of those bear hugs, kissed my head, and swooped out of my life, with the exception of postcard from Savannah two weeks later that read, "I'm here. Come visit me in the heat, darling girl! The Lord has work for me here! Love, Sister Roop"

I took Sister Roop's advice and talked to Grandma Delanie that afternoon, at home, by the Indian fountain, after her body was laid to rest. I told her about the funeral, and the funny exchange between Grandpa and Jim Dandy, my talk with Sister Roop, and how I would try to take care of Mom. I think Grandma understood what I was up against, that I had to get to Akron U, and I told her I would always carry her turquoise ring like a Saint Christopher medal. It would take me through college and through life, and she promised that when the air had that certain stillness and certain clean smell of this day, she was with me.

I knew I needed to get grounded and start working on my life, like Sister Roop did in Savannah, or I never would, so I made an appointment with an advisor at the University of Akron. It was an impersonal experience, with a phone call to the University, but at least I had decided and taken a step forward.

CHAPTER TWENTY-THREE

Jim Dandy insisted that he would drive me to the appointment at Akron U, although I had lined up a ride with a friend. "Can help you to get some money," he expounded as I got into the passenger side of the old Chevy. He was good at getting money without earning it, so I obliged and thought that maybe this would be his contribution to my education.

I had filled out the necessary financial aid forms and found out at the appointment, that with my grades and the education policies of the Carter administration still in effect in 1982, I qualified for a complete grant.

Walking into the warm, golden, pine-paneled room, my eyes went directly to a small book shelf lined with books, while I waited for the advisor to arrive. The last book on the shelf, clear as day, was a biography of Mahalia Jackson.

"That's a good sign," I told the advisor, pointing to her book. "I always look for signs."

"What's that?" she asked.

"Oh, I just saw the Mahalia Jackson book. She was my grandmother's favorite artist. And I just attended her funeral yesterday," I recounted.

"Oh, I'm sorry," said the lady whose nameplate read Mrs. Simmons. "I love the Negro spirituals and that tradition," she said. "How the people overcame so much." I liked Mrs. Simmons with that statement.

"I think Mahalia was a marvelous person and vocalist," I said.

"For sure," Mrs. Simmons said.

"Dumb n...," Jim Dandy mumbled. I knew what he said, and I hadn't heard him. I looked at Mrs. Simmons who got the drift from me.

"Best damn electrical contractor in the world, but I can't read," proclaimed Jim Dandy, pointing at himself, out of nowhere as Mrs. Simmons was closing the door to go over my grant details. "Never needed it, though. I can wire anything." Here we go again, I thought, the Jim Dandy Show.

"Never really cared about readin' either. It's dumb. Don't really see why I'd want to read when I did so well without it." He was taking chewing tobacco out of his gray hooded sweatshirt. He put it in his mouth as tobacco pieces fell onto a circular, impeccable, white rug by her desk. Mrs. Simmons put her hand over her mouth.

"Mr. Dane," the advisor admonished, looking at my application for his name, "we're really not here to discuss your issues. We're here to find a way for Delanie to attend college," she voiced in a business-like manner. "Some people—like you..." she plainly hesitated on the word *you*, "can do well without college, but in today's world—"

"My issues? What the hell are you? In today's world— whatta you, or that nigger minister, know about today's world? Nigger singers tellin' me how to live! I own a house and a car and two TVs!" he screamed as I was again looking for that hole to crawl into.

"Well, you want Delanie to have an easier life than you, right?" asked Mrs. Simmons. "And I really don't appreciate that language."

"Ya not gonna sit there and tell me how to talk to my own daughter. Thinks she's better'n me already," he said. "She is mine. No club foot, but has blue eyes."

"Delanie, let's just get this done," Mrs. Simmons said as she shook her head. I think the club foot reference confused her, and she just shook her head like she was trying to get water out of her ears.

"Add to it! Who, in their right mind, has a nigger woman minister? Ya gonna get her a job where they pay her to read books or be a philosopher or somethin'?"

"I'm so sorry," I interjected.

"This man has some real mental problems," Mrs. Simmons said.

That comment took him over the edge. His face changed. "I ken get along fine without one book in my house!" He reached across her desk and knocked a folder onto the floor. "Maybe if she'd get her head outta stupid books and marry that boy that she's screwin'...."

"Okay, Delanie, you need to fill out this form," Mrs. Simmons was telling me, standing and ushering me to the door. "Send this in the mail or drop it off by my office when you get all the information completed. If you have questions, here's my number. Just call."

"You wanna hear about her thinkin' she's better than me?" he asked, standing up on his tiptoes. "She doesn't have a God-damned club foot!"

"Mr. Dane, there is really no reason for his line of conversation," Mrs. Simmons again admonished. "Delanie has the necessary paperwork, and I think she can handle it from here."

"I will work on the forms and get them back to you," I told Mrs. Simmons, hurried. "Thank you. I'm grateful for your help."

"You are welcome, Delanie. I wish you the best here at The University of Akron." She nodded toward Jim Dandy in a knowing sort of way.

"What are puttin' in her head? You wanna hear how she thinks she bettered 'n me?" he repeated.

"Mr. Dane, I'm very busy right now. I don't have time for this."

"Don't have time? Payin' taxes so you can sit there and drink coffee and have this job, and you don't have time for me?" He went over to her wastebasket and spit juice into it. He was always spitting or smoking. He kicked the white rug and scrunched into a pile.

"Listen, Mr. Dane, because of Delanie, I don't' want to have to call security in here. Can we end this now?"

"Security? Ain't afraid of no rent-a-cop! Who do ya think ya are?"

In reaction, Mrs. Simmons picked up her phone, pressed a combination of buttons, and looked at me in confusion, shaking her head.

"Come on, Dad," I urged. "This could get ugly. Let's go. You need to come with me."

"Ain't goin' nowhere!" he professed. "Let some rent-a-cop come and try to take me outta here! I gotta club foot, but I think I ken take ya. I pay taxes for her to have this job!" He began to stomp his club, and he got that look in his eyes. The scary look. The look that someone was going to get hurt. "Not goin' to tell her how to be high falutin' about me."

Within a few short minutes, a short security officer walked into the office, holding a billy club. "Sir," he said quietly at first, "you need to leave the premises. We don't allow loud or disrespectful conversation in this building or on this campus. Will you go willingly or must I file a report?"

"Go ahead and mess with me, ya shrimp rent-a-cop, and I'll show you who's boss," Jim Dandy warned, pointing at him, sizing him up.

Maybe remembering the altercation at King Arthur's Round Table, thank God Jim Dandy followed me when I turned to go. The security officer allowed Jim Dandy to keep walking.

I wasn't sure what would happen on the way home, but I was afraid. I was afraid for anyone who crossed his path: another driver, an animal on the sidewalk, anyone or anything that was less powerful than him.

We approached a railroad crossing with the cross-bucks down, and a train was visibly approaching, fast. "Dad, please, let's wait." My heart was still pounding from the scene with Mrs. Simmons.

"A challenge, huh?" he asked the air, putting his foot down hard on the gas pedal as the old Chevy rattled forward with its loose fenders. My head flew back onto the headrest, and I closed my eyes. I just wanted to live to see the day that he was not in my life.

This place, the University of Akron, could be the way out for me. Like pieces of a puzzle, my life could be put into place. Maybe I could fit in here. I could continue to work at King Arthur's Round Table, commute to school when I found a dependable car, pay for the car and insurance, pay for my books, and of course, find a few hours here and there to make some new friends. I could endure a few more years in the dark house as long as I had a degree in the future and a new life waiting for me. I believed in education, hard work, and good behavior.

I would get out. I could get out. If there were a God in Heaven, it just had to be so.

CHAPTER
TWENTY-FOUR

How quickly life passes from common to cosmic. It had been exactly one week ago that I was talking on the phone to Grandma Delanie about worldly matters and today—right now—she understood other-worldly matters. If there is indeed a Heaven, she is there, looking down, and pondering the simplicity of it all. She knows the truth for which we are all searching: Are we reincarnated? Is there a Hell? Is there a Heaven? Will we ever meet again?

All of the scenes of the past few days had transformed me into a pile of broken, raw emotions. It was late July and hotter than a pepper pot in Texas, and in the heat of my upstairs bedroom, I knew I had to get myself together, buy a car and some textbooks, and come to terms with the reality of getting that college education.

Continuing, the Jim Dandy robbery thing was still hanging in the rafters. I was hoping the whole thing was finally put away, but it lingered because he was never officially charged with a crime, but I believed in my whirling paranoid mind that he was the accomplice who watched as Swartz drove away with the money. It would never be proved.

Jon conveyed the feelings to me of the whole King Arthur's crew one night when we were closing together. I wasn't in love with him or anything of that serious nature, and of course any feelings cooled off after Jim Dandy made more of an ass out of himself, but it was a romantic enough relationship, just interesting enough to compel me to go to work every night. After Grandma Delanie's funeral, he broke the news to me that it was his last night working there. "I'll be leaving in a few weeks for Indiana," he said as he was yet again scraping the grill. "Tonight is my last night." The words shot through my heart like Cupid's arrow.

I turned around, looked at him, and said nothing.

"I can take you home tonight, if you need a ride," he said over his shoulder. "I know you haven't bought your car yet." Surprised after the encounters with Jim Dandy that he would volunteer to take me home, I agreed because I did want to talk and say goodbye.

"We can talk on the way home," he said, "but I'll just pull in real quickly and you can jump out. I don't want to see him."

"He won't come outside if we are quick."

"Anyways, my mom said that it isn't safe for Jimmy to pick you up on the moped. She said she was worried about you when it's so dark." I liked how he sounded fatherly and protective, and his mom cared enough to worry about me.

"You know, you are both right," I said, "but feel better, I'm looking at cars tomorrow."

We pulled into the driveway of the dark house, he turned off the engine and pulled a Polaroid photo out of his wallet of the two of us at the putt-putt golf place taken earlier this summer. I was standing next to Alice in Wonderland's house, suntanned, and my hair was really blonde. I was acting like I was going in the crooked door, and I was laughing. "I really do think you are a cool girl," he said. "Could you write?"

"Yea, for sure," I said. "That's really a cornball picture of me."

"I want to remember you laughing and having fun."

His comment was important to me because I wanted to tell him not to remember me as the pitiful girl with a crazy-ass father, but I couldn't form the words without sounding pathetic. Instead, I took the high road and let him think what he inevitably would want to think. It was his mind after all.

"I am worried about you," he said sweetly.

"I'll be alright. Really. I am going to make it. You won't see me working at King Arthur's in five years. I'll be teaching school, living my own life, on my own...traveling, meeting people, buying nice clothes....I'll be out of the dark...." I almost added the word *house*, when at that exact utterance of the word, there was a tap on the driver's side window. As Jon cranked down the window manually, the barrel of a shotgun touched his ear and the side of his face.

Jon screamed, "You are a moron!" And then softer, "Del, you hafta get out of the car."

"Hands off! Ain't gonna buy no cow if ya git the milk for free!" screamed Jim Dandy. "I want to see yer hands!" Jon put his hands on the top of the steering wheel.

"What are you doing? We are talking. What are you doing?" I wanted to add the word *asshole,* but I stopped short.

"Marry her or git off my land and never come back," he pointed the rifle into the sky and shot it with a reverberation that recoiled to the stars and the outreaches of the universe. The sound descended back to the earth and jolted into the chambers of my heart.

"Get out of the car!" Jon repeated as he cranked the key in the ignition. I barely had time to open the door and roll out when he started reversing. I fell into the gravel driveway on my hands, cut my knees, and ripped my work skirt and my pantyhose. Jon pushed the pedal to the floor of the car, and it lunged forward like a tiger grasping its prey. He tore off down the long, dark driveway, stones flying in his wake. "I will write you!" I yelled with my hands cupped around my mouth.

He didn't answer with words. Just like that, he was gone. I would never hear from him again.

CHAPTER TWENTY-FIVE

With its confusing, cold demands and exasperating and exhausting speed, the world had changed. Dedicated and exhausted high school teachers, who knew and encouraged their students, were left behind on a slower plane of high school, a place with an unappreciated, friendly, we-care about-you attitude, where play mingled with learning. The lunchroom routine— Alana and Jessica—with their packed lunches and idle gossipy chatter, had moved to college campuses. The cafeteria ladies, making homemade pizzas and salads with smells that piped warm homey feelings into the school building, they were left behind. Those things, now of childhood, they were deposited in the past. Different sites, different rules, and different players now moved faster; they didn't care; they played by competitive rules. Potential and possibility were buried somewhere. Indifference was now the norm.

I could picture Alana, like me, standing somewhere alone on that vast Kent State University campus, looking about her new landscape and wondering what she was doing there in that equally faster, colder urban sprawl. Jessica, I had heard from some our other classmates, was surrounded by sisters in a sorority at Akron with paid-for, well-established, and built-in friends for support. She hadn't called me about getting together or catching up, but then again, I hadn't called her either; I would have to get a message through from her grandparents.

Just when I had been thinking about Jessica, about a month into that Fall Semester when the loneliness was overwhelming, I ran into her. I had just heard on the radio news that Princess Grace, a beautiful American actress married to a prince in Monaco, had died of the injuries from a car accident. Of course, my thoughts enlarged and coincided into musings about strange twists of fate. Princess Grace, like Diana, was another person who, as I saw it, had everything: beauty, money, fame, love, security. One wrong move of a steering wheel, and, like that, she was gone. We are all just mere mortals.

But I couldn't get consumed. I had to get on with my life that I still had for some reason. I parked my little white Ford Pinto along Fir Hill and was walking upward toward Olin Hall. As I crested the hill, I saw Jessica standing on the veranda of that huge old white sorority house where several Greek pillars supported the stately roof. She was flanked by two gorgeous and well-appointed sorority sisters who looked like they had stepped out of *Glamour* magazine. So much for my garage sale and sale rack fashion sense that I copied from from Mom's ability to put together an outfit on a shoe string. They were bookends wearing hot pink striped Ralph Lauren polos, short white tennis skirts exposing their long, suntanned legs, and pastel cardigans which were tied casually around their necks. Jessica, a little on the short and dumpy side anyway, shorter even than me, had changed in light of her new atmosphere. She had lost a ton of weight, got rid of the piled hair, and was wearing the same kind of preppy clothes as the other two girls.

"Jessica," I called as I waved and approached the imposing Greek columns. "Hey! It's Del"

"Oh, hi Del," she seemed happy enough to see me, but acted restrained with the Delta Gams beside her.

"Did you hear about Princess Grace?" I asked, thinking she was the Jessica I used to know.

"Princess What?" she asked like I was a martian or some alien from outer space. I forgot myself that I was that nerd who loved current events, and I actually wanted to discuss other people's reactions.

"Princess Grace was just killed in a car accident," I said. "She was that beautiful movie star. You know, she married that prince? Not Prince, the singer, but a prince..." I didn't know how to get out of this nerdy path that I had started down. The two gorgeous sorority sisters found me to be an interesting specimen, and they tilted their heads sideways and put their pointer fingers on their cheeks. I felt like a bug pinned to a piece of Styrofoam.

"Oh, really?" she was in a tough spot.

"Hey! Do you want to meet for lunch after my class in Olin?" I asked, hoping to talk one on one without the girls eavesdropping every word.

Jessica covered her yawn with her hand. Her sorority sisters snickered a little at me, and one nudged the other and whispered, "Did she say her name is Del? What a dork."

The other nodded her head positively, and they laughed together. "That is hilarious." I was the outcast. "Did you, like, know this princess?"

"No," I said shaking my head. "It was Grace Kelly. Sorry."

"I can't," Jessica uttered as if speaking to a child. I approached the steps to the porch while looking down at the concrete.

"She can't come up here," warned one of the sisters to Jessica, speaking loud enough to humiliate me, as if I had the plague or that new disease called AIDS.

"I won't come up," I informed them. "I have class in about ten minutes."

"We're getting ready for a mixer tonight, so I'm busy," Jessica proclaimed, half embarrassed, half proud. "Only sorority members can attend."

"Okay. I understand. Well, sometime? I come by here almost every day."

"Probably not," interjected the first girl who spread out her hands to encompass Jessica in a protecting manner from me. They started into the house, ushering Jessica inside.

The second girl turned her head sideways to me as she entered the house. "We don't mix with commuters." She smirked at me. "We're real college students. We live on campus."

I walked toward Olin Hall, more than a little hurt, I must admit, and as I sat down in the front row and took out my *Norton Anthology of English Literature*, and I asked myself: Did that really happen?

I started tallying up the losses of the past few months: Grandma Delanie, Jon, high school teachers, and now Jessica. I was alone at this lonely place and the old things that I had known and understood, they were at odds with this new existence. Here I was in this big city, this big competitive place, this concrete campus. In Akron, you had to be good to make it. Princess Grace no longer had choices, but I did. I was still alive for a reason. I would crawl forward, exhausted, half beaten, and I would prevail. I had no other choice.

As I sat down and made eye contact with Dr. Slocum, my favorite English professor, the most gorgeous man I had ever seen walked into my little cornball world. He was tallish, with brownish blonde hair, and he was wearing a faded gray sweatshirt that read "Akron Law 86." He looked at me in a perplexed kind of way, his head tilted sideways. He held the glance for about three seconds, and he then grabbed a note from Dr. Slocum, squinted squarely at me again, and left the room.

Maybe the tables, and at least a few heads, were turning, and I turned to the intro to *The Canterbury Tales*.

CHAPTER TWENTY-SIX

Goodness—and I know this is so oversimplified— balances the evil forces in life.

Call it Karma. Call it God. Call it cornball cosmic. Call it anything you like, but life, as cruel as it can be sometimes, does offer counterbalance. I believe in putting good things out there because, like a boomerang, they usually circle back and hit you, like that dodge ball always does in gym class—at least for me, square in the face.

Arriving that summer was Hal, after the past devastating losses, a win who was well worth the waiting.

Humming that new song about the city disappearing by the Rubber City's own Chrissie Hynde and the Pretenders, I was picturing how Akron, as she knew it, was all gone because it was now all paved up, and the green grass of the farming fields, now malls and parking lots. Akron was indeed changing; the rubber was hittin' the road. A few minutes later, the forces of the Universe must have been smiling on me. The chemicals, or atoms, or whatever they were, were circling around, and they were coming back my way. In my memory, I see the moment clicking like an 8-mm home movie to the tune of that song.

Hal was a glimmering, shimmering light countering the oppressive darkness that hovered in the corners of the dark house with Jim Dandy. Hal had a sense of humor that matched mine—corny and at times secretly tinged with evil—a fragile piece of himself also protected in a glass case on a high shelf. His life was no walk in the park either; he had his own demons to fight, and they were only slowly revealed to me that semester. Hal had a way of expressing himself, a voice that went up and down the musical scale, a laugh that robbed my seriousness—just lifted it up and gone—and an eye for the unusual among people. Characters, as he called them, were everywhere, and he pointed them out regularly, quietly, under his breath, but he was always on target, and he always made me laugh. He was an observer. "That guy over there, the one with the Flock of Seagulls hair, thinks he is a ladies' man," were the first words he uttered to me as he ushered his head in the direction, "but the ladies want nothing to do with him. I mean, do you?" I looked at Hal: his grin, his eyes questioning whether I would laugh or not, and I laughed and accepted his gift of laughter as we walked together on that mystical, rainy fall day back in 1982.

He was a floundering general studies major who had no idea what to do, where to go. I told him about my English classes, and he said that creative writing sounded like his "thing" because he wanted to write comedy, so he added creative writing that day, and unconsciously, at that point, we had charted a course together —literally.

In class, we found that we our sense of humor was so close, that we made eye contact across the table, wondering if the other was thinking what we were thinking; there were only twelve of us in the class. He wrote dark humor about people being killed on tractors and the goofy family members who only wanted the money. I wrote about the pain of trying to survive the darkness that encircled me and the waves that kept washing me out to sea.

We were young dreamers searching for answers—but also anchors to each other's drifting out to sea. We tried to dig out of the heaping stacks of sorrows piled onto our souls—not of our own doing, but from the misdeeds of a parent trapped in the hellish nightmare of his or her own flaws. Laughter saved us, and we shared its wonderful, priceless gift.

It took a few weeks after a discussion about one of his short stories about an alcoholic mother when Hal finally absorbed the silence, thinking, thinking, and then he broke the silence at a study session. "My mom is gone," he recounted, "but I am still alive. I live with the guilt she left me."

I waited, making sure I had the right question. "What is the guilt about?"

"My counselor told me," he conveyed as we sat in pleather booths in an open-all-night, family-owned diner, "that when someone causes enough pain in your life, you hafta make a plan to get rid of them. So, I was thinking about how to get her out of my life, and then she had a heart attack at forty five."

"That's not your fault, Hal," I said. "You didn't force her to drink."

"I know, but I was thinking about how I could get her out of my life," he said.

"You didn't do it," I said. "It sounds like she was trying to kill herself."

"See, her death—it didn't solve my problem," he proclaimed. "It might not be that easy."

"Well, this is going to sound terrible. And I don't mean disrespect to you, but I wish Jim Dandy, my father, would just go away. I wish he would—-," I stopped short. "I think about it all the time," I said.

"He must be a monster," he stated correctly.

"He is," I said.

"Was your mom a good person, Hal?"

"My mom was a heavy drinker. She died a few years ago when I was in high school," he said.

"I'm glad she was a good person," I said. "That would really cause guilt if you didn't get along."

"I miss her. She was a good person who got caught up in an addiction. Does Jim Dandy drink?" he asked.

"Jim Dandy prides himself that he doesn't drink. But he might as well. He is so freakin' mean, alcohol might make him nice," I said. "He's an electrical contractor, but he quits all his jobs."

"It changes a person's personality," he said. Then he shook his head like a bee had flown into his ear. He paused and his humor kicked in, "I'm sorry, but what kind of stupid name is *Jim Dandy?*"

"A very stupid name," I answered. "But it isn't so stupid because it describes him perfectly. He is a jim dandy asshole—not just a typical strict or overly involved parent. He is truly, truly crazy. He does stuff that I couldn't even explain. Like, you would say, 'he did what and why?'"

We were silent for a moment.

"Hal, tell me about her," I said. "Tell me everything you remember. I'd love to know about her."

He began to describe her physical appearance: she was thin with a brown hair. She wore very little make-up. "She chain-smoked cigarettes and always had a Coke can in her hand. She would slurp off the fizz of the Coke, then add Jack Daniels until she finished the bottle."

Then she would light cigarettes with the drinks, but she was kind. She felt helpless about the pain in the world. She wanted to help everyone, Hal said, and she couldn't. She loved animals—all animals—and couldn't stand to see them hurting, homeless, or hungry. That helplessness, Hal believed, created depression. But her soul, the deepest part of who she was, was kindness and love, he explained.

"Jim Dandy, on the other hand, sounds like he is the exact opposite of your mom," I explained.

"My dad gave up; I gave up. We had fought it for so long to get her sober," his voice was shaking.

I was left without words. We sat there in silence until his pork chops and mashed potatoes were plopped in front of him. I waited to dive into my house salad until the waitress returned with the Italian dressing.

"This food looks good." I was trying to change the subject, which was way over my head. I felt that drowning feeling again, only this time for Hal. We all have problems, I thought.

"Del, you know, you have to live your life," he advised. "That Jim Dandy ass has made you scared."

"I'm not scared; I know, I know where I am going."

"Sometimes you do," he explained. "I mean, I think you're great. You're on the right path. You are trying to get out, and I respect that. But he has shaped you into this girl who is so scared of trying things, new things, taking chances."

"He has?"

"Everyone told me that you are a serious girl," he said. "You're so smart, so driven. I've never seen anyone like you."

I just stared at him and blinked.

"Me? People—who—told you that about me?"

"Everyone always tells me that they are afraid of you. You drive through 'em like a bulldozer."

"Are we still talking about me?" I laughed. "And who?"

"The guys in our class. But I understand why you are that way. Some of the other guys, they don't know why you are so driven. It's like you have blinders on. It scares them away."

"It does? I scare people? I scare guys?"

"Guys have told me that they like you, but you are like 'get outta my way!'"

"Really?"

"Yea," he shook his head and looked away. "You're tough."

"I'm about as lost as they come, Hal. You know that. I have no idea where I'm going. What am I going to do with an English degree?"

"I don't know. One thing that I do know about you: you will figure it out. I have faith in you."

"Thanks, Hal." I remembered the other time I had no words just a *thank you* when Mrs. Tetley stood by me on stage.

"I've never been more sure of anything in my life," he stopped, held my gaze, and blinked a few times, and looked away. "That is —your ability to get out."

I took a stab with my fork at a nice chunk of iceberg lettuce. "Get out," I said, scratching my eyebrow. The light had gotten brighter.

Some people don't just come into our lives, they make an entrance.

CHAPTER

TWENTY-SEVEN

It was my second semester in college. The January snow was flying. The Ohio world that I knew was covered in white, like powdered sugar sprinkled on Corn Flake leaves; piles were still left in the yard. It was bitter, record-breaking cold: gas caps were freezing on cars; weather forecasters warned us to cover our faces when walking outside; and spit would freeze in mid-air. I tried it.

My beautiful white little Pinto, camouflaged in the snow and out to pasture in the long driveway, pampered and prepared to open the road and the sky for me, was ready and rested, in my mind, for my mission to school. I had recorded a new tape of Hall & Oates, and I was looking forward to my morning jam. That little four-cylinder car, with a toggle switch heater, could pump out heat and keep me warm on my way to campus. I was one of those fastidious record keepers, handwriting all oil changes, tire rotations, and any repairs in a booklet filed safely in the glove compartment. The Ford Motor Company called the Pinto, in a 1980 article in the *Beacon Journal,* "an automotive design nightmare" due to the placement of the gas tank near the rear of the vehicle. Many automotive reviewers called it a "dangerous little car." But for me, that roadster was my ticket out of the dark house. I didn't care. Dangerous or not, it was my sidekick, the white pony, saddled, ready to jump the fence, and help me to find the life that someday awaited free range.

I was tying my Chugga boots by the back door when Jim Dandy came into the house, his feet stomping heavily on the floor. It was very unusual for Jim Dandy to be up and out the door before me. He was wearing a winter coat over his underwear and his work boots. His bare white legs, freckled with blue veins and his stupid club foot, looked so much like my pasty white skin that I thought it funny, if not sad, that I did indeed share his biology. He passed by me as he headed to the coffee maker and filled a giant Ball canning jar half full with molasses. Then he added a cup of sugar and filled the rest with thick, black coffee which was the consistency of motor oil. He started stirring the concoction with a butter knife, click, click, clicking the sides of the jar. "What bullshit today?" He took a huge slurp of the motor oil, steaming hot.

"I have American lit, then U.S. History," I relayed, soon realizing that *lit* would confuse Jim Dandy. I was trying to take it back, rephrase it, when he was on the offensive.

"What's *lit?*" he said to Jimmy, who had just appeared in the kitchen for his morning cereal. "What's lit?"

"It's slang for literature," I said, knowing that I had to be as simple as possible for Jim Dandy. The appearance of smugness or knowledge often set him off. His mental state was fragile—especially in winter. "Stuff written in America, by Americans," I said.

"Lit shit! What a waste," he mocked. "Made up crap nobody cares about. Don't pay no bills."

"It really snowed last night. I hope the roads are okay." I tried to change the subject. "See you later!" I swung the wool scarf over my face, closed the back door, and crunched through the snow to my car, when I realized that it had been vandalized. I saw little cubes of Safety glass sprayed all around the car, sparkling like little diamonds on the snow. Through the continuing swirling snow, I heard the back door open; Jim Dandy, elevated on the porch in his underwear, was laughing, witnessing my reaction to the destruction. He was holding that Ball canning jar of coffee in the air, yelling "that'll learn ya to be high and mighty," and I began to swirl like the snow. Cars zoomed by our street and the people – commuting to work and being normal—wondered, I'm sure, why at twenty degrees below zero, a man was standing outside in his underwear in a snowstorm, but it was indeed real. I was, once again, victim to his attempt at my undoing.

"Why did you do this to my car, you—?" I yelled into the heavy, cold air. My broken, helpless voice, inaudible with really no force or strength, halted only a few inches from my face. Meanness and insanity defined him.

"That'll learn ya to be all high falutin'," he yelled across the driveway. "Lit my ass!" He went back into the house, slamming the door behind him.

Nobody would miss him if would slip on the ice, break his sick head open, and die. He had nowhere to go, nothing to do, except to destroy this humble piece of transportation connecting a person to goals. A needed B to get to C.

I went into the house, grabbed the phone, and dialed Hal. "Can you pick me up on your way to school? I have, I have, I need your help," my hands were shaking uncontrollably. "I have a minor disaster here." I could hardly construct a sentence.

Hal was there within half an hour. He saw Jim Dandy's goofy underwear-clad body on the porch, his club foot turned to the side, as Hal lept into the driveway in his maroon Volkswagen Rabbit. "What the hell happened to your car?" He asked the matter-of-fact question as he rolled down the window.

"I got up this morning and someone had broken the windows," I recounted as I was hopping into the Rabbit.

"Did you call the police?"

"Hal, it is too complicated to explain."

I didn't know how to tell him what had really happened. I reached my hand across his face, touched his shoulder, drew him into me, and hugged him near to my heart as mascara formed stripes on my face. "We need to get it inside somewhere or cover the windows," he relayed. "Did that asswipe...."

I will never forget Hal's rescue, his hilarious words when I needed them the most, or the smell of his clean cologne permeating through the warm air. He was a knight in his shining armor. He was rescuing this damsel in distress. He was my prince, and I felt like Grace Kelly.

CHAPTER TWENTY-EIGHT

If only Jim Dandy were gone, our problems would be solved. Poison, booby traps, starvation—nothing messy or bloody— just fast and foolproof. He was the one who needed to go—not Grandma Delanie, a person who added to the world. Unfortunately, he was alive and well.

Yes, I was slowly sinking into unhinged, and I was aware that I couldn't move forward if so much of my life was reacting to his negativity. Even with the humor of Hal, literature, and my job, fury had furrowed into my body. Small things were eating at me, and those small things weren't really to blame. I had spent my whole life, up to this point, swearing that I would never be anything like him, yet I was losing me as anger and helplessness continued to fester and capture my heart and my head. Hal was right; I was becoming afraid of life and challenges, and as a result, I was losing the self that I was trying to gain with education.

"You might need to talk to someone," Hal said it bluntly one day when he dropped me off after class. "That Jim Dandy asswipe is really putting you in a bad situation. I don't mind picking you up every day, but we gotta get your car fixed. You can't let him win, Del. You need that car."

"You're right," I agreed. "I have made calls, Hal, but I just don't have the money to fix it."

"Do you know anyone who could fix it?"

"It has to be done by a Ford dealership. They have to order the windows."

"Let me talk to my dad," Hal said. "He has a friend who is a mechanic. And, while I'm on this, you probably should talk to someone, a counselor. This stuff is making you a little crazy. I'm worried about you."

"I can't afford counseling, Hal," I said.

"We can talk tonight when I get off work," he said. "But maybe you should talk to your pastor or someone at your church."

His urging confirmed my speculations, but unfortunately, my best spiritual advisor, good and solid Sister Roop, had moved back to Savannah. The cost of long distance phone calls to Savannah made it impossible to call her, so I decided that the Mega Church of the Salvation at least had my affiliation as a child, and I could hitch a ride to the mall with Nancy the school bus driver and walk the rest of the way. The Pinto was parked in Elton Jenkins' barn, and Nancy, like Hal, was getting used to me hitching rides. The snow had stopped, and the day was a pleasant thirty-two degrees for January. Even with its vast membership of people swarming around, the mega church, I reasoned, had to have someone who could help me. On a journey to find peace, I embarked. Being a Tuesday afternoon, I stood at the end of the driveway knowing Nancy's route back to the school bus garage. She stopped — probably against policy—and picked me up in her empty school bus.

"Hey Kid," she said. "Heading to the mall again?"

"Yep," I said. "Can you give me a lift?"

"For you, anything," she said. "Get on board!" She dropped me off at the "end of the line," and I walked the rest of the way to the Mega Church of the Salvation where the marquis read, "The only way to heaven is through THESE doors." I ambled through the double doors of the giant modern brick building and hobbled, hurling the weight of my world—my hurting soul— inside.

I was prepared for a directive about leaving the dark house from someone—that advice always came, but that would require quitting school. That was not an option. I needed a strategy to deal with my maniacal lunatic father, if there were indeed a way. Dr. Faustus made a deal with the devil, but I wasn't about to sell my soul for that loser and lose my future. "Revenge is mine saith the Lord," Sister Roop once told me, "which is like Karma, Del. The getting even will take care of itself. You just gotta take care of yo'self, honey chil' 'cause you is all you got."

Looking at the huge monstrosity of a high-ceilinged room, gated around the perimeter with an ornately carved walnut fence to separate the staff from the served, my eyes searched for a kind soul. I thought that I had found one in a middle-aged white woman. She was holding a folder and wearing black half-reading glasses like a necklace. She wore her heavy make-up attractively, along with her very coiffed dark hair. She wore a pink and peach colored tweed suit and beige high-heeled pumps.

"What brings you here on this Tuesday afternoon?" she asked, noting the day of the week like a canned speech.

"Can we step into your office?" I asked, leaning my head in the direction of rooms in the back.

"O-kay," she voiced hesitantly, afraid of my straightforwardness. There was one gift in being short and female, I thought. Strangers were not afraid that I could hurt them physically— I'm too small—but I was beginning to use words, long and precise words, and I could shoot them out like a marksman.

I followed her to the tiny office with a sign on the outside of the door that read Female Assistant to the Pastor. Sister Roop ran Grandma Delanie's whole diverse and busy church on her own—

female or not—praise God— the word *female* on that sign bothered me just a little. Why didn't it just read Assistant to the Pastor or just Pastor?

Obviously, I was on the verge of something bad boiling inside. It wasn't the time to second guess the person who could possibly help me, so I went with it. She made it apparent with her body language, harrumphing, and looking at her watch, that I was intruding on her time. I sensed her frustration with my arrival, and I tried to get to the point. Thirst consumed my body. The spit in my mouth was thick, and I couldn't lubricate my mouth. She offered no tissues or water while water poured out of my eyes, but no water went in. "How can I help you?" she finally uttered, not sympathetic, head tilted down, eyes peering over the glasses attached with a chain.

"My name is Delanie Dane," I recounted. "I grew up in this church. It was—is—Jim Dandy's church."

"Is the person a cartoon character? The person's name is Jim Dandy?"

"Jim Dandy is my father," I said.

"Yes, well, he has a strange name, a very strange name, but our Heavenly Father lives in this church," she condescended as if I didn't understand, or was incapable of understanding, the difference between an earthly and Heavenly father.

"No, that's not what I mean," I tried to explain. "My biological father—my earthly father—h-h-he came here when he moved to Akron—with his parents, the Danes. But anyway, this is a weird and embarrassing story, but he broke all the windows in my car. Is there some kind of fund that I could borrow money to pay for the repairs? It's my car—I use it for school. I mean, I drive it to school and work. I think he was the one who broke all the windows—with a sledgehammer—not by accident."

"This Jim Dandy fellow did this? And how can I help you? It seems you need a mechanic, not me," she chuckled at her insensitive wit.

"I don't need you to help me with the windows," I continued. "I need a loan. The cost to fix the car is beyond what I can pay. I can pay installments."

"This isn't a bank," she said.

"I know that. Is there a loan system, you know, for church members or people who need temporary help?"

"No, we don't provide loans. You will have to go to a bank, dear."

"Okay. Let me ask something else. I have all this anger boiling inside me. It worries me. And I feel like I might explode. He does things like this all the time, and we just have to take it."

"Why do you have to take it?" she asked. "Why can't you stand up to him?"

"We're afraid, I guess," I choked out the words. "He rules by fear."

"I need to look up your file," she said in a business-like manner. "What's your name again?"

"Delanie Dane. You have a file on me?"

"We keep track of things like this, so we can check your tithing records."

"We're afraid of him," I tried to draw her back into my situation.

"Well, yes, I would be too! He sounds like he needs salvation."

"He is violent. He beats us up," I recounted. "He rules with fear. We are terrified."

"I need that file," she left the room.

When she returned without any paperwork, I was determined to get to the heart of the matter. "I just need to work on my anger issue. I just need to know where to turn. I just need a quick answer; that's all."

"It doesn't seem to be that simple here, does it?"

"It could be simple. The Dane family goes way back in this church. Where do you go when you are angry? Who do you talk to?"

"I cannot advise you. I would call the police," she said.

"Yes, there is that, but he would get away with it. He gets away with everything."

"You don't know what the police will do," she said.

"True," I said. "That is true."

"I am not a counselor. One thing I can say is that coming in here and spilling your guts is not what we do. It is not healthy to expose your problems to the world and other people. I have learned that much. Don't go around talking about your problems. Chin up!"

"Are you saying that I should keep it bottled up inside?" I asked. "Can't I talk to, say, another minister?"

"We really don't deal in loans and such. We rely on the literal words of the Bible," she lectured. "The Bible, one of the Ten Commandments, in fact, speaks of, and I quote 'honoring your father.'"

"I didn't do anything to deserve this. He is just crazy!"

"Well, I wasn't there. I can't vouch for you or uh, what's his name? Jim Dandy," she pronounced his name like he was a cartoon character. "I don't even know you."

"Well, I just wanted to talk to someone who could help me. Who could give me some hope, some guidance, you know?"

"Young girls come in here and strut around and think that because they go to college, they know everything. Well, listen, I didn't go to college, and I did just fine."

"Am I strutting around?" I asked as she got up and slammed the door.

"Yes," she said. "You came in here with all eyes on you."

This Female Assistant to the Pastor was taking this conversation in the wrong direction. I didn't say anything to her about college or her personally. I didn't bring an attitude. I wasn't strutting, I was crawling. She was bringing her own insecurities and attitude into my story. I couldn't steer her back to answer a simple question of dealing with anger. I valued the "Praise the Lords" and tight body hugs from Sister Roop more than ever.

"I'm lost," I admitted. "I just need to talk to someone, I guess."

"Do you know the Lord Jesus Christ as your savior?" she cross examined. "He will take away all your sins, and you will find peace. Are you born again?"

"Well, I pray and I believe in God, but I need to talk to a person about my anger. I need to get my car fixed. Being born again is not really the problem right now. My freedom has been taken, and I need to go on with my life."

"It sounds to me like you don't know the Lord Jesus Christ as your personal savior. You need to attend a service and find salvation," she continued, again avoiding the answer to my original question.

She didn't get it. We were going in circles. She was chasing me; I was chasing her, but really, we didn't want to catch the other person.

"He doesn't want me to go to school. He wants me to stay there forever, as his pawn, as his little slave, so he can torture me. I need to get outta there, I know that. I need to talk to someone who can help me."

"We offer salvation and the path to salvation. God offers guidance."

"But God doesn't talk," I said.

"He talks to me," she proclaimed smugly. "Read your Scripture, young lady. Your earthly father, this Jim Dandy fellow, must have a reason to punish you in such a way. You might start by calling him *dad* instead of *Jim Dandy.*"

"He isn't a dad to me," I said. "He is a bad person."

"Well, there you have it," she said. "Some might consider it harsh, but I am sure he has a justifiable reason to do such things. Was there some transgression that you committed to make him so wrathful? It is the job of the earthly father to punish his children as he deems it necessary."

She rattled off these words like she said them all the time, like a saleswoman demonstrating a product. This woman was as heartless as Jim Dandy. She was so caught up in the mega church files and tithing records and being born again that she couldn't see a real human being standing in front of her.

"Listen, my dear," she went on. "Calm down first. This isn't made up. It's in the Bible, written by God in a lightning bolt. We all have our problems, and we deal with them. We keep them inside and hide them from the world. That's just what we do. Toughen up! I can tell you that the Lord's wrath is equal to the transgressions you have committed."

"First of all, God didn't write the Bible in a lightning bolt. A person did. I think Paul or Mark or somebody wrote some of it. And secondly," I asked, "do you really believe this stuff you are saying? Don't you ever question things?"

"I believe every word of it. I never question the authority of God. I never question men."

She must have seen the disgust on my face, because she just stared at me while I digested this idea. She had made the statement that she had "never questioned a man" and that disgusted me.

"Did you say that you never question a man?" I repeated.

"That is correct," she said. "Men have dominance over women. The Bible says it to be true."

"Oh, I think I am going to be sick. Thank you, but this isn't what I expected," I said quietly, and I left her office and headed toward the bathroom. The room was illuminated automatically when the door opened, and the terrible gray fluorescent lighting in the mirror cast an ugly spell on my ash white skin and my greenish blonde hair. I had a rash of new pimples popping up on my chin. Ironically, for the first time, I understood Jim Dandy's frustration of paying for something with taxes or tithes, and the recipient of the money absolutely misses the point.

It seemed like I could always speak to God in bathrooms: when Jeff Farnsworth called me "Fatty" or at the National Honor Society luncheon, bathrooms were my sanctuary. It was actually quite simple. Not a person came or went into that bathroom, so I was able to experience tranquility, an urban soliloquy, in the center of this busy, huge, labyrinthine mega church. It was just God and me while I drank water out of the spigot, splashed it on my gray face, washed the anger off my hands, and prayed. I sat on the cushioned sofa, looked at my torn and ragged cuticles, took deep breaths, and asked God what to do next.

A sense of peace came over my body. A message came down, out of nowhere, and strangely enough, I felt sorry for Jim Dandy. He, in his pathetic stupidity and meanness, was missing out on so much life. He was missing out on friendships and connectivity with others, with life, with the world, with hope. Then I was mad at myself. Why didn't I just stay home and pray at the Indian fountain? Like Grandma Delanie had said, the answers didn't come down like winning the Lottery. "Answers, chil', don't come down like a lightning bolt outta heaven or on your timetable," I remember Sister Roop's voice, "but the answer would come. You gotta believe it. She's with you all the time."

I was sitting there in a house of God, asking for help, but instead I was villainized and ridiculed by this woman who hadn't walked in my shoes or any shoes except for those beige pumps. If she had walked in my shoes, she would believe that Jim Dandy is right because he has male equipment and I don't. I couldn't roll with this type of religion. I needed to be alone with just God.

It was just another case of me being me, but of course I then connected this situation to literature. In his slave narrative *Autobiography of Frederick Douglass*, Douglass described how the hypocritical slave owners whipped their slaves in the name of God. My struggles were miniscule compared to Frederick Douglass' struggles, I knew that. As I looked at it in comparison, it gave me pause. I realized that in Akron, in Ohio, in the United States, in the world, there were much bigger problems than the stupid windows in my Pinto. Life with Jim Dandy was my burden, and as I thought of the size of it and the other pain being endured out there, it shrunk. I would have to go on, forge ahead, and move forward, for just a little longer because, as far as I could see, there were no other options. The anger, I suppose, would have to come along for the ride as well because I had no money for a counselor, and the Mega Church of the Salvation wasn't open to helping me.

I could go back to my life one more time. I had no other choice. I would have to continue my quest.

I could hear the choir going up the musical scale downstairs as I headed toward the door. I would have to walk home or borrow that Assistant's phone to call Hal or Jimmy's moped. I didn't want to ask her for any more favors. It was about five miles back to the dark house, so it would take me about an hour to get back. I would just have to hoof it. About ten minutes into my walk, Elton Jenkins and his mom, who were on their way home from a doctor's appointment in a nearby office, saw me trudging along, turned their car around, and asked me if I needed a ride.

"Why are you so far away from home by yourself?" Elton asked.

"I was doing some spiritual searching," I told him and jumped in the car. "Thanks for the ride!"

CHAPTER

TWENTY-NINE

"This funkadelic asswipe..." Hal leaned over the tabletop jukebox to George, who was his usual low key and dry-humored self, as we waited for pizza at Parasson's. "...is supposed to be her dad. The idiot took a sledgehammer and broke out all the windows in her car. For no reason. Who does that?"

"Why would he do that?" George asked.

"He does insane things," Hal said. I was embarrassed, but I allowed him to explain.

"Well, if I do something he doesn't like, he gets even," I said. "I can't prove he did. Maybe it was vandalism."

"What would merit that?" George questioned.

"His stuff doesn't make sense," I said. "It isn't anything normal like staying out late or getting caught smoking. In this case, he said it was because I think I am 'high falutin'."

"High faluting? Who does this kind of stuff?" George wasn't looking for an answer to his question. "Those kinda guys don't mess with people their own size. They only pick on people smaller than them."

"Yea, an old friend of mine used to say that," I said, thinking of Sister Roop saying the same thing.

"Well, that's true," George said. "I don't mean disrespect; he's your father, but I question his motives."

"He is a real ass," Hal retorted.

George was right. "No disrespect, Delanie, the guy must be depressed—no joke, I'm serious."

"I know. I am beginning to see that," I said.

"I have a friend in the auto repair business. We can probably get the windows fixed for a lot less than a Ford dealership. Let me do some checking," George said.

George might be the answer to my prayers.

Jim Dandy was sleeping on the floor in mud-crusted jeans and a ripped flannel shirt when George and Hal pulled in the dark house driveway early the next morning driving George's "work truck," a 1960 turquoise Ford Econoline with a wobbly bed and a big rusted chrome bumper on the front. It was one of those dated vehicles that, I swear, had a face that looked like the Little Engine That Could with a determined expression.

It was still too cold to drive the car without windows. George towed the Pinto with the Econoline, while the plastic garbage bags taped to the window frames shook violently in the backdraft. We were off to Sonny's Garage, a friend of George's from high school. "The energy you put out into the world comes back to you," George pronounced in his measured monotone voice as we squished together on the front-seat bench in the Ecoline. "It will come back around and get him someday."

"Like Karma," I suggested.

"Who's Carmen?" he asked.

"Karma, Dad," Hal said. "It's a Buddhist belief that the energy you put out is what comes back to you. Kinda like circular energy."

"I don't know what you are talking about, but I that reminds me of Chinese food. I would like some good lo mein," George smirked, turning off the radio.

"Well, you sure don't know how to make a frozen pizza!" Hal interjected.

"I fell asleep," George offered. "You are never going to let me live that down, are you?"

"The fire alarm woke you up," Hal deadpanned back as if they were a comedy team on a late-night talk show.

While they bantered, I chuckled at them, but I was worried about cost. I had a paycheck coming, but that really needed to go toward my tuition installment. George read my mind. "This should be easy. Sonny said you could make payments," he said. "The worst part will be getting the glass out of the way."

"Maybe I should have vacuumed it," I said, stupidly.

"Nah, Sonny's got a car vacuum. He can work magic on cars," George assured me.

We dropped the car off, and the laughter continued with the two goofballs. They lightened my spirit, and I was grateful to have them in my life. George's hankering for lo mein could not be quashed, so the three of us went to a little family-owned Chinese restaurant in a plaza where we ordered and drank hot tea out of tiny porcelain cups.

After pouring tea for all of us, George raised his little cup. "Here's to getting the Pinto back on the road." We made a toast.

"Del, don't let him sweet talk you into believing that he is perfect," Hal argued. "He is a slob. You wouldn't believe his eating habits."

"I am not a slob," George defended himself, swishing a noodle onto the table that was caught in the fold of his shirt.

"That is disgusting," Hal said as George plopped it into his mouth.

"Look at that stain," Hal pointed out. "Who is gonna get that out? I'm sick of pre-treating all your shirts."

"Quit nagging," George croaked back as more sauce dropped onto his shirt. "I'll save that for later." He winked.

"I need some of that Shout stuff at the grocery store," Hal said convincingly. "See what I mean? He's a slob?"

They didn't know what they had. They were healthy and refreshing and hilarious. They were not aware that their banter— supportive and demonstrative of unconditional love— spread to me. It comforted me like a soft blanket.

I carry a pocket planner to keep track of my work and school schedule. On the bottom of every month is a quote. The quote for January 1985 was from Alexander Graham Bell. It read, "When God shuts a door, he opens a window." The point was not lost. The windows were broken, but the doors of my heart were open wide with thanks to my friends.

CHAPTER THIRTY

Not just with stupid ass Jim Dandy, but with darling heart Hal, I felt like I was walking on broken glass. Hal's perfect face, his voice, and his clean smell permeated my mind. Awkward and skinny with those oversized Clark Kent glasses, he was not the guy that every girl swooned over, but that didn't matter to me. I remembered the striking good looks of that guy in Dr. Slocum's class wearing the Akron Law 86 shirt; he was a guy to swoon over, but Hal's heart was solid gold— not hollow. He understood me— from the very beginning. No games, no lies, just truth and grit. I felt safe when he was around, but I didn't know how he felt about me. I didn't want to rock the boat because things were chugging along rather smoothly; we had agreed, silently, to be mutually supportive friends. We hadn't talked about *us* and that was fine, until the discussion came up one night at a Zip Strip bar, when this loudmouth guy in one of our classes posed, after too many beers, the question about how long we had been "seeing each other."

"We're just good friends," Hal piped in after a long and awkward pause.

"We have so much fun together," I added, trying to calm the waters. "We understand each other." These things were true. We were drawn together as we were testing the trepidation of trust that we both needed to explore in the opposite sex. Our chemistry was possibly too simple and too pure for the complex world where we co-existed and moved among mortals.

"Sure," continued David Norbin, a scrawny guy with a too-big, nosey nose, who sat squarely between us in Shakespeare. "You guys just keep telling everybody that bullshit. But I know. I can see it."

"See what?" I had ventured, stupidly, onto the shaky branch of some pitiful sapling that was just sticking out there and ready to snap.

"Everyone can see the chemistry, the energy," David pointed out.

"That night at the Rubber Bowl, you guys just kept laughing and laughing as if nobody else was around. It was all inside jokes," piped in Leslie, a heavyset girl with a guy's haircut.

Everyone just snickered and we did too, blowing off the steam of the gawky conversation. The elephant in the room was announced. It had smashed its way into conversation, and it continued thrashing its way into our tranquility, never forgetting the question, even after we left the party.

"Let's get some late-night Luigi's pizza," suggested Hal who always "got the shakes" when he was hungry —which was most of the time.

After a long silence, with only the hum of the road and the Rabbit's shifting gears to be heard— a rarity with the radio off— we drove toward Luigi's, an open-all-night pizza place on North Hill; I let it air out a while, and then I finally took a stab at the gaping hole.

"Hal, I don't know what is going on. David made it very uncomfortable."

"You know, we need to pick up your car tomorrow," he interjected quickly, changing the subject completely. "Do you want to tell me why he smashed your windows?"

I loved the way he used the word *we,* and it took me on a little ride around the Milky Way.

"You wouldn't believe me if I told you. His reasoning, if you could call it that, doesn't make sense to other people. To me and my family, it is just what he does. I realize that normal people don't have the windows smashed on their cars on a daily basis."

"Yep," he said. "I know you didn't do it. I know that mutant freak man Jim Dandy did it. But why?"

I left out some parts, so not to overwhelm him, but I told him little bits, fragments, cubed Safety Glass chunks, about life in the dark house. Being perceptive, of course, he already knew. "That dude is a freakin' monster. Jim Dandy! What a stupid name for a stupid ass guy! I can't even come up with the words, Del!" His descriptions cracked me up. "Don't tell the psycho that I said it! He might kick my ass!" He stayed deadpan as I laughed.

"Well, yea! He is a monster, and I wouldn't tell him. I hate the son-of-a-bitch!"

"You gotta get outta there!"

"No duh on that," I said. "Just a few more years, and I'll have my degree."

"He doesn't help you at all with school?"

"Not a penny," I answered. "But I can't afford rent. Well, you see what he did to the car? That's about all he ever does for me: cause pain."

"He's a flaming asshole!"

"Yea, Hal, I know!" I yelled emphatically.

"You could call the police on him for that, you know?"

"It is possible, Hal, that someone else did it. So what are the police gonna do? It would only make it worse," I acknowledged.

"But who would do this to your car?"

"I don't know," I said.

"You need out!"

166

"I don't want to take out loans. I am so afraid of that—any, everything."

"Other than that, his stupid ass, what are you afraid of?"

"Academically, I can do this. I'm not dumb, but the other parts —financial, emotional, social—that stuff is such a challenge for me. I don't know how to put it together, so I can be the person I want to be. I struggle understanding where and how I will fit in. It's just too much," I said. As I spoke, all of this was swirling around in my head like snow driving down on the Pinto's headlights.

"I can figure that stuff out," he explained. "That's the easy part. It's the academics that strangle me." He put the car in park, and he swung open the door. The red and green sign was illuminated and flashed *Luigi's* off then on. The door dinged our entrance as the old-fashioned automated band on top of the bar played its usual polka song. The owner, holding menus, seated us near the swinging saloon-style kitchen doors. The vapors of melted mozzarella cheese mingled with yeast and basil and oregano tomato sauce, erasing the complexity of the issues that brought us there.

"That's why we are here together," Hal finally concluded, clinching it perfectly as he unrolled the napkin containing his silverware. "Things work out the way they do for a reason."

"You and your dad helped me so much," I said.

"I'm glad we could help," he said.

"The stars kinda lined up, huh?" I took a sip of the Diet Coke that the waitress had brought.

"We all have goofy families, Del," he acknowledged. "I had to get some counseling when my mom died. My disgust for her haunted me. I had so much anger that I couldn't direct."

"You said that before, but I never picked up one ounce of anger," I said. He was so optimistic. He was like a child's bouncy ball, springing right back up at you.

"I still have anger, Del," he said.

"You're so easygoing," I explained. "Now me, I'm angry."

"Who wouldn't be—living with that psycho? Did you talk to your minister?"

"I tried, Hal, but it didn't go very well," then I recounted the Female Assistant to the Pastor story, and he just shook his head.

"Some people are ignorant," he said. "They don't get it."

I was chewing. "How did you get help?"

"Counseling helped me a lot," he said, shaking more parmesan cheese on his pizza. "But it is expensive if you don't have insurance. But sometimes just talking helps, like we're doing right now."

"Okay," I concurred. "You're sorta my counselor."

"If it makes you feel better, you don't project any of this to the world either," he said. "You seem like you have it so together. Remember when I told you that?" As he was chomping on a piece of buttery garlic bread, he was cracking open my shell, scaling that ornately-carved wooden fence, swimming in the moat and ah, my heart was right here. He was digging me out.

"Oh, I'm a good actress. I cover it up," I proclaimed. "I could win an Academy Award."

"You have such a get-out-of-my-way attitude," he gestured, making stop signs in the air. "Like watch out!"

"Yea, you told me that," I managed to laugh and cry at the same time. "But I don't see it."

"Hell, yea," he insisted. "I was afraid you would run me over with your car when I first met you."

"Me?"

"Remember how we met around Thanksgiving? I told my dad, 'I met this girl and I think she was one of the Pilgrims. She's so, uh, serious and focused.'"

"A Pilgrim, huh?"

"You're a tough little thing," he was emphatic. "All laced up with your bonnet but ready to work."

"Well, I have a confession," I joked. "I thought you were the turkey!"

"Really?" he questioned. "Why?"

"Strutting around like you were so cool, but you are searching just like everyone else."

"You got something there," he admitted. "Let's order more food. George has no food at the house! You know he thinks he runs a diet clinic. I'm skinny enough. He is so cheap; he hates to buy groceries!"

"I think he is great."

He consumed a large regular Coke, a huge cheese-stacked salad, another piece of garlic bread, and a large lasagna. I daintily dined on a salad with only vinegar and sipped a Diet Coke. He continued to complain about being skinny; I gained two pounds.

There are some things that we can escape in our biology. Metabolism is not one of them.

CHAPTER THIRTY-ONE

It was still and dark in the March outside. Toilet flushing inside was punctuated with whimpers from Mom, and it interrupted my jam session to this great new Michael Jackson song called "Billie Jean." In his sequin jacket, black loafers with white socks, and one tendril hanging in his face, he was everywhere on MTV, moon dancing his way across the screen. I had a feeling that my moon-dancing was about to be over—again.

"Mom, are you still sick?" I announced myself entering the bathroom behind her because we all startled so easily. She was bent over the toilet, hugging a wadded up, faded, and bleached-stained hot pink bath towel to her chest.

"No, Del, I will be alright," she said.

Nausea traced itself from my stomach to my mouth with her utterance of those words. I had seen enough movies, taken enough high school biology, and had witnessed a few friends who exhibited these symptoms. I swallowed hard. "Mom, you have the flu, right?"

"Del, I can't even think about it right now. Don't make me talk right now," she was holding her stomach. "I'm late for my period."

I answered with silence.

"I just can't think about it now," she reiterated, but I was left to think about it. "The Saturday morning cupcake truck needs to be unpacked. I have to take out the garbage, and I can't call off sick. We need the money."

"I will take out the garbage for you," I offered. "But we need to talk—about, about a plan. Do you have a plan?"

"I've never had a plan, Del. That's the problem!" No truer words were ever spoken by her.

Arms folded at my chest, I nodded a *yes* and *no* at the same time when Jimmy came into the room.

"Another baby?" he asked bluntly. He was a high school kid, and he got it. He got it better than she did. Meanwhile, Jim Dandy could be overheard downstairs watching boxing on TV and screaming "get him" like the boxers could hear his stupid screams.

The solution had been legal since 1973 and although emotionally painful, it may be a better option than giving birth—in this hell hole, in this dark house. In the fantasy world of my mind, babies don't live in dark houses. They live in pink rooms, with the perfume of baby powder as a music box lifts little chimes through the air.

"He is the most worthless person in the whole world," I whispered.

We all just stood there, and Justin tiptoed in. "You guys act like you did when Grandma Delanie died. It will be alright."

"You guys are going to have to step up and help more." She was now using the hot pink towel to wipe her tears.

"Us? What about that worthless piece of ...Jim Dandy....downstairs?" I could feel the anger overflowing.

"It just happened," she tried to explain. "You'll have to change your schedules to help out more; I still have to work, or we will lose the house."

I knew that this problem would land on my lap. I couldn't let a newborn baby lie in a wet crib and cry, while that freaking monster smoked cigarettes in its face. I couldn't do it, and she knew it. She had put my life, my future, in peril. I hated her at that moment, maybe more than I hated Jim Dandy.

I started spinning out into the universe. There was the Milky Way Galaxy. There was Polaris and the moon and oh, I waved as I swooped by Sirius and Betelgeuse. On my way back to earth, I saw Kathie, confused, running with me to the rusted and dirty Chevy Caprice. I saw Jimmy on the sidelines, confused, trying to decide whether or not to go onto the football field. I saw Mr. Camparti, confused, looking at the turkey remnants on the medieval chandelier. I saw a picture of myself, confused, looking out at my little Pinto, windows smashed, parked in the driveway, as it filled with snow.

Everything was confused and confusing. We were all weighted down as I crash landed back in the dark house like Dorothy after the tornado. All of this, more stuff added to my list, was swirling around like black cinders rising from an orange fire. I could picture Jim Dandy holding a pitchfork laughing maniacally about this new predicament that he had helped to create.

I hadn't answered any of the three phone calls that I knew were from Hal about picking up my car. Jim Dandy was too consumed in his boxing match on TV to answer it—thank God— but he was able to scream about the God-damned phone.

I turned off "Billie Jean" from the turntable, and I saw Hal pull in the driveway a few minutes later. I called out the window that I would be right down. I was one hundred years old. "Hal! I can't believe I can even function," I uttered when I reached Hal's Rabbit. "I just found out that my mom is pregnant."

"With that mutant freak Jim Dandy?" he stated the obvious. "That is a disgusting thought."

"Yea, I get nauseated just thinking of him in any way," I said.

"Who will take care of it?" he asked.

"I'm smart enough to know how not to have a baby. You'd think she be would too, huh?" I said sarcastically.

"Let's get outta here and get your car," Hal suggested, looking around like he was on a surveillance camera. "The garage closes at noon. We can talk on the way over to Sonny's."

While some college girls were partying and trying not to get pregnant themselves, I was now trying to figure how to balance all of this added stress of my mother's pregnancy at forty-four.

Who was I becoming in all of this? What had happened to the faith that I had for so long? What had happened to that girl who believed that anything was possible? What had happened to that girl who naively believed that Santa would make it all better? She's gone, and she has changed places with this angry, frustrated, scared girl who thinks now about abortions and people dying. Back then, I traveled miles and miles in my mind, in a book, with a movie, with a song, with a friend. Today, that girl is swept away with the flood of worry, too much, too heavy, much too young. With Hal there, I felt safe in his car and decided that I needed to redirect my energy toward him, this wonderful friend by my side. He was there and it was now. I didn't want to lose him, or what he meant to me, so I tried to get back into the present time—or at least I pretended to do so.

I looked at him from the side and realized that he had the most perfect profile.

CHAPTER THIRTY-TWO

"A sociopath," explained Dr. Philip Longworth, my psychology professor, as he was writing notes on the freestanding blackboard at E. J. Thomas Performing Arts Hall, "really only cares about himself. He has very little feeling for those around him, nor does he care how these actions might affect those around him. Sociopaths tend to be incapable of truly loving anyone. They have early histories of juvenile delinquency, but they 'get by' by conning others."

We were mid-way into Spring Semester, and I was jolted back to scholarly things as my mind became absorbed in his topic on this particular day.

There's a name for it! I couldn't breathe. I was trying to take in air.

As I tried to fill my lungs with fresh oxygen, I looked around to see if anyone had noticed my dramatic reaction to the lecture notes, and there, three rows in front of me, sat the gorgeous stud muffin, the Akron Law 86 guy from last semester. Today, he was wearing a rag-wool sweater and didn't seem to notice, thank God, that I had noticed him again. I watched him listen to Dr. Longworth and write in his notebook.

I exhaled hard as Dr. Longworth went on: "They have shallow emotions. They lack remorse or shame. They have a grandiose sense of self, and they have a poor work ethic, but they survive by being parasitic. They can usually find someone to support them. And here's the clincher: They can be charming, if they try."

I was wiping away the tears that had started rolling down my cheeks. I was hoping that nobody saw me, of course not Akron Law 86, as the tears wouldn't stop. "He's a sociopath," I whispered to myself. "He's a freakin' sociopath."

"Okay, see you guys on Thursday," Dr. Longworth said. The rest of the class started filing out of E.J., and I collected my books slowly—still in a daze. Without thinking, I automatically went to the front of the huge lecture hall where the bearded professor was gathering his materials.

"Do you have a question, my dear?" Dr. Longworth asked, obviously not knowing my name out of three hundred other students.

"I just figured out that someone I know is a sociopath," I uttered. I don't know why I told him; I guess I was obviously interested on a higher level than the other students, so it was something that I felt compelled to communicate. I put myself was out there like a hand ready to be shaken.

"Amazing, isn't it, when we at least find a name for the problem?" Dr. Longworth concluded.

"Amazing," I repeated. "I always thought he was mean for mean's sake. But he's sick. Is it treatable?" I asked Dr. Longworth.

"It's almost impossible to treat. I'm sorry," he said authoritatively. "Sociopaths are know-it-alls...."

"Yes!"

"So, it is hard to reach them. They insist on being the one with all the answers. They are very convinced and convincing that they are always right, when quite often, they are dead wrong."

"Oh, yes," I wanted Dr. Longworth to continue.

"Occasionally talk therapy works, but the sociopath has to want it to work. They have to see their problem. The therapist must maintain a low profile because as soon as the sociopath picks up on the authority or a knowing attitude, all progress will be lost."

"So that is why he hates me to be smart," I muttered under my breath.

"What was that?" Dr. Longworth asked.

"Well, the sociopath that I know hates me to be smart. He continually degrades me and tries to keep me….stupid, under his thumb. He gets mad if I use a big word," I recollected all the clues. All of a sudden, it all made sense.

"That sounds exactly correct," he concurred.

"So, it is best to always let him win?" I asked.

"Well, yes. In his mind, let him think that he is always right. Even when you know that he is dead wrong to avoid fights."

"I have to get to my next class," Dr. Longworth said kindly, "but I'd be glad to talk to you in depth, say, tomorrow, if you have time?"

"Yes, I have a break between ten and eleven. Will that work?"

"That sounds great. Stop by my office."

As we were finishing our conversation, Akron Law 86 approached Dr. Longworth and interjected, "Excuse me for interrupting, but Dr. Longworth, do you want the overhead installed for tomorrow?"

"Yes, Ray, that would be great. I'll be using it all this week," Dr. Longworth replied. "I'm sorry I didn't ask. What is your name?"

"Oh, I'm Delanie Dane. I should have introduced myself sooner."

"Oh, that's fine. Hello, Delanie. This is Ray Cooper, my student assistant."

"Hi," I said, waving my hand in front of my face like a windshield wiper. I was trying to avoid saying something stupid, sneezing, running into a wall, or knocking over Dr. Longworth's freestanding blackboard.

"Hi," he blushed. "Are you a psych major?"

"No. English. I am an English major."

"I'm pre-law," he explained. "Well, actually political science. This is my last semester, and then I'm starting law school."

"That's cool." I was racking my brain to think of something not-too-sophisticated yet not-too-nerdy to say. Cool? That was really the best word I could come up with?

I needed to get away from there because I was starting to talk myself into a panic, worrying if I had used the wrong word, the wrong verb tense, or a Jim Dandy non-word, when talking to the splendid specimen Ray Cooper or the brilliant brain Dr. Longworth.

"Well, I hafta get to my next class," Ray Cooper said. I was relieved to leave.

"Okay, Delanie," Dr. Longworth concluded. "I will see you tomorrow at ten?"

"Sounds great. Thanks, Dr. Longworth. Nice meeting you, Ray." I managed to stumble off the stage without breaking a leg.

"Nice meeting you too!" he yelled, hands cupped around his mouth.

Two major breakthroughs in one day: I learned that the antagonist of my life could officially be called a sociopath. I also learned that Akron Law 86, who was real and in my psych class, could officially be called a Ray Cooper.

Things were getting names.

CHAPTER THIRTY-THREE

When I arrived at his office, Dr. Longworth was typing on one of those boxy, newfangled computers with a rainbow-colored Apple on it. He was listening to classical music on WKSU with his office door open. I was apprehensive about telling anyone the truth about my life in the dark house. He would be the first person who would know about Jim Dandy's darkness—from my mouth. After all, people might look at me and judge me. I didn't want to be seen now by a professor as a pitiful girl with a crazy ass father. I didn't want to be attached to any stigma. But I needed information.

"Delanie," he said, starting to stand up when I appeared in the doorway. "You are the only student I have ever had with that name. It is lovely."

"Thank you," I said. "Delanie is my mom's maiden name," I offered.

"Hmmm. I knew some Delanies at Firestone High School," he said.

"Really?"

"Yes, I went to school with Linda Delanie," he stated.

"Are you kidding? Linda Delanie is my mom. She is Linda Dane now."

"She was a beautiful girl," he said. "A nice girl. Great dimples."

"Yes, she is an Irish beauty," I replied. "I wish I had her height. Looks like Vivien Leigh in *Gone with the Wind*, when she takes off her glasses."

"She does," he said. "She was a nice girl. Very funny, as I recall."

"Yes, I would like to think that," I said.

"Did...she...marry...Jim Dandy Dane?"

"Yes," I said.

"Oh, it is very clear now," he recalled.

"It is?"

He went on without addressing my question. "I even remember your grandmother—a great lady." He said nothing of Jim Dandy being *great* or even *nice*. The obvious omission and the way he spaced Jim Dandy's name told the complete story.

"You know my grandma?" I realized my verb tense was incorrect. It should have been past tense. "My grandma just recently passed away." I felt tears coming.

In an office nearby, someone was smoking. It must have a Pall Mall cigarette because I intimately know that smell, it kept me awake at night, lying in bed with Jimmy and Justin beside me, worrying that Jim Dandy would fall asleep, and we would all die in a house fire. At school, we had to sign a sheet that we had told our parents about the health risks of smoking, and that we had asked them specifically not to smoke in bed.

"She needs to stay outta my life—damn teacher," Jim Dandy said, the belt thrashing my legs and arms. "My business in my house!"

I was recalled from my flashback when Dr. Longworth cleared his throat and moved to an upholstered chair by the window. "I'm really sorry to hear that about Mrs. Delanie...She was a class act."

"I know."

"Have a seat," he waved to a comfortable chair. "Linda Delanie and I were pretty good friends."

I felt a little weird—especially now that I knew he knew Mom—telling him the story of the dark house. "I read an entire book last night about sociopaths, Dr. Longworth," I said. "I was amazed at how perfectly he was—is—described."

"Are we talking about Jim Dandy?"

"Well, you know, since you know my mom, I'm kinda embarrassed, but yes." The words fell out of my mouth with the force and strength of Niagara Falls. I didn't know this girl who was talking; I was just along for the ride in her body. I was in that barrel, going over the Falls, hoping to survive, but in a sense, it was so liberating.

"I knew Jim Dandy Dane," he admitted. "You have probably pegged it correctly. A textbook case."

"Did you know him well?"

"They're fairly easy to spot," he went on, not directly answering my question. "Sociopaths live among us. They are quite cunning and deceiving—until we finally—like you—figure it out. Some people never figure it out. The victims think that they caused the problems. They think that everything is their fault."

"Yes," I was dumbfounded and mesmerized at the same time.

"I understand why the people around the sociopath feel that way," he explained. "But really, when you stop and think, he is the one in darkness. He has the darkness, but you don't have to share it forever, or at all."

He paused. "But with education, you can begin to find your way out of the darkness. It is important that you, and the rest of your family, get away—detach—from him as soon as you can. Even if it's not physically, but emotionally and intellectually, you need to see how sick he is, and how that sickness affects you."

"I know. That is the goal of my life—right now," I said. "He is a heartless person, and I never knew that there was a name for what he has. I just thought it was a bad personality. Is it a disease?"

"No, it is considered a disorder, a personality disorder."

"Do people become sociopaths as result of their childhood, or are they born with it? Is it genetic?" Were these words coming from my mouth? I wasn't floating down the river anymore. I was controlling the words: intelligent and well-thought out.

"Those are good questions. Many psychologists believe that at least fifty percent of the disorder is genetic," he continued.

"Could I..."

"But not to worry, you did not inherit it," he answered my unasked question. "I can see that you are quite aware of the world around you, and you know how you impact it."

"The other fifty percent, they think, is due to upbringing and never having boundaries, never being responsible for the actions or decisions and how those decisions affect other people," he walked over to a pitcher and poured a glass of water. "Want some water?"

"Yes, I would love some water," I answered. "That is amazing," Dr. Longworth had hit a bullseye.

"Here is a copy of a research project I am working on," he said as he handed me a folder. "I'd love to have you participate. I'm looking for people who know sociopaths. Their input is important to the project."

"I'd be glad to help," I said.

"And tell your mom that Phil Longworth said 'hi.' We were in the same English class our junior year in high school." He remembered her that vividly over twenty years ago?

"I will tell her." I was wondering what she would have to say about this news flash.

CHAPTER

THIRTY-FOUR

We had seen the daffodils and tulips and the showers of April. Mom was definitely pregnant. She had to tell Mr. Reynolds at Marathon that she would be off work for a while, and she was worried how he would take the news. How would we survive without her paycheck for that period of time? At forty four, the chances for birth defects increase greatly, not to mention that she would be sixty-two years old when the baby graduated from high school. Heck, I would be forty when that day finally arrived!

"Mom, have you thought about the whole child-care thing?" I asked one Saturday morning while I was folding towels beside her.

"You will not be able to go to college this fall," she said. "Then when you go to work, Jimmy and Justin can take care of him until I get home from work."

"What about that ass hole?" I asked, blatantly, openly, and unflinchingly. The words just tumbled out.

"He won't do nothing," she agreed. "And watch your language."

"Anything," I corrected unwittingly. The grammar correction went over her head. She thought was stating my support.

"We're talking about a newborn baby, Mom, wearing diapers, weighing less than ten pounds, drinking bottles, learning to walk. Why does he get away with doing nothing?"

She avoided the question like it wasn't even there. "Del, you and Jimmy and Justin will have to step up and help out more. I don't know what else can happen. I can't quit work, and we can't afford a babysitter."

The conservative, closed-minded mega church already had damned me to hell, so I couldn't go any lower. I didn't just blindly accept their dogma. I read too much literature, news, and sought different opinions. The Female Assistant to the Pastor hated my guts. I couldn't be a worse person in their eyes. Could I go to another deeper level of hell, like the murderers suggested by Dante in *The Inferno*? Maybe Dante flashed forward and met Jim Dandy when he penned the epic?

"Mom, do you remember a guy named Phil Longworth from high school?"

"Phil Longworth? Were you in my yearbook again?"

"Why? Is he in your yearbook?"

"Oh, I think he had a crush on me our junior year. We were in the same English class." She also pinpointed that English class twenty-six years ago.

"He is my professor. My psychology professor. I wish you would have married him," I stated, aware that Jim Dandy was not within earshot, off the couch for the first time in three months, working on a car part for some vagrant guy. I was also aware of the truth of this hard-hitting statement.

"He was very smart," she acknowledged. "He always wanted to be a counselor or something like that. He was kinda boring."

"Well, he became a professor. He isn't boring."

"He always wanted to read books. He was boring."

"Well, he said to tell you 'hi.'"

"Don't mention his name to your dad. He used to make fun of Phil."

"Why?"

"We went out with a group of friends once. He asked me out, but I thought he was a goof."

"You should have gone, Mom. He said you were beautiful. Your life could be so different. And here he is, my professor." I didn't dare to mention the fact that we talked about sociopaths. I didn't mention Grandma Delanie either, but that clue helped me to figure that they probably had been on a date.

"A professor. That sounds so boring." She was so ignorant. I thought to myself that boring would be so much better than this recipe of psycho and meanness she got with Jim Dandy.

"Mom, have you ever thought about how your life could be different? Have you ever thought about changing your life?"

"No," she confessed. "He won't let me leave. Jim Dandy told me once that if I ever left him, he would find me and take you kids."

"He wouldn't kill you." I only half believed myself.

"There is no telling what he would do," she whispered. "I might not ever see you kids again."

"Mom, have you ever thought about the possibility that Jim Dandy has some kind of disorder with his mind?" I tried to put it in understandable terms for her.

"I think he has some kind of tumor on his brain, and every time it moves, he has a mean streak," she explained.

"Well, he is sick, Mom. It isn't just a mood." I tried to keep it understandable for her.

It still went over her head. I should have known that the conversation had gotten a little too deep for her. "Okay," she changed the subject. "Could you fry up that hamburger in the fridge for Jimmy and Justin?"

That was the end of that conversation. It couldn't go any further. We had hit a dead end.

So, I fried the hamburger.

CHAPTER THIRTY-FIVE

Burden and worry were continuing to consume my soul, but I forged onward. The advancing life, innocent of the creation of these problems, was merely a bundle of cells growing, so unaware of the heap of troubles into which he or she would be born. Here I was, the oldest of these siblings, trying to plow on and care, while trying to remain on my own course. These thoughts were churning around in my head when I realized that I was headed in the wrong direction, literally.

I was walking to my car; I had to park in an out-of-the-way lot that day, and I couldn't stop my mind from creating one disaster scenario after another. I didn't have that new virus AIDs at least, but what about the baby? What if the baby had some terrible disease? What if Jim Dandy shook it to death when I wasn't there? What if a meteor struck the earth? On and on, my mind kept going in circles. Thirst struck me and exhaustion overcame my body as I ducked into this weird, out of place, small yellow and orange squarish brick building near the parking lot. I was in search of a drinking fountain; I didn't know that I was on a wayward path.

"Hello!" a woman greeted me and looked up at me with eyes as green as an Irish shamrock.

"Oh, hi." I was taken aback by the immediate welcome. "I am sort of a lost soul out there. I was wandering around just looking for water; I'm so thirsty. I hope I haven't bothered you."

"No, no, you haven't bothered me," she said.

"I was just lost in thought. Do you ever do that?"

"All the time," she admitted. "There is a water fountain around the corner. It's real cold and good." She was wearing pince-nez reading glasses. Her silver hair was cropped short in a pixie style and she wore small silver heart earrings. "I'm glad you're here. It has been rather quiet. I could use some company."

"Where exactly am I?" I asked.

"This is the campus ministry," she stated. "My name is Jane. We do some counseling and ministerial work for the Akron students."

"It sounds like something I could use," I agreed.

"I believe that things happen for a reason. All those who are searching are not lost." She shuffled a few papers in front of her.

"Well, I'm lost," I felt comfortable letting down my burden with her. "I'm scared. I'm confused, and most of all, I'm angry."

"You don't seem to be angry. You're good at covering it up," Jane smiled and her eyes twinkled.

"Yes, I'm a great actress. Nobody would know what I have inside. Anger, resentment, confusion: everyone thinks I have it all together. They don't have a clue!"

"Well, I can try to help. I'm just a volunteer here; we're nondenominational. Do you have church home?"

"Not really," I said. "I grew up in that famous mega church, but it's not really my place." I didn't feel like explaining Sister Roop and Savannah at that moment.

"Well, it doesn't matter. You are here now. What is on your mind?"

I gave her the list: the sociopath, the unborn baby, Hal, Ray Cooper, the future for Jimmy and Justin, and I could go on.

"What do I do?" I couldn't stop talking; I felt like I had met the first solid person I could talk to since Grandma Delanie had died, and Sister Roop had left for Savannah. The words just flowed, like water, without a stutter, without worries about uncomfortable sentence construction, without bad grammar, without a flinch or concern for judgment. These kind green eyes, squinting from reading too much, held so much empathy. She got up and hugged me. I felt safe; my thirst was quenched.

"Well, right now, you need to take care of you," she said. "The baby isn't here yet. There is a very important, but simple teaching that you need to know. It is called serenity. I think you need some! I'm going to teach you a prayer, and I want you to practice it. It will soothe your soul."

She began quoting a famous prayer, "'God, grant me the serenity to accept the things I cannot change...'"

"Whenever you get in a dither over this or anything else for that matter, remember that you cannot change other people; you can only change you and how you react. You didn't create the problems, and you can't cure them."

"That is so intelligent, yet so simple. Why couldn't I see that?"

"Because you are overwhelmed. But God knows your heart. He knows what you carry, and He will help you to find a way out."

"How will I know the right answer?"

"Maybe you won't know immediately, but you will know," she promised. "You're on the right path."

She told me the same thing that Grandma Delanie had said. The answer won't just pop out of the sky, but I will know it when it comes. I talked to Jane for two hours—realizing that I had missed two classes and had to leave to go straight to work. My soul had been massaged. I couldn't change Jim Dandy or the fact that Mom was going to have this baby. The Hal and Ray Cooper things would work themselves out. With the reassurance of Jane, I felt that I could handle whatever came my way because she told me that I was smart; she reminded me that I had good friends around me, and that I was willing to work hard to do what had to be done.

I tried not to let this stuff overcome me or take me down anymore.

Jane made me understand that I could only control my life. They had their own lives and choices to make.

I shouldn't feel guilty about my pursuit of my own happiness. It was my life after all.

CHAPTER THIRTY-SIX

What else but fireworks would bring explosions?

"I have to tell you what is going on," Hal said one night as we were walking back to the Rabbit after watching the July Fourth display in downtown Akron. "I don't know what to do next."

I thought he was referring to me or numerous other topics we had discussed.

"You don't know what to do?" I repeated his words.

"Right," he replied, and we kept walking. I skillfully allowed the silence to force him to speak.

"Hal?" I said, turning to him, thinking that this was maybe that one romantic moment we had been waiting for.

"Del, this is new territory." He grabbed my hands, and then he let them go. He turned and unlocked the car.

"What is going on?" We got into the Rabbit.

"Do you want some tacos at the drive through?" he asked. "I went to high school with his girl. Her name is Carrie," he said after getting money out of his wallet. "She was there for me when my mom died. She stayed with me that next night. She was there for me. Yesterday, she called me and told me that her dad is dying. She wanted to get together and talk. So, I did."

"Okay. I'm glad she was there for you," I said, "and now you can be there for her."

"After my mom's funeral, we had fun together. Her dad is well connected. She asked me to go out with her a few times, so I did. Then she promised me a pretty good job, but before anything happened, she left for Maryland."

"Why did she leave for Maryland? What kind of job? I'm so confused."

"Mr. Meyer, her dad, owns Meyer Industries. She said he always has jobs that need filled, and they are pretty good jobs," Hal said. "She left for Maryland for about a year. I don't know what she was doing up there."

"Well, is she back to go to Akron?" I asked.

"No, she just wants to talk about things. She was doing some drugs for a while, and now she says she is clean."

"Oh," I said, intrigued that Hal would get involved with someone who uses or used drugs. "But she isn't doing drugs anymore?"

"That is what she says."

"Well, that's good," I said.

"It's just that I feel guilty going out with her, seeing her, and not letting you know what is going on," he said.

"Well, you have to help her out," I said. "She was there for you." I hated myself for saying this, but I couldn't tell him 'You're mine and I love you. Why would you let anyone else into our realm?' We were, as it stood, friends and friends only, but I was also worried for Hal. He was vulnerable to manipulative people—especially females—and usually these females were aware of their power over him. I believed this vulnerability came from the difficult situation with his mom, just as Jim Dandy, also being an opposite sex parent, created problems for me. I felt that our friendship was based on our mutual, yet unspoken, agreement to watch out for each other. My charge was to protect him from girls who might lead him away from his dreams, and he did the same for me.

"If you feel something for Carrie, you have to decide the nature of those feelings, plus the job thing," I managed to sputter out. I was once again pulling out my hidden acting talents. "You need to go out with her," I said. "You need to see her and help her through this. It's worth it to find out. Just be careful."

"I didn't want to go sneaking around on you," he confessed. "You deserve the truth."

"You need to make your own decisions." I hated what I was saying. I wanted to say the exact opposite, but it was his life and his lesson to learn. Like Jane had said, I could only live my life and Hal needed to live and learn his own. "I don't own you."

"Are you okay with it?"

"Sure," I lied. "I know. I'm so dependable and good. I wish I could just throw that part of me away and be like everybody else. Why can't I be possessive and freak out on you?"

"Do you want to freak out and be possessive of me?"

"Uh, yea," I said.

"Really?"

"You're not mine to freak out on," I said. "Right now, we need to keep doing what we are doing."

He sat there in the driver's seat and stared straight ahead for a few minutes, and I watched him. He shook his head and shrugged his shoulders. He eventually turned the key in the ignition, and we headed to the new Taco Bell drive through. We ate in the car because I had a ton of reading to do for my summer class the next day.

Jim Dandy had been low key for a while, but I needed to get back to the dark house. He was actually working. He was wiring a house for someone, so he had been too tired to pick on anyone lately, but Emily Dickinson, in her exiled world, was calling me back. She was not one of my favorites anyway. How could this unmarried, socially-isolated, and fragile recluse understand the human heart enough to give advice to those of us who were out here in the world, living, fighting the daily turmoil of best male friends who decide that they are infatuated with some rich girl (who pops in and out of his life)? Emily, I could tell you a few things. But yes, there I was in this pepper pot, and Emily was perfectly cool and untouched on the pages of my literature book. Maybe she had it right.

I loved Hal. This realization threw a total wrench into the situation.

CHAPTER

THIRTY-SEVEN

My life needed an overhaul. I was constantly the victim, and I was sick of it.

I resolved to be a little more forceful, since all these other girls seemed to get what they wanted, and I was always left there holding the metaphorical bag. Hal had been doing this disappearing act with Carrie through most of August, so I decided that if I saw that Ray Cooper stud muffin on campus in the fall, I would approach him and make conversation—even if he might think I was dork. I decided to participate in life, and not just watch it go by. If I failed, and he thought I was a total cornball, I could rest knowing that at least I had tried. It was a brave move for me. What did I have to lose? I knew I couldn't have a re-do on life like Michael J. Fox in *Back to the Future*, so I had to do it now.

It was about a week into the fall semester, and there was Ray Cooper, heading toward Olin Hall, unshaven and wearing a suede jacket, faded jeans, and those same Frye boots that were all the rage in 1985: this was my chance. I must do this, I thought. That song by Foreigner, "I Want to Know What Love Is," kept playing on the radio, in stores, everywhere, and thus repeating in my head as I hurried toward the door, trying not to slip, fall, and make a complete idiot out of myself, timing my convergence to appear as if it were nonchalant happenstance.

"Ray!" I yelled from about twenty yards away, helping fate just a little bit. Where the valor came from, I still don't know, but desperation sometimes speaks out of an unknown part of me. Of course, I had spent the summer cheering for myself after the lonely summer without much Hal. "Wait a minute!" I was wondering if I were possessed by Carrie's assertive voice. It worked for her. She had called Hal out of the blue and re-entered his life, and blink, Hal was missing in action.

"Hey, Delanie," Ray Cooper replied, smooth as silk. He had remembered my name.

"Do you remember me from Dr. Longworth's class?" I asked, breathing hard from my little jog to catch up, realizing later it was a stupid question. His reply indicated his remembrance.

"Sure. How did your project with Dr. Longworth turn out?"

"It went well," I said, wondering if Dr. Longworth had revealed the details of his research into sociopaths and how my father, Jim Dandy, was one of them. But I continued, hoping the answer was no, trying to overcome the boulder on my shoulder of my father. "I just loved his class," I said. "Are you assisting him again this semester?"

"No," he said. "I'm not working. I'm working on my grade point average, so I can get into law school. I need a straight A semester."

"Hey, I wanted to ask you," I said, trying to keep the conversation going as long as possible. "Are you Ashley Keith's cousin?" Where this question came from, I have no clue. Ashley Keith was Jessica's *Glamour* magazine photo sorority sister who wore the preppy skirt and sweater and made fun of my name.

These smooth, glossy words about Ashley's imaginary cousin just rolled off my tongue like a woman possessed, but I was happy with this temporarily new assertive Del. At least I was talking to him.

"No," he said. "But I know Ashley, though. She is a Delta Gam," he said. Oh boy, I was in trouble with my unplanned sputtering of words, a completely made up story from, again, that unknown place, the devil on my other shoulder.

"How do you know her?" he asked.

"She is in a sorority with one of my best friends from high school," I said, returning to some truth and reality. "I think she has a cousin named Ray, but I might be confused. You kinda look like him."

"Who is your high school friend?" he prodded.

"Uh, her name is Jessica Overton. Do you know her?"

"I know Jessica through Ashley. Didn't Jessica go to Western Star High School?" he asked, latching onto the high school topic which was more interesting –and real—than Ashley's non-existent cousin.

"Yes, with me. Class of '82," I said, hoping to steer onto solid ground.

"Do you know Mr. Cooper—the math teacher?" he posed.

"Yes, I had him for geometry."

"He's my dad," he laughed. "That big dorky math teacher."

"Really?" I asked. "I can't believe it! I loved him!"

"Yea, he's a little bit of a nerd," he joked. "But I guess dads are nerds, huh?" I didn't want to answer that question. How I wished that mine were a nerd.

"Oh, my gosh! What a small world! He had such a dry sense of humor. He cracked me up. He might be the only math teacher who liked me. I actually understood geometry."

"I will tell him that I know you," he said.

"Don't ask him about me. I'm the girl who confused circumscribed circles. I mean, not really the circles, but the word, I mean. It's a long story."

"Were you the one who said in a proof that circles were 'circumcised circles'?"

"Yea, how do you know that story?" I could feel my face turning even redder. My new assertive self was wondering why I hadn't just remained the safe little wallflower.

"He came home and told us about this girl—and I guess it was you—who just raised her hand so confidently and answered the answer to the question was 'circumcised circles.' I guess it is math humor!"

"Yep, that would be me," I was amazed that this teacher, one who I am sure thinks I am an idiot, is Ray Cooper's dad. Things like this always happen to me, I swear.

"My dad is a very shy guy," he said, enforcing my observation of him.

"Yes, he seems like it," I admitted. "Tell him I said 'hi' and that I miss his class!"

"Aren't you an English major?"

"Well, isn't that a good thing given my background in circles and all?" I asked, thinking this was a witty comeback.

"Maybe...." he acknowledged.

"Those math teachers could use a little more comedy, don't ya think?" I asked rhetorically. The words were rolling off my tongue.

"There isn't much joking around in math," he agreed. I walked inside the door that he was holding open for me.

"I actually did understand geometry. I guess 'cause it's visual. The rest of math was—is—a total loss on me."

"Are you always here on Thursdays?" he asked.

"Yep, I have a ten o'clock here."

"Next week, after your class, let's meet at the Chuckery. I want to hear more stories about my dad," he insisted. "I want to kid him about it before I tell him that I know you! I'd do it today, but I have an interview for an internship."

"Okay, that will be fun! I'll try to think of some stuff about him!"

I had just broken the ice; I didn't fall into the river, run into a wall, or completely embarrass myself. He asked me to meet him next week, a move in the right direction. My utterance of circumcised circles was purely innocent, I kept telling myself, and

Mr. Cooper knows that I am not a mean-spirited or disrespectful person. Right? But this conversation with Ray Cooper was a turning point for Delanie Dane.

I actually owned my own words, and I had an angle. My words and my confidence, they moved things along quite nicely.

CHAPTER
THIRTY-EIGHT

It is a rare occasion when the weather and our lives work together—especially in Ohio.

Making sure to wear the best outfit I could pull together, I met Ray Cooper at the Chuckery the next Thursday. I was having a bad hair day though: the humidity was so high that my hair was flat—not a good thing in the 80s. But guys, I have been told by Justin, in their own worlds with their own priorities, didn't really notice the size of girls' hair. "It's for girls to impress other girls," Justin explained to me once when I was freaking out about my hair going flat. "Guys really don't care about your latest fashions or your giant hairdos."

"My dad said to tell you 'hi,'" Ray Cooper said as I made my way to the table where he was eating a piece of pepperoni pizza. I was only pretending to feel confident with my freaking flat hair.

"Did he remember the 'circumcised circles' stuff?" I asked, blushing.

"Yes, and he remembers you," Ray said. I could picture how Mr. Cooper, recounting the story to Ray, face bright red, would deliver the ending of the story with the clincher, with his straight-faced and dry sense of humor, "Be careful, Ray. That girl knows her angles." Then he would walk away, and Ray would wonder about me. That might be a good thing.

"Yes, he just laughed and said you were smart," Ray said.

"Well, that's good," I said. "In spite of my air-headedness, I was a pretty good student."

"I have an extra ticket to see Journey at the Coliseum tomorrow. Are you up for it?"

What had just happened?

"That sounds great," I said. I decided that I never took a day off work—never—and Mr. Camparti would understand if I told him right away that "something had come up."

"Do you have a car?" he asked. "You will have to drive."

"Yea, I can drive," I accepted, afraid to ask why he couldn't drive. There was something about him that told me not to dig too deep. Asking too many questions might bring answers, and I really didn't want to know the answers. I wanted to linger in this fantasy for a while. He was gorgeous and asking me—me—to a concert and I would leave it there, at that.

I was happy to say that I had retained some of my tan because September was unusually warm, and I had been reading my assignments by the Indian fountain. This meant that my hair was blonder than usual, and my curves were in check because I had been exercising and eating no junk food. The clincher, however, was that I had a date, a real date, with the most gorgeous man on campus at The University of Akron, circa 1985.

In terms of looks, Ray Cooper stood out in a crowd. I was excited to see and be seen with him at the Coliseum. Everyone would be at the Journey concert, and those Western Star classmates would be wondering how pitiful little Del, the scrub woman who works day and night at King Arthur's Round Table, could manage to finagle a date with this specimen, this Ray Cooper.

Ah, this was my chance to be like everyone else.

I picked Ray up at his fraternity house, and this plan actually worked out well because he didn't have to encounter Jim Dandy. I arrived in the Pinto, and I didn't ask Ray any questions, again sensing that it might kill the current vibe. Then there were my geometric skills. I figured that a second triangle needed to be constructed, in addition to the first triangle with Hal, Carrie, and me.

I treated him to Pizza Hut then we jumped on the highway and headed toward the Coliseum. As I shifted gears, Ray kept the Journey eight-track tape playing "Don't Stop Believin'," "Wheel in the Sky," and my favorite "Separate Ways." It was one of those illustrious early fall evenings in Ohio when the air was clean, not heavy or humid, so my hair was extra poufy, and the sun was gleaming with the golden slant that made everything seem like a dream, even illuminating my skin. I was a little uncomfortable that he drank a few beers in the car as I drove, throwing the empties casually in the back seat, but it was a trade-off of coolness that I had to accept. I stuck to my usual Diet Cokes; I wanted to know that I was safe behind the wheel and aware of my comments and actions in the company of Ray Cooper.

As the opening band checked and re-checked their microphones, this glorious feeling of coolness multiplied when a few snooty girls from high school descended upon us as we stood in the concession line to get Ray a few more beers. These were the girls who always had the top-notch guys and excluded everyone else–including me—from their social circles. "Oh, there is that Delanie Dane girl," mocked Mary Anne Renecki, arriving intoxicated with another girl from Western Star, just as Ray was showing his ID to the bartender.

"Hi Mary Anne," I said, hearing my name and turning to make eye contact. "How are you?"

"I'm great," she bragged, pushing her overly processed hair off her shoulder. "I'm planning my wedding. I'm getting married to a guy with lots of money! He sells cars. What about you?"

"Well, nothing real exciting. I'm finishing my degree in English at Akron. Working...."

"Who is this?" she asked, like she had missed him at an exhibit.

"This is Ray Cooper," I said.

"Hi, Ray. Del does pretty well for herself, being a little waitress at the Steak Pit, doesn't she?"

"Seems like you do too, marrying a rich car salesman, ooh," he said, swigging one of the beers. I wasn't sure if he was being serious or facetious, but it was an interesting exchange. The other girl with Mary Anne just stood there and took it all in.

"Ray's dad is Mr. Cooper, the geometry teacher," I explained.

"Oh, my gosh! He absolutely hated me," Mary Anne stated to her friend, being overly dramatic. "I was a terrible student. But not Delanie here, Miss Honor Student. But wait! Didn't you make some comment about penises once?"

"Well, not really about penises," I said calmly. "I confused the word circumscribed with circumcised. Those are circles that go around other circles. Huge difference a few letters make in meaning! I wasn't thinking. I was in my own world," I admitted, realizing that I do go there quite often.

"That's right. I was there. It was a classic! Ray, I'm surprised your dad would let you go out with a girl who talks about penises in class! I remember Mr. Cooper turned bright red!"

"It wasn't really about penises," Ray corrected again.

"Yes, she wouldn't really know what to do with one," she laughed. "Would you, Del, honey?"

"Aren't you going to college, Mary Anne? I thought you got a scholarship?" I asked, navigating this conversation in another direction.

"Yea," she said. "Not using it. Remember? Marrying a rich guy?"

"Well, I'd use it," I warned.

"Not working—ever," she repeated. "No need for school. I will just be spending his money, doing what I want. Tough life, huh?"

"Well, good for you. See you later. We hafta go," I said, ushering Ray away from her mouth.

"You wouldn't know what to do with one, huh?" he said, swigging more beer.

"That was really uncalled for," I said. "She is such a bitch. Always was...."

"What language from you?" he said in a friendly mocking manner.

"Well, if ever someone deserved it, it was her just then. That was terrible."

"Are you really that much of a goody-goody?" he asked. "Or do you just play the part?"

"Well, she doesn't know me very well," I explained. "I was new to the school as a sophomore. I have a few things that they don't know about."

"Like what?" he asked.

"Let's just keep a few things a mystery at this point, okay?"

"I was wondering why you only drink Diet Coke?" he asked. "Do you smoke?"

"I always want to be ready to drive my car—and to know what is going on," I said confidently. "And I guess I'm a nerd because I don't smoke either."

"So, you are a goody-goody?" he dug deeper. "Goody Two Shoes, like the song."

"I wouldn't say that," I explained. "I'm just a dorky, responsible girl, I guess." I wanted to say something about Mary Anne Renecki's scholarship and how she should use it – I would. I could feel anger boiling inside me like rice cooking on an unattended stove.

We sang along and danced to Journey. By the second encore, I walked Ray back to the Pinto, holding him up as he staggered and vomited a couple of times, once outside the door in a trash can, another time in the parking lot by my car. Mary Anne and that other girl passed us on the way out, and she yelled across the parking lot, laughing. "Hey, Ray, I'm available for a few weeks before I get married!" He didn't hear her; he was too sick. He passed out in the passenger side of the Pinto. I was glad he had already puked, so my upholstery was not in jeopardy.

By her comment, Mary Anne Renecki must have thought he was gorgeous, and it did feel equalizing. In fact, it was delicious. During the long bumper to bumper ride out of the parking lot traffic, Ray woke up a few times, gave me directions to his house in Akron, then passed out again.

I didn't want to ring the doorbell at midnight, so I deposited him on his front porch and hoped that he would be able to go to his room before his parents found him there in the morning. Mr. Cooper wouldn't blame me, or think less of me, I reasoned, because Ray was so drunk when I dropped him off.

This new girl, with an assertive voice, was starting to make a few appearances. I liked her.

CHAPTER THIRTY-NINE

I didn't tell Hal about Ray, but he found out.

David Norbin, our Shakespeare buddy, along with Mary Anne Renecki and a few others from Western Star, had spotted Ray and me together at the Journey concert, but I assumed that David was the one to pass the exaggerated gossip to Hal.

"I told you about Carrie," he said over the phone the next afternoon. "Why wouldn't you tell me you were seeing someone? Especially that guy!"

"I was going to tell you, but we have been busy and working. The concert was only yesterday."

"Well, I told you about Carrie before I even went out with her."

"I know. I wasn't thinking. I'm sorry."

"What if we ran into each other? How would you want me to react?" he asked, making sense.

"I knew you weren't going to be there. You were going out with Carrie."

"You think he is just so gorgeous, I know you do. I see how you stare at him. It is so obvious."

"I stare at him?" I asked, embarrassed.

"Yes. It is really disgusting," he said. "Just because he is going to law school...."

"Wait a minute," I tried to explain, but Hal jumped in.

"It just makes me sick. He isn't a very good guy."

"Oh, and Carrie is, with her calls in the middle of the night?" I said.

"She can call me if she wants to," he stated.

"Well, what's good for you is good for me," I retorted. "Hal, I'm sorry all around. I thought that you had Carrie, why couldn't I go out with Ray Cooper? He asked me out, and I said yes. That's all."

"Oh, is that his name? Ray Cooper?" Hal asked in a mocking way.

"Yes, his name is Ray Cooper," I replied.

"Norbin said you were all starry-eyed over him, or more like drooling," Hal said.

"Starry-eyed? He is reading too much Shakespeare. Hal, Ray was drunk the whole night. I didn't even see Norbin, so how does he know? It wasn't much fun."

"He said you were having fun," Hal retorted.

"David Norbin doesn't know, by just looking at me, whether or not I am having fun."

"Well, anyways, what can I do about it? I am going to the Sun tonight for Halloween. Do you want to come along?" he asked.

It was a caramel-colored, crisp Halloween Saturday, and I decided that the scene would just be starting when I got off work at ten o'clock. "Sure," I said. "I'll meet you there after work." I decided against spending money on a costume for a one-night event. I changed into jeans and a navy blue t-shirt because I just wanted blend into the woodwork.

Hal wore a straggly wig, added a 1970s Goodwill shamrock green leisure suit along with the loose-fitting light green polyester pants and hilariously called himself "Uncle Alvin." Carrie conveniently showed up about ten minutes after I arrived, perfectly dressed like Madonna from the *Like a Virgin* album cover. She was wearing a sequined, form-fitting tube top with a tulle pouf skirt, accented with five or six intertwined necklaces, and elbow length lace fingerless gloves. She definitely stood out in the crowd with her disheveled bleached blonde Madonna hair. This costume spoke volumes. She was a risk taker, and I hated that I decided to be the conservative wallflower. I felt like some boring old lady next to Carrie's loud shouts of *oh my God* all the time, her uproarious laughter as her head went back, and her dominating and intermittent shouts of *shit* and *damn* that turned every head in the bar. She was a flirt with money. She opened her wallet and revealed hundred-dollar bills which she waved at the bartender after every round of drinks that she bought. I brought five dollars for one drink and a Diet coke that I could keep refilling as designated driver. She was one of those girls who immediately clicked with almost every guy in the place, and although she wasn't an Akron student, many guys came up behind her, grabbed her shoulder, or whispered in her ear for which she would laugh hysterically. With my relatively contrasting Puritanical ways, she kept pulling her shirt down to reveal her cleavage and I, being the nerd that I am, kept thinking about England. She wasn't Hal's type, and I knew it right away. Hal, being a guy, didn't get any of this, and he would have to learn in his own guy time.

The lyrics to "Misled" by Kool and the Gang were making me uncomfortable as that outdated 1970s disco ball flashed squares of light around the ceiling, and I thought, but wouldn't swear to it, that Hal was having the same reaction to the song. Ray Cooper arrived about twenty minutes after we started talking. He casually approached our table and formed a square out of the existing triangle. Carrie bought him drink after drink, and they, ironically enough, seemed to hit it off right away. Hal and I danced a little, but I left the dance floor when "Crazy for You" by Madonna hit the speakers. It was Carrie's Halloween costume moment and she could demonstrate to me—and anyone who cared to look—her, I couldn't help but believe, pretend feelings for Hal. I smiled, but rolled my eyes behind her back, returned to the table, ate two tacos to look busy, then acted like I was interested in watching everyone dance.

When I was about to pretend exhaustion to get out of there, Carrie deposited Hal back to the table, grabbed Ray Cooper by the hand, pulled him out of his seat, and returned to the fast songs on the dance floor.

"She's so confident. She's always got money," Hal shouted across the table, moving his thumb across his fingers in the money symbol, while Carrie and Ray attempted to moonwalk to "Beat It." "Her dad pays her credit card every month. Whatever she wants, he pays for it. No limits."

I wondered if some of his new expensive wardrobe was funded by Carrie's credit card and her dying dad. "Wow, she's lucky," I said, picturing Jim Dandy handing me a credit card, and I laughed.

"He buys all her gas, pays her insurance," he said as I rolled my eyes.

"That's great, Hal," I said, feeling defeated, wishing he would just shut up, thinking I needed to leave.

"What about Lover Boy there? Does he spend lots of money on you?"

"Hal, we've only been out a few times," I replied. "And to tell you the truth, he doesn't work. His dad was Mr. Cooper, my high school geometry teacher, and I think he is pretty strict with money. I usually pay for everything when we go out. He doesn't have a car. I always drive."

"Oh," he said, shaking his head.

Then he said something interesting. "I want to warn you that she is pretty intimidated by us."

"Well, we are great friends," I said.

"Yea," he said. "She said that I talk about you too much. She freaked out the other day and yelled about it."

"She did?"

I didn't know what else to say.

"I'm surprised she came here, knowing you were going to be here. But maybe that is the reason she came here. And then she spends all the time with that Ray Cooper. Makes no sense," he said.

"She's a flirt, Hal."

"She is," he said. "She has it made."

"Yea," I said. "Ray seems to like her."

"She is probably trying to make both of us mad," Hal stated.

"Boy, that is a great strategy," I replied.

"She brags about how she doesn't need to go to college," he said and for a moment, I felt sorry for her because education builds character. Ah, how beautiful it would be to get an English degree for the education of it. Some people just don't know what they have.

"Hmmm," I said. "I think education is more than just getting a job. It is understanding the world. It is important."

"She thinks I should drop out because of that job at her dad's industry."

"That would be the worst thing you could do," I said. "Hal, don't you want to be a college graduate? Don't you want to have a degree? If you drop out and work for her dad, she will own you."

Just then, Ray and Carrie returned from the dance floor. "What are you guys arguing about?" she asked coyly with one hand on her exaggerated hip.

"We aren't arguing," I said. "We just have to yell because it is so loud in here."

"Oh, yea, right," she said. "Let's get back out there, Ray. They're playing that song we like about Del."

"It is her song," he said, looking over his shoulder at me and chuckling. It was, of course, "Goody Two Shoes." Hal looked at me, perplexed, and frowned for me.

I was the center of the circle, but I felt more like a square.

CHAPTER FORTY

I was doing dishes in the kitchen when I overheard Mom discussing my destiny with Jim Dandy. "Delanie is going to have to quit that college crap," she told him, possibly unaware that I could hear them. Here were two idiots who screwed up their lives, and they were trying to maneuver mine: It wasn't going to happen.

"Yea, big waste," he said over a car chase scene on TV.

"With the baby coming, she can stay home and take care of it." She didn't know that I could hear their conversation. She always played it both ways. She'd tell him one thing and then turn around and tell me another. Sometimes she seemed to know right from wrong. She just couldn't stand up for the right thing, especially if it was a difficult situation, or if Jim Dandy were involved.

"He's gonna get away with the cash," he yelled and laughed at the TV. "Cops can't get him. He's too smart."

"Well, Dandy, Delanie can watch the baby," she said, trying to direct him to something that actually mattered.

"Don't care what she does. Haf all this to do." He always talked about "all he had to do" which appeared to be nothing except creating misery, watching TV, and taking up space.

Mom didn't reply. What could she say? Jim Dandy was worthless, but as I predicted, she thought that I would be there to pick up the mess; I would drop out of college to take care of this baby. It was nearing Thanksgiving, and the baby was due around Christmas. Even though I had a long haul ahead of me, two to three more years, quitting was just not an option. I knew that if I dropped out, or took a semester off, I would never go back. Mr. Camparti told me this; Dr. Slocum told me this, and Mrs. Simmons told me, "Some people take time off and end up regretting it their whole lives. They get caught up in life, and they never finish their degree." I wasn't going to allow Mom's lack of planning to alter my path out of the dark house. Like Jane had told me, my life was important; I was getting that damn degree come Hell or high water.

"It's nothing but a waste of money anyway," she reiterated, hoping he would engage in something beyond the TV, almost trying to get him stirred up. "It's settled: Delanie can take care of the baby while I work."

"I don't care!" he yelled. "Figure it out! Tryin' to watch this guy. He's gonna kill the cop. Shut up about it!"

I decided I needed to walk to the Indian fountain to think about a few things.

~

Two weeks later in early December, I drove Mom to the hospital in the middle of the night while Jim Dandy sat in his underwear and watched TV. "Got stuff to do," he said when I asked him to come along with us. "Big day tomorra."

I appreciated the paper cut-out Santas and decorated tree that blinked off and on red, green, yellow, and blue. It attempted to add holiday cheer to the sanitary white walls of the hospital. I occasionally watched a little of that new CNN News channel in the waiting room about the Christmas celebration at the White of

House of President Reagan, who had recently been re-elected for four more years.

I signed the papers that I was Mom's emergency contact, and I stayed with her until the doctors made me leave for the delivery. She listed Jim Dandy's name on the birth certificate, making me sick to my stomach, and then she signed her name to the live birth of Jennifer Denise Dane. She had no names picked out; I suggested the name Jennifer because Mrs. Tetley's first name was Jennifer.

The baby appeared healthy, but she was small. I saw her, so helpless and pitiful, blue and cross-eyed, and I went into the bathroom and threw up—hating myself for only thinking about the heaps of problems that this child would add to my life. I said a prayer in that sterile, stainless steel bathroom, understanding that I was selfish for thinking about this baby as an added burden. Fortunately, Jennifer would have a loving mother, two brothers, and a sister who would always, in spite of their own struggles, do their best to care for her. The four of us were, after all, good people.

I called Jimmy and Justin in the morning; Justin was getting ready for school. I told him that we had a new baby sister, and we tried to act excited. Jimmy hadn't come home in several days; Justin didn't know for sure where he was staying, but he would try to leave a message with Tom's mom.

"She isn't hearty like the rest of my kids," Mom said, swaddling the bundle, as I shifted into fourth gear in the sputtering little Pinto. The lyrics to Madonna's "Papa Don't Preach" appropriately consumed my attention for four minutes. Jennifer was also blue-eyed, leaving Justin still the only brown-eyed person in our family, and she was very quiet, not making a peep all the way home. A couple of times, while we stopped at traffic lights, I checked to make sure she was still alive. She didn't seem to want to live.

My heart just ached for the diminutive thing, so undeserving of the piles and piles of hell on earth that Jim Dandy would heap her way. Tears tumbled down my cheeks, blinding me as I drove on. At least Jimmy, Justin, and I had the advantage of being raised by

Mom. Now that she was working so many hours, Jennifer would spend most of her time with Jim Dandy or Justin. She would endure Jim Dandy's increasingly worse behavior, and now the four of us, we would be starting over with the introduction of this fifth human victim thrown into the dark house.

"You can't go back to school, you know," she said as we were pulling into our driveway.

"I'm not taking time off school," I said a little bitchy. "This isn't my baby, and I'm not sacrificing my future."

"What am I going to do?" she screamed. I wanted to tell her that she should have thought of that about nine months ago, but I held my breath on that comment. She should know how not to make a baby. But it was an uncomfortable discussion anyway, and I didn't want to throw more confusion on the pile of worries that I could see in her tired eyes. She was in a tough spot, I knew that, and for her and this baby, Jim Dandy's crazy behavior were more than not graduating from college. I could move away someday. This wasn't my life forever.

"Not to be mean, and I love her, and I feel sorry for her, but I didn't have her. I will do my best to help, but I won't take a semester off school. I am a junior; I will graduate in two years, and I'm not putting it off. That's how people never go back."

Jim Dandy was standing there, winter coat over his underwear, a lit cigarette hanging out of his mouth. He had tied an extension cord around Mickey's neck like a collar. The December wind whipped through the empty trees and Jim Dandy was thumping Mickey, over and over, with the plug end of the extension cord. "Knocked over my ashtray," he said. "This'll learn him."

"Stop it, you asshole," Mom yelled across the driveway, swaying the tightly bundled baby in her arms. "Do you want to see your daughter?"

"It's a girl?" he asked. "Another slut."

"Welcome to your new life, Jennifer," I said under my breath. "You will learn to hate him more than any words could ever express," I told her telepathically. Justin came bounding out of the house. He surmised the developing scene, made eye contact with me, shook his head, and he looked toward the Indian fountain.

"Jimmy isn't here. I told Tom's mom about the baby," Justin whispered to me. "She said she would tell him."

"Hi, Little Jennifer," he said approaching the baby and smiling. "I'm your big brother. I'm not the youngest anymore."

"Well, do you want to see the baby?" Mom asked Jim Dandy again, pitifully.

"I can see her from here," Jim Dandy said, spitting chew juice about three feet. "Should put that in a juice spitting contest," he said.

"Her name is Jennifer Denise," I said.

"Girl. Another stupid mouth to feed."

Anything other than this behavior from Jim Dandy would have seemed abnormal.

CHAPTER FORTY-ONE

Onward to the quiet and quaint, orange and yellow brick building, carrying my heavy heart, I opened the door, continuing my spiritual quest. "Jane?" I called.

Since Grandma Delanie had been elevated to a higher plane now, and Sister Roop, grounded in her mission in Savannah, also walked among those searching for something more here on Earth, I needed guidance in my journey, and I was hoping Jane could pass on more of her wisdom.

"Hello?" greeted a booming voice, coming from the other side of the building in what I learned was the kitchen area. An older, heavyset man, looking to be of Italian descent, came into the anteroom, wiping his hands on his apron. "I'm making the sauce for the spaghetti dinner. Are you one of the volunteers from the church?"

"No, I'm sorry," I said. "I'm Delanie. I was wondering if Jane is here today?"

"I don't know anyone named Jane who volunteers here," he explained.

"She is the little lady with silver hair," I continued. "She has beautiful green eyes. Is she a minister of some sort here?"

"I don't know her," he repeated. "I know about all the volunteers. Nobody named Jane. But I'm Jim Ignotti, spaghetti supper volunteer. I am the one with the recipe." He smiled.

"Nice to meet you," I acknowledged. "It smells good. I love homemade spaghetti."

"You are welcome to stay or come back later. We're here until about seven. We make the sauce from scratch. I use basil from my garden."

"I have to work tonight, but I might join you sometime. I really wanted to check in with Jane. I wonder where she is?"

"I will ask around and see if anyone knows someone named Jane, but I have been doing this for couple of years, and I know just about everyone. I don't know Jane," he repeated. "It is odd."

"Where do you work, is it Delanie?" he asked.

"I work at King Arthur's Round Table at Rolling Hills Mall," I said. "We are in the same business."

"You work with ol' Camparti?" he asked.

"Yes, he's my boss. I love him!"

"An Italian boy from North Hill," he explained. "Great guy! Tell him ol' Ignotti said 'hi,' will you?"

"Sure! That's hilarious. Small world. Tell me something funny about him," I asked.

"Used to speak Italian with my mother before she passed. She loved that. We grew up together in North Hill. He was a language major at Kent State, you know?" he smiled as if recalling those times.

"I knew he was a language major," I said. "So, he speaks Italian?"

"Yea, he needed native speakers, and she was his native speaker, his guinea pig. Always loved that about him. She said it brought back the old country."

"How cool," I said. "He is a great guy."

"Sure is. Come back next week and stay for some spaghetti—on me. It's actually my mother's family recipe!"

"I will see about getting a Wednesday off work so I can do that," I said. "Will you check around and see if anyone knows Jane?"

"Sure will. Make sure you come back next week and bring a friend. It is on me," he said. "If someone is at the door, tell them you are with Jim Ignotti."

I could use some fellowship and the comforting warmth of an upbeat meal with others, so I penned it in on my calendar.

CHAPTER FORTY-TWO

I am not, nor have I ever been, a risk-taker. I hate that about myself. I decided I would have to go back to the dark house, once again putting education above my health.

Today, I can sit here and wait for this train, I thought, or I can race it, like Jim Dandy used to do when I was a kid—and still does for that matter—scaring me out of my mind.

But I decided to wait, be patient like always, always me waiting, never waited on, wait and wait for the world to change, knowing that I will miss catching Ray outside Olin Hall, and I will be late for my first class. Today this waiting, it could change my life.

Just remembering Jim Dandy racing trains, in that clunkity old Caprice, while the whistle screamed a warning, made me breathe hard. I was still wrestling with buried anger and negative thoughts of him that kept flooding my mind, boiling like a maelstrom, almost all the time, as if he were there in the flesh at every twist and turn of my life.

Ray hadn't called in about a week, and it was late January, and my birthday came and went. No calls, and I held fast to the waiting game, on advice from Mom. Although one stupid decision changed her life markedly nine months before I was born, her advice did make some sense, and she even used some logic: "If he likes you, he will call. Don't act desperate. Don't call him. Play hard to get."

But I was desperate, and unfortunately, the guys weren't lining up at my door.

The need to be loved, even if just on the surface, or at least to feel loved, was consuming me. "Don't You Forget About Me," by freaking Simple Minds kept echoing my thoughts, but apparently Ray Cooper had forgotten about me. I was too serious about him. I thought too much about my future, and I just didn't take chances. He thought I was boring, and I guess I was.

It was a painful and long week, but I kept waiting, listening to Mom's advice, letting the ball stay in his court. Hal was still seeing Carrie, and reaping all the benefits of her dad's open-ended spending policy. He called me about once a week, and we talked on the phone—mostly about her dad's terminal disease, but not too long because Carrie was always on her way to his house, or they were going somewhere—usually an expensive restaurant that in our old lives—we couldn't afford.

A few more times, since I had been seeing Ray, Hal and Carrie met Ray and me at the Zip Strip bars. Hal wasn't happy about Ray; I wasn't happy about Carrie, but neither one of us had the footing to complain, so we smiled and laughed, danced and laughed, while we were both, I believe, dying inside. I could feel the tension.

One night, before this dry spell with Ray, while Ray and Carrie drank too many beers and danced together, rubbing against each other a little too close on the dance floor, Hal broke the ice. "In terms of Carrie," he yelled across the table at the Trolley Stop, a bar in the Highland Square area of Akron, "she's not very intelligent; she's not a very hard worker; she doesn't understand me like you do." I moved in closer to make sure I had heard him correctly.

"Did you say, 'She doesn't understand you like I do'?" I repeated, knowing that that was indeed what he had said, stirring the ice, then sipping my Diet Coke out of that little straw.

"She makes fun of my dad. She says he should pay for more. She calls him *cheap*, and it pisses me off. He's not a millionaire like her dad is."

"She's a privileged girl," I said. "Her life is worlds away from ours."

"I saw her dad the other day. He seems perfectly fine. I just wonder if he is really sick, or if she is using that as an excuse to see me."

"Who would do that?" I asked. "I mean, who would make up something like that?"

"Do you want me to answer that question?" he asked me rhetorically.

"No, not really. Because I don't want to put you in a tough spot," I said.

"Thanks!" he yelled across the table. "Thanks for not making me answer that."

"We are the same," he said, taking a huge bite out of his taco. He waved his hand so I would continue to listen while he chewed. "The work thing and getting our degrees. It's fun to have money to spend, but not if it's with the wrong person."

I just looked at him and blinked, squishing my mouth in a confused expression. "I know what you mean."

"Did you ever think that you might be chasing this Ray guy because your dad is a dick?" He confronted me with a truth that might have been taken from my playbook. His psychoanalysis of me was also interesting—especially considering he was doing the same thing with Carrie.

"Uh, maybe. Why?"

"Girls sometimes look for substitutes when they have *daddy issues,*" Hal said.

I couldn't find any words to match my thoughts. Yes, he nailed it. Yes, his was a parallel situation. Yes, I was a little pissed—like he is entitled to run around with Miss Rockefeller Ass while I sit and wait for him? I didn't say anything, and I let him continue with this line of reasoning.

"She is fun. She likes to party. Look at her with Ray up there," he finally said. "They should maybe be together!"

"They would be perfect together," I said, half serious.

"Oh, are you having problems with him?" Hal asked, also smirking, "Mr. Stud Muffin?"

"Haha. We're different also," I said. "He likes to drink too much and then pass out. I seem to be his chauffeur."

"I know you think he's hot," Hal said. "But that does scare me a little bit. There's something about him that I don't quite know for sure. He's a little too cocky....You, well, never mind."

"What?" I asked, tilting my head. "What?"

"I think you're right. Ray and Carrie would be good together!"

"Hal, are you having problems with Miss Privileged?"

"I don't know," he said.

"Hal, just don't get in trouble with her. That could clinch it for good," I said.

"Yea," he said, yelling over the song "No Parking on the Dance Floor."

"Oh, here they come," I said.

"What are you guys talking about?" Carrie asked, approaching Hal, as she leaned her hipbone into his shoulder. She bent down and proceeded to lick his ear.

"How great you guys dance together," I said. "You guys are great out there!"

"Del, you have to get me another drink," Ray said. "The bartender won't serve me anymore."

"Then maybe let's stop," I said.

"No! Get me another beer!" he said urgently, then he added. "I'm sorry. I was just kidding. You're right."

Hal raised his eyebrows and eyed me from across the table, even though Carrie continued to stick her tongue in his ear and stroke his hair.

"I'm going to get Ray home," I told Hal and Carrie. "He needs to get out of here. One more drink and it could mean trouble."

"Us too," Hal said. "It's late, Carrie. Let's go. Del, do you guys want to meet up with us for some late night Luigi's?"

"She needs to get him home, Hal," Carrie said.

"No," I said. "But thanks. I've got to take Justin to his game tomorrow and watch Jennifer in the morning."

I walked Ray to the Pinto as he stumbled and fell twice. I helped him up, buckled him in the seat belt, and wiped the tears that were trickling down my cheeks as I shifted the little Pinto into second gear and headed out of the parking lot.

Physical attraction, I was learning, wasn't all it was cracked up to be.

CHAPTER FORTY-THREE

On the home front, things were shifting and getting settled. It was a tough time, but we were doing the best we could do. Justin would get home after school, pick up Jennifer from the neighbor's, and then take care of Jennifer until Mom got home. Elton Jenkins' mom, bless her, saved us; I think she intuitively knew the threat of Jim Dandy, so she agreed to watch Jennifer most days for basically peanuts. Jimmy had moved out of Tom's basement, and he was living in a rented room somewhere in Cardinal City. He didn't have a phone and luckily for him, he missed the happenings of the dark house. I hadn't talked to him since the day after Jennifer was born.

Hal and I were talking a little more about our situation after that night at the Trolley Stop. Ray was still hovering in the picture, despite the games that he played with my burdened heart. In medias res, Kathie called me one night. With long-distance phone bills and her new boyfriend, she told me, she hadn't been able to call. I understood because I had allowed us to fall out of touch as well. I too was tangled up with my own complicated life and the pathetic life of my little sister. In fact, Kathie didn't even know that Mom had had another baby.

"Del, my dad is very sick," she said, sobbing. The sound of her voice told the story. "He wants to see you."

"Sure, Kathie," I said. "I'd love to see you and your dad. Where is he?"

"He's at Akron General Hospital, in the cancer ward," she said.

That statement clinched it. I knew that Andy had wrestled with cancer years before and was in remission, but sometimes, cancer comes back with a vengeance. I knew we were talking weeks, not months, by the tone of Kathie's voice.

I left school early the next day, skipping out on a Western Culture discussion group, and headed to Akron General. Kathie was not there yet, and Andy was asleep when I entered his room. He had lost a lot of weight—he was never a big guy to begin with—and he looked old and weak. I said a silent prayer upon crossing the doorstep, and he opened his droopy brown eyes just as I looked at him and approached the bed. He looked exhausted, like the old picture of Christ carrying the cross in Grandma Delanie's old Holy Bible.

"Del," he said as I came to the bed. "Del, Del. It's good to see you. It's like old times!"

"Hey, Andy!" I said. "Are they treating you okay here?"

"Yea, okay," he said.

"Hospitals are so sterile," I said. "They're clean, but they're so...."

"Quiet," he said. "Lonely. No music, Del."

"That's it," I said. "For us, we like music and laughter and people talking...."

"Barbra has a new song called "Memory." Have you heard it?"

"I love that song," I said. "I was wondering if you had heard it because you love Barbra so much!"

"It's my favorite song right now," he said.

"Andy, I have an idea," I said. "I'm going to try to get a cassette player in here so you can hear it." I left the room, called Kathie from the nurse's station, and told her to stop by and get Andy's cassette player because I had the cassette in my car. We beamed the song into the hallway and into the nurse's station. An older nurse, of whom we thought might yell at us, told us that this was her favorite song, and she came in singing and gesturing like she was performing live. We all laughed as she pretended to be on stage.

"You always have fun ideas, Del," he said.

"Well, just add music," I said.

"No," he said. "In life. You always kept going. I knew you would make it."

"Oh, well, thanks," I said. "But I haven't 'made it' yet. I still have one more year of college, and from there, I don't know what else."

"You're gonna graduate with a college degree?" he asked, almost amazed at the prospect.

"I hope so," I said. "My senior year could be the hardest."

"You were never one to find trouble or to take the easy way out. You saw something that you wanted, and you went for it. You were always willing to work for it, to earn it. I know you've been through a lot."

"Let's not talk about me," I said.

We got quiet as Streisand belted out about the "old days" and not giving up. Then she urged us to remember the old times.

I knew that I might not be able to talk to Andy again. My life was just so jam-packed with worry and work, that I had almost lost touch with these two people who had meant so much to me. I was so consumed with Hal, Ray, Jennifer, my school ambitions, and the dark house to squeeze in Andy and Kathie. They were an integral part of my past, and I was too caught up trying to grasp my future.

"Del, you know all the neighbors on Eclipse kept talking about how you would make it?" Kathie said. "I was a little jealous, I have to admit. You, you have a plan, and you don't let anything get in your way."

"I really don't have a plan," I replied.

"It's better than mine," Kathie acknowledged. "You are so serious—and driven—about everything."

"Sometimes," I broke off my thought, "sometimes, I need to let go a little bit more and live now. But I'm just too obsessed to take a break. I'm afraid that if I pause, I won't be able to get it back."

"You never let..." Andy stopped mid-phrase.

"What?" I questioned.

"Del, how is your mom? How is Justin?" he asked.

"They are fine. Did you know my mom had another baby?"

"Kathie told me that," he said. "I'm surprised at her age."

"Andy, it was not planned, and really, it has been a burden. Jennifer is healthy, but to be honest, we didn't need another baby. Mom is working lots of hours, you know, and Justin, the neighbor, and I take care of her. It is sad."

"Justin is doing okay?" he asked again.

"Justin is great. He is my sunshine. He is such a good person."

"I'm glad," Andy said. "Tell me about his hobbies and his talents."

I thought this was a strange topic of conversation, but I began to describe Justin's compassionate nature, his love of music, his heart of gold. As I talked, I wondered how Justin could be Jim Dandy's son, but then again, I was Jim Dandy's daughter.

"You never had an excuse," he said firmly, taking a different approach. "Joe and Rosie told me about some of the things that they heard with Jim Dandy. When Kathie came home that night....at Christmas...."

"Del, I'm sorry that I told." Kathie turned her eyes away from me. "I was worried about you."

"Oh, you can't help what you saw. It's just embarrassing," I admitted. "It...is...a...part...of...my, my life."

"You can't help what someone else does." Andy summarized it well.

We all sat there quietly for a few minutes, listening to Streisand's words, knowing that the song was a retrospective of all the years we shared on Eclipse Avenue. I struggled for words. Kathie left to check on his dinner tray. It was Andy who broke the silence. "Del, now that Kathie is gone, I wanted to ask you another favor." This was intriguing. "Can you make sure that Justin is okay?"

"Justin? My brother?" I asked.

"Yes." He stopped short and then he mumbled something else.

"Make sure he's okay?" I repeated his words. "Justin?" Just then, Kathie walked back in the room.

"You acted startled when I came in," Kathie laughed. "What are you guys talkin' about? It's like you're up to something. Are you guys talkin' about the dictionary again?"

"Oh, nothing," I blew it off. Just then, an attendant came in pushing a dinner tray. I decided not to say anything else to Kathie about Justin in case Andy was dreaming or hallucinating. I needed to mull this over.

I stopped the Streisand cassette which was becoming obtuse. It was droning on. I needed silence.

"Oh, how is Mr. Sunshine?" the aide asked, straightening the blanket covering him. "Everyone here just loves this guy!"

"He is pretty good today," Kathie said. "Did you hear the new Barbra Streisand cassette? That might have cheered him up."

"I know he wants to talk music and books with everyone," the aide chuckled. "I know he loves Streisand. He talks music all the time with the other nurse June. She also loves Donna Summer, Barry Manilow, and Olivia Newton-John. One day, I had to come in here and get her, we had a new patient, and she was talking music with Mr. Sunshine."

"Don't get him started on Sinatra or Fred Astaire and Ginger Rogers or Judy Garland or Henry James' novels..." Kathie lectured.

"I bet," the aide confirmed. "I need to get this food down him. If you girls want to have some dinner yourselves, I can feed him. He might eat better, and you can talk after he eats."

Kathie and I bought dinner at the hospital cafeteria for the sake of convenience. I told her about my dilemma with Ray Cooper and Hal, and she told me about her boyfriend Paul who wanted to move into Andy's house because his mother had kicked him out. "He is looking for a job," Kathie explained, "but isn't having any luck." The fact that he didn't work and wanted to move in worried me. If his mother kicked him out, he must have some baggage, not to mention the fact that Kathie was in a vulnerable state. I thought of my mother and the quicksand that she had created with Jim Dandy Dane when Juan left for South Carolina all those years ago. I thought of vulnerable women and how overbearing men could take over their lives.

"Kathie, don't do anything fast right now," I instructed. "With your dad in the hospital, you need to take your time and think things through. I know I'm not in the best position to offer advice, but don't make any serious moves right now."

"But Paul says that he really needs to get married right away," she explained. "Like he loves me so much, he needs to be married now."

"Kathie, that doesn't make any sense. If he really cares about you, he's not going to hurry you. And he's not going to make you do anything that you don't want to do." Those words echoed into my own soul when I realized that I was preaching but I wasn't practicing. Ray was so good looking that I too didn't want to make anything the least bit challenging for him. If I had an empty house, I'd let him move in. He said he didn't have a job so he could get good grades, but he managed to get drunk all the time. If I made it too hard, he might walk away, and I needed someone in my life. Maybe Hal was right. I didn't want to look too closely at my own precarious situation. Who was I to give Kathie advice?

With Ray, I was flirting around with a gorgeous but grotesque human being. He drank his courage. I knew he was dangerous; I knew that I was walking on the wild side, but he was so delicious; I knew that I was such a pushover. I wanted to walk where the other girls walked: I wanted to see and be seen with him. I wanted to be wanted. I really wanted to be loved; love was so absent from my life. I wanted to keep the truth hidden, just like everything in the dark house. I wanted to keep up the appearance of love, of having a relationship, even though, when exposed to the light of day, it was merely a façade. I knew all this deep down inside, but I didn't want it to come to the surface into the light of day. It would wilt, dry out, fly away. It might melt like ice sparkling in the sunshine. I just had to be careful of the fall out, that I didn't fall too far, or fall in—like quicksand.

We walked back up to Andy's room to say goodnight—and goodbye. I might not ever see him again. The man who meant so much to me in my childhood, in those golden formative years, the man who taught me self-respect and confidence and laughter, the first real dad I ever had, was dying. I hugged him and told him that I loved him. I paused and looked over my shoulder at him. His eyes were closed.

Andy died the next day.

CHAPTER FORTY-FOUR

"God is the father," Jim Dandy screamed as I was reading Andy's obituary aloud to Mom in the kitchen, a few days later, about a week before Christmas, 1985. "This guy isn't a father," he continued. I noticed that Mom's reaction to Andy's death, later that evening and alone in her room, was dramatic. His death affected her gravely, even though she hadn't seen him— that I knew of—since we had moved to Western Star six years ago. Although I tried to keep the subtleties of her reaction hidden, I was unlocking a discovery into another prison in which my mother had lived for all these years. There was more to the story that I hadn't known. As she sobbed and cried with me, she revealed something deeper—without words—a secret that I would never be able to communicate.

"How could they call him 'a father'? He wasn't a father," Jim Dandy continued screaming, moving toward the boxing match on television, carrying a plate of fried chicken smothered in gravy. I felt his reaction was overkill, even for Jim Dandy. It was jealous rage. "He didn't work; he just walked around and picked up sticks in the backyard," he continued ranting.

"He was Kathie's father," I spoke calmly. "He was a dad."

"God is the father," he screamed again. He picked up an empty pop bottle and threw it toward me. I ducked, and it smashed against the wall, leaving a huge dent. "Those Catholics start with 'God is the father' and that Mother Mary bullshit."

"Told you and Jimmy and that Justin to call me *dad* and not *father*. Was some wimpy, limp-backed wussy." Jim Dandy continued, as if he were some dictionary scholar. He had this thing up his ass about the difference between the words *dad* and *father*. His argument, based in his study and interpretation of the Bible (which was none because he couldn't read), says that God is the father and men are dads. He was neither. So out of sheer disrespect in my own mind, and the piss poor job he did as a father, I decided that from then on, in my writing and in my mind, he would be called Jim Dandy or father but not dad. To his face, however, I called him dad to avoid a punch in the face. He was a father, a sperm donor, a contributor to one of those newfangled paternity tests that were now available.

His theology continued. He was moving into his theory of women in the ministry. "Catholics believe in that Mother Mary crap," he continued. "Can't pray to a woman! These stupid women minister know-it-alls..." Dr. Longworth's description of misogyny kept echoing in my mind. Jim Dandy hated women who command their own lives, women who were smart, women who had any power, women who saw through his gorgeous blue-gray eyes, his piles of blonde hair, women in general. He hated me for all those reasons. I knew and understood it.

Along with powerful women like Margaret Thatcher in England or Sandra Day O'Connor of the Supreme Court, I began to list the dads that I knew or had known: Andy was a great dad. Alana and Jessica both have stable dads. Hal has a kind and helpful dad. Ray Cooper, for God's sake, has a dad. I did not have a dad. Instead, I have a monster, a menace, a hopelessly mean demon. Not only did he proclaim to know it all about fatherhood, he hated women. "You are so much like Lizzy." He was gritting his teeth referencing his sister. "She was a bitch too."

The rant woke up Jennifer, and Mom asked me to bring the baby to her room. "How is Kathie handling everything, Del?" she asked as she rocked Jennifer.

"Kathie will probably marry her boyfriend, Mom," I informed her. "I don't think he's good for her."

"Why?" she asked.

"He wants to hurry and move into Andy's house. Maybe already has. That just seems suspicious to me," I explained, "for him to be in such a hurry."

"I know how that feels," she said. "You feel like you have to do something right now. You feel so alone, and you do stupid things." This was powerful statement from my mom.

"I wish I could take her in and provide a place for her. I wish I could provide a safe place for everyone I love, when they need it," I said.

"I know you do," she said, thinking clearly today. "Someday, I think you will be in that position."

"He doesn't understand emotions. I don't want him to hear us," she whispered. "Andy was such a good guy. Does Kathie even know what a good dad she had?"

"She knows, Mom. I know that she truly loved him. I did. He loved everything and everyone with his whole heart: people, music, books, animals," I said.

"He made everything special," she established.

"Yea." I was waiting to see where she would go with this.

"Jim Dandy," she stumbled for words, "he gets in these moods all the time and he's a son-of-a-bitch. I, I, I wish I could get away...." She paused. "But I'm afraid. He'd take you kids. He told me that if I left him he would take you kids and I'd never see you again."

After the robbery, the altercation at Jimmy's football game, and even the cheerleading bologna event, I believed that Jim Dandy could do anything. Nothing would stop Jim Dandy when he had his mind set on something sinister. Mom's fear was real, but nobody wants to test a sociopath to see if they're real. The proof of their threats could indeed be death.

What she didn't understand was that Jim Dandy "wasn't in a mood." He has a disorder, and he wouldn't someday, magically, transform into a wonderful prince of her dreams with those gorgeous blue gray eyes and his ability to act a part, to be charming on occasion. Sociopaths just exist, Dr. Longworth taught me, and they can't be rebuilt, talked down from the bridge or out of their mood, and magically transformed into Andys or Georges.

Justin, in his room jamming to "Brothers in Arms" by Dire Straits, turned off his music and came into the room where Mom and I were comforting each other. "Hey, Del, I heard about Andy," he whispered. "You know, I didn't know him that well, but I saw how good he was to you and Kathie. I know he was special to you. I thought he was a real good guy. He was a good dad."

"He was." I was unable to say anything else. With his entrance into the room, the air got so heavy. Words became impossible to utter. Mom couldn't utter a word; she just sat there and looked at Justin's smaller stature, his kind and soft words, but the realization came to me when I looked into Justin's brown eyes. The mystery was solved.

I thought back to the Eclipse years, in the occasional times when Jim Dandy was working. Mom took pie or cake across the street to Andy and Kathie, how the four of us sometimes sat on the patio, listened to music on Andy's transistor radio and laughed about the junk our neighbor sold at their garage sale or a skit from *The Carol Burnett Show*. There was that night that she came home late, I was about six years old, when Jim Dandy was wiring a building, and I stayed with Jimmy. Justin was born the following summer.

I began to piece it together, and I thought about the biology lecture when Dr. Stevens explained that two blue-eyed people almost always have blue-eyed children. Mom, Jim Dandy, Jimmy, Jennifer, and I all have blue or gray eyes.

Justin, on the other hand, has brown eyes. This was the missing piece of the puzzle.

Andy's concern now made sense, but I would never be able to verbalize what I had discovered that night in Akron General Hospital.

CHAPTER FORTY-FIVE

Six-month-old babies cannot make concessions about their waking and sleeping hours. Somehow, in Jim Dandy's crazy-ass mind, he believed that little Jennifer scheduled her sleep and wakefulness to bother him. That's how he saw everything in the world—as if everything circulated around him, and people planned every move according to his dislikes. He began "learnin' her" and punished all of us every night by waking her at three a.m., so she "would sleep during the day" according to plan, and essentially not interrupt his television shows.

He continued these rants of rage by setting the stove alarm every night for three o' clock, something he never had to do for anything productive in his life. He went to her crib, shook it until she woke up, and when she would start screaming, he would proceed back to his stinky couch and go back to sleep. Then Mom, Justin, or I would take turns comforting her, and we would try to get her back to sleep. When she continued to wake up every morning around eight o'clock—his plan backfiring—he would kick and pound on the crib. "Worthless piece of shit," he screamed, kicking so hard that a picture fell from the wall. Justin and I tried to intercept the best we could before she would wake up on her own. On days when I didn't have an early class, I would get her, bring her into my bed and cuddle with her. Justin often did the same thing.

I knew his behavior was child abuse. The child could not communicate what was happening. Justin and I carried this guilt around with us, wondering if we reported it, would anyone be able to do anything? Justin and Mom looked to me for advice, but I didn't know if anything could be done. If the authorities did do an investigation, the result would probably be removal of Jennifer from our home. Mom would be devastated, so Jim Dandy's routine continued, pitifully, for about three months when it finally stopped because it wasn't producing the desired result. The failure of this strategy, however, didn't help his mental stability. If anything, he continued to get worse.

I was still chugging along with my classes. In current events, CNN had reported that the sunken *RMS Titanic* was found in the North Atlantic Ocean by two French explorers using sonar radar. I stopped by the student center to watch live coverage of the divers as they found ghostly candlesticks and baby dolls from that fateful night. I had always been fascinated by the story of the *Titanic* and loved to hear Mrs. Hershberger, my eighty-year-old neighbor, recall how she and her family were moving to the United States from Germany when their ship, the *Frankfurt*, sailed within sight of the *Titanic* back in 1912. She was seven years old, and her father held her to the deck to see distress rockets launched from the unsinkable ship in the distance. They would wake the next morning and learn of the deaths of hundreds of people. Life is a series of misses and near misses.

Back on land, my ship was still afloat, but barely. It was the fall semester of my junior year of college. I had purposely scheduled my classes for afternoons so that either Justin, Mom, or I could be with Jennifer most of the day. We agreed that we should avoid situations where she would be alone with Jim Dandy.

She was still small and fragile for her age and Jim Dandy's nightly rages, I'm sure, propagated her failure to thrive in those early months of her life. I wondered how they affected her developing brain and her ability to feel secure.

When I cared for her in the mornings, I would see her little lungs' desperate attempt to take in air in the smoke-filled room where the dragon puffed one homemade, highly potent cigarette after another. It was bad enough that we all had to inhale his toxic air, but it was agonizing to watch this little urchin labor to breathe the poison. I would clean out the mucus from her nose, and it was black. She was officially *asthmatic* and her doctor's visits were irregular, due to our lack of health insurance coverage and Mom's busy schedule. Medical care, we all agreed, was not as important as food.

Even though I did all I could for the baby, I had to accept the situation. It continued to eat me alive, consume my mind, inflame my emotions, and detour my personal goals.

The dark house was darker than ever.

CHAPTER FORTY-SIX

I was walking to Olin Hall, on a warmish day right before Halloween, when I was confronted by Carrie, standing near the same elevated place where I had talked to Jessica that day my freshman year. She was fixed in a pose, arms folded under her breasts with her 1980s blob of giant blonde hair blowing stunningly in a balmy breeze. Weather, it seemed, was always on her side. She looked like a movie star, waiting for the cameraman to start shooting the scene. She obviously was lingering for me to arrive at this designated spot in my life.

"Hey, Delanie," she shouted as I crested Fir Hill, carrying my heavy *Riverside Shakespeare* text, being well aware that the sidewalk, the pathway of my life, was uneven, and any little thing might cause me to trip and lose focus.

"Hi?" I uttered with the question mark after it.

"I thought that maybe we should talk about it," she was urging me toward her in a confrontational way.

"Talk about what?" I asked. "I have to get to class, Carrie."

"Delanie, I know you will never have much use for me," she retorted. "With your English teacher brains and your little curvy attitude, I would love to hate you, but you're not mean...."

"Thanks?" I replied, also with the question mark after it.

"Why do you want to keep Hal from me?"

"Carrie, I'm not keeping Hal from you. Hal is his own person," I spoke forcefully.

"What is this power you have over him? The only thing I can think of is you want him for yourself."

"He doesn't like me that way. He told me that himself."

"Well, he sure can't keep you out of the conversation," she concluded, dropping her hands so they dangled about her waist. "What about Ray Cooper? Isn't he enough for you? He totally blows Hal out of the water!" She started walking toward me, in an aggressive way. I was, frankly, afraid.

"Carrie, Hal and I are just friends. We agreed on that a long time ago. We're Platonic friends. You have more power over him than I do. That's for sure. I'm, I'm not trying to keep him from you."

"Hell, if you're not," she retorted. "Hal keeps saying how 'Del wouldn't do this' or "Del wouldn't do that.' I'm so sick of hearing about it."

"Well, I don't tell him what to say," I said.

"You might as well," she replied. "It's all about you, all the time. Who do you think you are? Some kind of saint?"

"Carrie, Hal can make his own decisions. I don't try to manipulate him. He's his own person. And no, I'm not a saint. Believe me, I have my own issues to grapple with—or, I should say, 'with which I grapple.'"

As I corrected the grammatical structure of my sentence, she stumbled for words herself, looked away, and then narrowed her eyes on me. "It's very hard to have a relationship with someone who is in love with someone else." She had broken the ice, tackled the heart of the matter. My mouth flung open. This was news to me.

I turned and started walking to Olin Hall, my chugga boots kicking little dots of black mud onto the back of my cream-colored corduroy pants. With much longer legs, she easily kept pace beside me. "I think he is in love with you. It's all up to you, Delanie. What are you gonna do with it, with him?"

"Well, Carrie," I countered, "your timing is amazing. This is amazing to me. I love Hal with all my heart and soul, but we have an agreement that we were friends first."

"Sure," she said. "You have freaking Ray Cooper. God, isn't he enough for you?"

"Carrie, I don't have Ray Cooper. Ray Cooper is also his own person. Ray Cooper is not a very good guy to me."

"He is so hot though," she said.

"Hot isn't everything," I had verbalized my feelings. "Hot isn't everything."

"I think it is," she said.

"Well, then why do you want Hal? Take freaking Ray Cooper. You guys get along."

"Hal is a challenge. Plus, my dad likes Hal, and I want to keep the money coming," she admitted.

"Oh, hmmm, does Hal know that?"

"I shouldn't have said that. I like Hal, but you guys belong together."

"We do?"

"He makes me sick. He talks about you all the time," she said.

"But why, you don't know me very well, why would you come all the way here—to campus on this gorgeous day—to tell me this?"

"I came here to beat you up," she bragged. "I've got about six inches in height on you—I knew that—I came here to scare you. To scare you away. And then when I saw you there, carrying your book in such a nerdy way, I couldn't do it. You're not very big, and you're really not a bad person. I guess you can't help how he feels. I mean, you're not cool."

"Well, thanks, I guess. I know I am a nerd; I just have to accept it. It's who I am."

"That's for sure," Carrie replied as she pushed her giant hairdo back into place.

"Thanks, on another level," I said. "Back in junior high, I thought I was the biggest girl in the class, so to hear that I'm not very big, that makes me feel good! And Hal and I, whatever is going on, it is happenstance."

"Happenwhat?"

"I'm just rambling," I said. "I'm sorry about your dad."

"Oh, that accident. He didn't get too upset," she said, missing my point.

"I don't know what you mean by an accident. I'm sorry that he's sick. Hal said he is dying."

"My dad ain't dying," she said.

"Your dad isn't dying?" She took my repetition as a correction of her grammar.

"Oh, excuse the hell outta me. Isn't," she said. "You talk like an English teacher."

That made me smile. I talk like an English teacher. I like this girl! "Well, my mom told once that love is love and no matter what someone does, love can't be manipulated. If I love Ray, then I love Ray, and you can't change that by telling me he's ugly or whatever."

"So, you do love Ray?" she asked.

"No," I said, "you can't convince me or change my mind how I feel about Ray or Hal or anyone. Marilyn Monroe could walk in the room, and if Ray loves me, it won't matter. Don't you see?"

"Marilyn Monroe is dead," she retorted, missing the point. "Thank God."

"Yes," I blinked, giving up on trying to further explain the point.

"I only understand about half of what you say," Carrie reacted, thinking she was taking a potshot at me.

"Well, I'm trying to understand why you are here," I said.

"I just thought you should know, I'm stepping out of this." With that, she clapped her hands together, and then spread them in the air like she was under arrest. "I'm gonna let you two nerds be together."

"Carrie, I really appreciate you a lot," I smiled. "If I didn't have class, I mean *a class*, I'd offer to buy you a cup of coffee or tea."

"Well, a beer would be a better offer," she laughed, slapping her hip. "But I know your type, coffee is about as crazy as it gets!"

"Well, once in a while I get a caffeine buzz on Diet Coke—and watch out!"

"You're such a dork," she said, thinking she had hurt me.

"Hey, at least I'm a dork without a bloody nose," I laughed.

"This ended way differently than I thought it would," she admitted. "I'll be at the Sun, having that beer since you mentioned it, if you want to stop by after class. But probably not?"

"Thanks, Carrie," I concluded. "I'm a nerd and there is nothing I can do about it."

"You two really do belong together," she yelled over her shoulder.

I walked toward Olin Hall, rethinking—accepting this revelation of me, and this new place in my life.

CHAPTER FORTY-SEVEN

"What do ya know about babies being borned?" Jim Dandy questioned me, standing in the doorway of my bedroom. "I think they call it *genetics.*"

I was reading, in my room with Mickey by my side, the creepy passage that young maidens "should not loiter in the glen/ In the haunts of goblin men," from Christina Rossetti's "Goblin Market," when Jim Dandy caught me completely off guard.

I swallowed hard, flipping my *Norton Anthology* upside down to mark my page, thinking that this might be headed toward Justin and Andy. "I really don't know much," I professed, not wanting to have this conversation. "I'm an English major."

"Is that baby mine?" he asked.

"Yea, you're on the birth certificate," I said matter-of-factly, hoping, but knowing, this explanation would not be enough.

"Know that," he ascertained. "She my kid— genetically? Saw a show about genetics. Says that blue eyes is not common. Blue eyes make more blue eyes."

"Well, she has blue eyes," I stated the obvious.

"I don't know if that girl is mine. I know you're mine, you look just like me. And Jimmy. He likes to hunt. Now that Justin, he's got brown eyes and he's kinda a pussy."

I didn't want to get into his choice of words, nor did I want to debate the meaning of the word, so I took it as a given. "Well, sometimes people are different than their parents," I said.

"I know. Look at you, reading them stupid books, but ya look like me," he said. "Think your mom has been running around," he alleged. "Saw something on TV about eye color. That Justin has brown eyes. Whatta ya think about that Justin?"

I wasn't about to tell him what I thought about "that Justin." I wouldn't tell him what I believed if he tried to beat it out me— which he might do, but at this juncture, he needed my intelligence. My thoughts are my own, at least he couldn't control my thoughts like Big Brother in *1984*.

He continued. "Know you're my kid," he presumed. "Got your mom pregnant that night. Plus look just like me—only a girl, even though read books. And Jimmy, well, I think he's mine because he likes to hunt, but that Justin, I don't know where I'd get two kids who like books."

"People are all very different," I said. "You are different than your parents, and mom is different than Grandpa and Grandma Delanie."

"That Justin, he's skinny, kinda girlish," he presented.

"He's a good person," I said, making his argument. Then I backtracked. "He looks like you," I lied.

"Don't think he's mine," his voice trailed off.

Please go away, I thought. I wondered if the TV show talked about the new product on the market called paternity tests, but I wasn't about to bridge the idea.

"Gonna find out," he said. "Gonna find out if that stupid girl is mine—and that God-damned Justin."

He turned from my room, and his feet stomped away into the darkness.

CHAPTER FORTY-EIGHT

Like a shaken Pepsi bottle, the anger and fear exploded.

It was out of control.

I was out of control.

And, of course, I was the wrong place, at the wrong time.

"Clean your own serving line!" as I threw the bar towel on the ground. I was shaking uncontrollably, and I couldn't catch my breath.

"Del!" Mr. Camparti yelled back across the serving line in the empty restaurant. "What is going on with you? Get in my office!"

I just stood there, looking at Mr. Camparti, watching the other employees watch me, and I knew that rage and fear were taking over my body and my soul. Jim Dandy was taking over my life. In my greatest fear, I was becoming Jim Dandy. This last threat of paternity testing by Jim Dandy had sent terror through my veins. As if that weren't enough, my last semester tuition was due; I didn't have enough money to pay it; I was probably going to lose credit for the classes I was taking; and the tires on the Pinto were dangerously bald. I had had strep throat and missed four days of work; I had a doctor's bill that I couldn't pay, and I desperately needed sleep and food. The world just continued to spin out of control, and like William Butler Yeats said, but of course not about me, "the center cannot hold."

In addition to all this, Jennifer cried every morning when I tried to go to school or work, and the guilt was eating me alive. Mom would just close the door and leave, knowing that either Justin or I would care for her. Justin was almost at his limit as well: I could see it in his eyes. He was trying to finish his sophomore year and have a life of his own as well.

"Delanie, what the hell is going on?" Mr. Camparti asked as he closed the door to his office.

I was still shaking, trying to get my breath, and stuttering fragments of words. "I can't even say it all...I just can't even, even, even..."

"Just take it easy," he whispered. "Here, get a Diet Coke. Let's talk about this. You melted down out there, and it's not like you."

"There is just so much," I wiped my eyes. "And it is all happening at the same time. I probably won't graduate."

"Why won't you graduate?"

"It's just too much." I wished that I hadn't exploded on him of all people. My anger was directed at the wrong person, and I knew it.

"Are your grades bad?"

"No, it's not my grades, Mr. Camparti. The main thing right now is that I don't have enough money to make my tuition installment, and I'm going to lose my credit hours."

"I can give you a loan," he spoke calmly. "You can pay me back as you can. You have to graduate. You're so close."

"You don't have to do that," I replied. "It's not your problem. I'm sorry for exploding on you."

"It is my problem when you are stressed like this. You've been with me here for, what, seven years? You're like family. Who stays here that long? Nobody. I'll help you out. I'll give you a check for the balance and that will be handled."

"Let me get back out there and finish closing," I urged. "Sarah is out there doing all the work."

"She's fine," he said.

"No, seriously, let me get back out there. The tuition thing helps a lot. I need to work and think this through." I went back out to the serving line and continued closing. I apologized to Sarah and the new broiler chef. I knew that I needed to talk to a true blue minister, someone who could guide me and help get the weight off my shoulders. After paying my tuition with Mr. Camparti's check, I decided that I would try to find that Jane lady at the nondenominational church. I had to get my head on straight, or I was never going to wear a graduation cap on it.

Mr. Camparti came out of the office with his checkbook in his hands. Nobody else was around. "What are we looking at?"

"I'm short about two hundred dollars," I answered. "This will at least keep my credits in place. I will pay back every penny. Thank you!"

"You can pay me back at your own pace, and I'll just keep track of it."

"You are an angel, Mr. Camparti," I replied. "I really think you are one of the greatest friends that I have. Thank you."

"I want to see you get that degree," and he winked.

"I'm so embarrassed," I confessed. "I usually keep it together," I said.

"I know you do," he acknowledged. "You are fine. You're just stressed. I understand."

I drove home thanking God once again for the friends in my life—Mr. Camparti, who I had really thought of as only a boss. I hurried upstairs, avoiding Jim Dandy, took a shower, got snuggled into bed with Mickey at my side, when Jim Dandy came into my room, and stood there abruptly in the dark.

"Need me a book. Ken ya get me one from one of them libraries?" he asked pitifully.

CHAPTER FORTY-NINE

I opened the heavy wooden door of the student ministry building; it was more like a closet, where I had met Jane last year at about this time. The sun was gloriously shining and the smell, once again, reminded me of that musty church basement smell (mixed with Pine Sol) that I remembered from church bazaars with Grandma Delanie.

I was still walking on the wild side with Ray Cooper, with Hal trailing in Ray's domineering and dominant footsteps; I was unaware of where the next turn would take me in this game of checkers we were playing. Some people might think otherwise, and although exhilarating, it was a scary adventure to be twenty-two, single, and totally open to what the world had to offer. The twists and turns toward the unknown should have held some fascination that I didn't quite appreciate, but my reaction was to the contrary. I continued, making small installments to Mr.

Camparti, to pay off his handshake loan. This semester was coming to a close, and my degree was on the horizon.

"Jane?" I called, entering the serene chapel. "Jane? Are you here?"

In the same place where Jane had been reading, sat an older heavyset man with gray hair and a five o'clock shadow, listening to classical music on one of those newfangled CD players, while he was writing in a three-ring binder. "Excuse me," I interrupted, "but I keep trying to find Jane, the little silver-haired lady. I only met her once, but she helped me so much."

"Jane?" repeated the man, as he removed his glasses and refocused his eyes to see me up close.

"She helped me with some issues in my life about a year ago. She seemed to understand things. Do you know how to get in touch with her?"

"I'm afraid I don't know anyone named Jane who fits that description," he said assuredly. "But I am the campus chaplain, Rev. Hampton. Perhaps I could help you?"

Maybe she was an angel, I thought, because she is never here and nobody knows who she is. "Well, you seem busy. I don't want to bother you. I really need some guidance in my life. I have some confusion and anger that I can't seem to let go...."

"Well, helping students, that is my job. I am the campus chaplain. I'm sorry to hear that you are having problems," he sympathized. "These are difficult years: college, starting a new life, relationships."

"My life," I offered, "is falling apart."

"What is going on?" he asked, walking toward a small refrigerator. "Have a seat."

"I have a baby sister," I began. "And Jim Dandy, uh my father, is abusive to her. She cries all the time when I leave. I feel guilty when I leave her because I don't know what he does when I'm not there."

"Well, first of all, it isn't your life that is falling apart. It is someone else's, so think of it that way."

"That's true. It is not my baby," I replied. "It is really painful to watch."

"Yes! But on to this issue: Can you call the police? What type of abuse is it? Is it anything that can be proved?" he asked, pouring two cups of water into mugs from a glass pitcher he kept in that little refrigerator. "What does he do to this poor child?"

"I don't know if there is anything that could be proved," I said. "Probably no physical marks, but of course there are psychological marks on all of us that nobody sees."

"Yes," he offered. "So many people carry marks from emotional abuse, but we can't see them."

I had hit the tip of the iceberg, I thought, and his words rang so true. He was the real deal.

"My mom—she works all the time—at a gas station. She has to work, because my father doesn't work. We have no money. It's my brother and me...."

"Paying bills on low-paying jobs is so difficult," he said sympathetically. "So many women have problems with child care when they work. Is your father unable to work?"

"He can't get along with anyone," I explained. "He's mean. Just plain old mean. He gets fired from every job he ever gets. He is talented and smart, but he can't function in the world, like other people do."

"When you think about it," Rev. Hampton was reaching inside his heart, "that, in itself, is sad. A perfectly healthy man who can't work, can't provide for his family because he obviously has psychological problems...."

"Yes. You have nailed it. I believe he is a sociopath. Dr. Longworth described a sociopath in my psychology class, and I think he is one."

"Dr. Longworth knows his stuff," Rev. Hampton acknowledged. "He's a smart man."

"Why do some people get away with this stuff, and the rest of us have to continue to pay the price?" I asked. "Why does God allow that?"

"Would you like to live your father's life instead?" Rev. Hampton asked me rhetorically. "You could get away with things?"

"No. He's a miserable loser. He doesn't have any friends. No laughter, no joy, no social interaction. Just the TV and being mean to people, really. That's his life."

"Sad existence," he took a sip of his water. "That is why you should pray. You should pray for him—and his miserable life. You can't move forward, my dear, until you drop the anger off."

"Is that the answer?" I felt tears being created in the recesses of my cheek bones. They started flooded out into my eye sockets as goosebumps took over my arms.

"You can't carry that nasty stuff around with you," he reasoned. "Anger? It will eat you alive."

"Yes," I was sipping water in as it was flowing out of my eye sockets.

"Think of all the things that you do have. You have a brain, a good brain. You have compassion, the ability to feel all these things. You must have friends, a pretty and smart girl like you?"

"Yes, I do," I said. "I hadn't really thought about it like that."

"Look at what you *do have*," he emphasized the words *do* and *have*.

"You're right."

"Make a list," he said. "It's called a gratitude list. You will see that he is such a small part of who you are. Get away from that old thinking. Don't let it drown you anymore."

"What am I going to do with my life?" I was adding to the burden already sitting on the table. "I am going to graduate from college in a few months. I have no idea what I'm going to do with this degree when I get it. I've worked so hard to get here, and you know what? It isn't magical. I'm scared; I'm confused, and I really don't know where I'm going next."

"Let's take one thing at a time. God has a plan. It might not be in your time, but trust that He has a plan. You have all these worries rolling around in your head. Let's try to empty that head of all the worries. Take them to God or your Higher Power. Every new college grad goes through this. It is normal."

"Really?" I questioned in wonder.

"Sure. I thought I wanted to be a stock broker. Can you imagine? Trust me on this. And one more thing: pray for that miserable man, your father."

I had searched so hard, so diligently, for so long, and it seemed that the answer was pretty simple. I just needed to be led, lovingly, by someone in whom I trusted.

So, I got in the Pinto, looked out the windows, and I prayed for Jim Dandy.

CHAPTER FIFTY

I walked in the door of the dark house, and it appeared that Jim Dandy had been waiting for me to arrive. "They give out different books at the library, right?" Jim Dandy asked.

"Yea," I said, trying not to laugh at the ridiculousness of the question. "Why?"

"I want to find out if that God-damned Justin is my kid," he said. "And that stupid baby."

"Well, a book won't tell you that," I said, lying, knowing that if he understood genetics, he would know that Justin was not his son because of his brown eyes. So, this is what I get for my prayers?

"Del, don't lie. Saw a show about eye color. Two blue-eyed people are *recessive*," he actually used the word *recessive*. I think my mouth dropped open. "Can't have no brown-eyed baby. And that damn Justin has brown eyes. Now tell me 'bout that?"

"No, I think they can," I knew that I was skating on thin ice. I was terrible liar—even if the person being lied to was stupid.

"Stuff called DNA," he paused after saying each letter. "It's in your blood, your spit, everything. Can prove if you were at the crime with it. They can use a hair or spit to prove it."

"I know that God-damned Justin is not my kid," he stomped his club foot down. "He's a pussy boy, and I don't have pussies. Jimmy is my kid. You, you're my kid because you look like me—even though you read books and no club foot, but one of ya should have the foot. I don't know about that God-damned stupid baby."

The sentence about the foot cracked me up so much that I was afraid I would laugh. Jim Dandy was trying to be serious, and he thought he was scientific.

"Want a book 'bout genetics, and want ya to read it to me," he said.

"It's actually complicated," I said.

"Gotta know some professor-like guy like that who could tell me if that Justin is my kid?"

"No," I said, as I felt myself float out of the room. How was I going to get out of this? "I am an English major, and my professors don't know biology," I said. "You need a biology professor or someone who understands genetics."

"Goin' up there to see what they know," he said.

"That's probably a good idea," I said, hoping he would never get himself dressed, make an appointment, and drive to the university to ask such a blatant question.

He could also get a library card himself and check out a few books, but that would require energy, wherewithal, and abilities to communicate and read.

CHAPTER FIFTY-ONE

I tripped on the sidewalk, that same place where I had encountered Carrie a few months earlier, spilling, admittedly, the weird contents of my purse asunder: teabags (I bring my own to save money in restaurants) in a plastic baggie, the turquoise ring from Grandma Delanie, a coupon for free French fries at the Chuckery, a photo of my dog Mickey, and of course, a feminine sanitary pad. As I was trying to scoop everything back into my purse, Ray, looking exceptional attractive, was approaching me, arms extended, as if someone had planted him there at that exact moment just to see the spectacle I had presented.

"Hey! Let me help you," he bent down and grabbed the photo of Mickey, cut into a heart shape. He promptly tore it in half.

"Why did you do that?" I asked, grabbing the sanitary pad first.

"You should be carrying a photo of me, not some stupid dog," he said.

"You really are a klutz," he laughed artificially. "My dad was right in what he said about you. And why do you have a photo of your dog and not a photo of me?"

"What did your dad say about me that was mean? He wouldn't say anything mean about me. I was a good student."

"Well, he said a few things that weren't so flattering."

"He did?"

"You know, you're always off in la la land. You need to focus on what you're doing, rather than daydreaming all the time. Those stupid books you're reading. What the hell?"

"I know," I wasn't even listening to him. I was thinking about what a dick he was. I was thinking about how he sounded like Jim Dandy.

"How about going to see *Cats* tonight at E.J. Thomas Hall?" he asked. This was an offer that was unlike a Jim Dandy offer. "I have some good tickets. Isn't tonight your night off work?"

"Yea, but Hal wanted...."

"Hal? I thought we talked about putting that skinny dork behind you. You need to focus on me, and what I want." He was pointing to himself over and over, forcing me to recall the repetitious hand motions of Jim Dandy.

"Okay, you know, I have wanted to see *Cats*. I'll call Hal after class and cancel our plans," I said, realizing that seeing a play was a cultural experience, and it was thoughtful of him to ask.

"Now, that's my girl," he said loudly, waving as he walked away. "Hold on to your purse, Klutz Girl! I'll call you and tell you the time you can pick me up!"

I was perturbed to change plans because I was trying to gain some lost ground with Hal after the Carrie fiasco, but he would understand. I would tell him that I wanted to see *Cats*, because he understood the concept of living on a budget—unless Carrie was around—then money was not a consideration.

"Del, I think you are making a mistake," he told me after class when I called him. "He is a big drinker, and he just uses you for rides, don't you see it? Besides, the new Janet Jackson album is out, and I was looking forward to dancing. Did you get those shoes you were talking about?"

"Hal, I have been wanting to see a play, any play, like people do, and I can't afford the tickets. He is not using me. He really cares about me." Deep down, though, I had an inkling that Hal was right, but I didn't want to admit it to myself or especially to him. I had a sinking feeling in my stomach when I hung up the phone.

"Well, okay. We can dance this weekend," Hal hung up dejectedly. I felt terrible leaving him in the lurch that way, but he had left me alone many nights when he went out with Carrie.

"Pick me up at the frat house," Ray told me when he called me later that night, last minute.

"What about dinner?" I asked. "It would be nice to go out and have dinner, rather than serving dinner to other people all the time."

"Well, we really don't have time, now," he reasoned. "I can bring you some brats that the boys threw on the grill."

"Uh, Ray, I'm a vegetarian," I said. "Don't you know that?"

"Oh, yea, well, you need to give that up. It's stupid, and it just makes it difficult to feed you."

When I arrived at the frat house, two other guys were there, ready to hop into my car. "Oh, I forgot to tell you," he laughed, "Steve and Joe are going too! Jump in, guys! The Pinto is a little small, but it's a ride!"

The three of them had already been drinking, and I was angry that it wasn't a date. Ray was so inconsiderate. Hal was right; I was being used for my car and my position as designated driver.

"Let's see if we can get this four-cylinder car to climb the hill. Let's see if Del here will have a drink," Ray said condescendingly. "She's such a goody two shoes like the song."

"What made your parents buy you a Pinto?" Steve asked, hitting the back of my seat. "These things are junk."

"My parents didn't buy it for me," I corrected, in a bitchy tone. "I bought it myself, and it was what I could afford."

"Well, why would you pick out a Pinto?" he laughed. "Aren't there other cars that aren't so, uh, dangerous—and dorky?"

"It's a good car," I said. "Very dependable. I like it. What do you drive?"

"When I'm home, I have a BMW," Steve bragged. "But not at school."

I just swallowed, breathed in, and shook my head in the dark—I didn't reply to that comment.

Cats, based on the works of the poet T.S. Eliot, focused on the peculiarities of cats and Eliot's love for them came through. Since I didn't have to buy the ticket, all the better. It was a night out on the town, but I wasn't happy that two frat boys joined us for the play. Why would they be interested in a play when all the beer was at the frat house? I didn't mind fun and making fun, but I didn't want to be watched, monitored, and mocked like some freak as part of the entertainment. And that's how I felt with the other frat boys making snide comments to me as Ray just sat there and laughed like I was the third wheel.

I had looked forward to dressing up for the play, something that I didn't get to do too often. I had just bought an adorable multi-colored boyfriend jacket with shoulder pads, giving the illusion of a very slim waist. I also wore a solid black skirt and those black patent leather pumps—the ones I was telling Hal about—with red cut-out hearts and blue diamonds in the toe box. My hair, I was so glad, was extra big because the humidity was low, and as a bonus, my skin was flawless.

We were headed for E.J. Thomas when Ray said, "Stop at Wanamaker's."

"Is that a restaurant?" I said.

"Uh, no, it's a bar—something you wouldn't understand."

While there, he drank two more beers, and Steve and Joe each had one more beer while I drank two Diet Cokes. "Grab some popcorn," Ray laughed at himself, pointing to the giant claw-footed bathtub, the bar novelty, which held freshly popped popcorn. "You said you were hungry."

The Donna Summer song, "Last Dance," had picked me up and taken me back to Kathie's front porch that summer of 1979, before I moved off Eclipse Avenue. We had loved that song together and sang it into the mirror in her bedroom, pretending that the toilet paper rolls were our microphones. We danced in the driveway, and Rosie cheered our performance from her front porch. "You guys are so cute!" she yelled from across the street. "I wish I were young again! Keep dancing'!"

Ray interrupted my reverie, by knocking on my head like it was hollow, and he said, "Are you in there?" His friends laughed hysterically at this little antic, and I could feel the anger boiling inside of me. "Oh, I was just remembering...."

"Oh, let me guess. About some goofy friend or some goofy old dead guy from years ago?" he mocked, referring to my stories of Kathie, Andy, and Eclipse Avenue.

"No," I said, anger in my voice.

"Well, snap out of it." He clicked his fingers with an edginess in his voice. "You are such a ditz. You're always on another planet. Earth to Delanie, Earth to Delanie."

"Did your dad, Mr. Cooper, teach you to treat people like this? Because he wasn't a dick like you are," I said before I could even think. The words just spewed out there, onto the bar top like a Thanksgiving cornucopia, while Steve and Joe stopped laughing and just looked at Ray for a reaction.

"Yea, he did," Ray said. "He said you were a little bitch."

"I don't believe you," I felt overpowered, undervalued, used, and alone. Every hair on my arms was standing at attention, waiting for my voice and the words to form.

"When did you decide to talk like some slut?" he asked, his voice rising. I could hear my girl Donna Summer still in the background singing about needing someone beside her. Someone to guide her. I understood what she was saying, and this guy wasn't doing the trick.

"I generally don't talk like..." I couldn't finish the sentence. Who was it that I needed beside me? A voice whispered in my head, and it kept repeating, "Not this creep beside you: Quicksand."

"Never mind," I was purposely acting overly sorry and afraid. "I'm sorry. Let's go to the play." He didn't' pick up on it. I wanted to see the play, I really did, and putting up with these shenanigans,

I thought, was worth the ticket price—especially in my financial dire straits.

We piled back into the Pinto, and the song was also playing on the radio in the Pinto. Donna Summer urged me to do the "Last Dance" with Ray Cooper that night. I thought of how I should be dancing with Hal. I thought of how I had left him in the lurch. I thought of how I had left Kathie and Andy and Jennifer and Justin. All for plans with this moron of a man, this shell of a man, who was the son of my beloved geometry teacher Mr. Cooper, who would never say that I was a bitch. Mr. Cooper didn't act that way. But his son, Ray Cooper, was the perimeter formula, not the area formula. He went around the edges and didn't cover the insides. The apple can fall far from the tree.

As I drove toward E.J. Thomas, I felt a lightness of being guiding me. Grandma Delanie's turquoise ring glimmered on my hand on the steering wheel as we whizzed under the streetlights that were dancing on the Pinto's windshield. I could smell nearby Rizzi's Pizza waft through the air, and there was Kathie, in my mind's eye, wanting to dance a "tango" down her driveway on Eclipse Avenue. We too, at one point, reluctantly did our "Last Dance" together.

"Hey!" Ray was once again knocking on my head. "Is anyone home?" He started patting down my extra poufy hair.

"Yes, there is a lot in there, but you wouldn't understand," I mumbled now, under my breath. "In geometry, they're called *givens* and *proofs*."

"What?" he mocked.

"Let's just see the play," I said.

"Why are you talking about geometry?" he questioned, unaware that I was speaking in allegory.

"I talk in circles sometimes," I said with a smile in my voice. Like a storm cloud, I was gathering strength.

"You're just plain weird," he uttered.

"Yea, I am." I winked up at Andy and Grandma Delanie whose presence I could feel surrounding me.

"I don't wanna pay for parking. Park the car on the street." Ray commanded. I squeezed the Pinto into a parallel parking space, re-poufed my hair in the rearview mirror, and got out, determined to see the play like a normal person.

Ray and I were seated side by side, but Steve and Joe, beside Ray, kept getting up to get more beer. I had no idea why they wanted to tag along until I realized that the tickets included an open bar. They obviously weren't interested in the play. I tried to watch and listen, watch and listen, while they laughed, passed beer over each other, spilled beer on my jacket and my shoes, and then got reprimanded twice by an usher for being too noisy during the show.

Ray leaned over, with the malted smell of beer on his breath. "Someday," he said, cupping his hand to my ear, "when we go on business dinners, and I'm trying to impress my clients, don't wear those shoes. They're trashy."

He was talking during "Memory," my favorite song, breathing down my neck, his beer breath breathing on me. Floating above the stage, in my mind, singing this song to me, for me, pointing toward an escape hatch where there was a light beaming down. My angels were there.

"Hey, dimwit," he said.

"Shhh, Ray, please, I want to hear this song. It's my favorite."

"Don't shhh me," he said.

"Please," I said. I again was acting the part.

"Joe thinks those shoes are pretty stupid looking," he said.

"What?"

"You heard me!" he began to yell. "Don't wear those shoes again. They're slutty."

"I wasn't talking to you," I said to Ray. "Did you say something about my shoes? Don't you love 'em?"

"No, they're ugly," he said.

"Daylight," I said back to him.

"What the hell?"

I thought of red-haired, dimpled Mom, statuesque, an Irish beauty, wearing her cat glasses, and my gorgeous, yet grotesque, father in those pictures from 1963. They were sitting on the hood of a small Chevy car. He was tall. His full head of blonde hair blowing crazily in the wind that day. This was before he started growing the crazy ass beards. His freckles, golden on his flawless tanned skin, and those cool, blue gray eyes, were so dazzlingly there, hiding evil and misery. He was wearing a white dress shirt and a skinny black tie looking so 1960s. In this photo, he was working as an electrical contractor.

"Quicksand," Mom had called her life. I looked over at Ray: So damned handsome and rugged, but, I thought, "at what price? What lurked behind those eyes?"

I was glimpsing night. The songstress belted out something about a new day beginning.

I put my ankles on the seat in front of me. I started *foot dancing*, showing off my shoes—the ones that Ray hated so much. "Those shoes are slutty," he said again.

"What's wrong with my shoes? I love these shoes! These are my dancing shoes! Hal loves 'em!" I was shouting at this point.

"Put your feet on the floor," he shouted. "Put your fucking feet on the floor!"

"These shoes?" I was, in my own head, on stage and acting a part. I had already made a pact with myself. "Oh, God, you'll never see these shoes again!"

"That's my girl," he concluded proudly.

"Of course, dear," I repeated like a 1950s housewife.

"But please, let's not talk about that fag Hal! Next time, Bitch, I might have to pick out your clothes and shoes. Let's see: Ray will pick out the clothes, got it?"

"No, I don't 'Got it.'" I swallowed hard. Words, like life buoys in a rough sea, started circling around my head: Last Dance, Daylight, Bitch, Quicksand...

I knew that the night would soon be a "Memory."

Swirling, swirling to the ceiling went my shoes, popcorn for dinner, beer spilled on my jacket. I could see these things raising up to the escape hatch on the ceiling.

The "Memory" song continued in my head.

"I'm sorry, Ray," I announced pitifully, acting the part. "I won't wear them again. I'm sorry that I disappointed you." The words, out of my old war chest of expressions that I used with Jim Dandy, covered my heart like a bandage, so I could think while things and words continued to swirl like a reverse drain of water. They poured to the ceiling: cheerleading uniforms, Jimmy trying to run out on the football field, cigarette smoke, Mickey being hit with an extension cord, thawed turkey chunks hanging from chandeliers, broken windows on the Pinto, a newborn baby screaming in a crib....

Andy and Grandma Delanie, the way I remembered them, were floating above me. I heard Mom's voice repeating, repeating "it's quicksand...it's quicksand, it's just like quicksand..."

"This is quicksand," I uttered calmly. "This is quicksand," I repeated, standing up.

"What?" he asked. "More weirdness from the Circumcised Circle Girl."

"No," I stated simply. "This is the solution to the equation. It's a given."

"What?" he asked again as I started to scoot over him.

"I need to go to the restroom. Can I get you a beer while I'm out?"

"Yes," he said proudly. "That's my girl."

I scooted over the two frat boys, and one of the idiots pinched my butt. I didn't react. I just kept scooting toward the aisle.

I approached the bartender, who was wiping down the counter. He was a kindred spirit in a sea of Rays and dickhead friends. "Can I borrow a quarter from your tip jar?" I asked. "I don't have my purse with me. I desperately need to make a phone call."

He took a quarter out of his jar—one server to another—and handed it to me.

"Any time," he said.

"I work at a restaurant, too," I said warmly. "I'm a good tipper." I walked away.

The pay phone was right outside the restroom. I got inside the stall and prayed. "God," I repeated over and over. "God grant me serenity. Be with me."

I went to the pay phone, hands shaking, and dialed a very familiar number. "Hal?" I spoke into the receiver.

"Del, where are you? I thought you were at *Cats*?"

"I'm at *Cats* alright," I stated. "And they are alley cats—in trash cans, clawing at me...."

"What? You aren't making any sense."

"I'm making perfect sense. I know exactly what I am doing."

"Are you okay?" he asked.

"I need you to pick me up, outside E.J., by the fountain, right away. I'll explain when you get here." The list kept rolling in my head: Quicksand, Bitch, Daylight, Last Dance, Klutz, shoes, "I must think of a new life...."

"Give me twenty minutes," he said and clicked down the phone.

"Hey, do you need help?" the bartender asked from the behind the stately bar as he continued to wipe the counter.

"This mouse is getting away," I mumbled. "Thanks for being there."

He shook his head up and down and smiled.

I went directly to the fountain outside E.J., in bare feet, carrying my shoes so I could run, and I listened to the water cascading up then down. Hal pulled up in his VW Rabbit right at that instant, shoved the car into park, got out, opened the door for me, waited as I got settled in the seat, and he closed the door. "Do you want some Luigi's" he asked when he engaged the car into drive.

"I'm starving," I laughed.

"I love the shoes!" he pushed the accelerator.

My head gently hit the headrest as we roared with laughter. "Why are you carrying them?"

"I had to get away, Hal!"

"Yep," he said.

We drove away while Boston warned, "Don't Look Back."

CHAPTER FIFTY-TWO

The rain was gushing down; the windows were fogged. Everything was moist and musty: the carpeting, the countertops, the sofa cushions. Jim Dandy's cigarette smoke was almost a solid. It was the spring of my second senior year in college when a lady from Western Star Children's Services knocked on the door. The lady was there, she said, on referral for a child abuse case, an anonymous report, and she wanted to see Jennifer Dane. Mom was there, and brought out Jennifer who, at the time, seemed to be comfortable and healthy. Of course, Mom and I were there, and it appeared that Jennifer was just fine. The lady filed a satisfactory report, and Mom signed the documents.

A few weeks later, when Mom was getting ready to go to work, she found Jennifer dead in her little crib, blue, and not breathing. I was home when she was discovered, thank God, and Mom bellowed hysterically, yelled for me to come into the room, screamed for God to make her breathe again, shouted obscenities at Jim Dandy, and then she fell to the floor, sobbing.

Mom, whose emotional strength was constantly challenged by constant mental gymnastics that were required for life with Jim Dandy, would never be the same.

Justin came running into the room, thinking it was just another fight. I called an ambulance, and the EMT pronounced Jennifer dead at the scene in the dark house. "It appears to be SIDS," announced the bearded male EMT, writing on a clipboard. "That's sudden infant death syndrome," he defined the acronym, looking for the light of understanding in my eyes.

Jim Dandy moseyed in from the other room, TV gunshots blaring loudly in the background, smoking yet another homemade cancer stick, a cloud of smoke enveloping him like volcanic ash after an eruption.

"Cigarette smoke," explained the EMT, "is highly linked to SIDS." The disrespect was evident in his voice. "Do you want to sign the death certificate?" he asked me, a little afraid, I thought, sensing that I would be an easier person to deal with than Jim Dandy.

"Let him sign it," I uttered to the EMT. "He is responsible...or I mean, the responsible party."

"No, my daughter will sign it," Jim Dandy said, pointing at me. "Didn't bring me a book. Maybe he knows about DNA," Jim Dandy said. A rush of adrenalin pulsed through my veins. This was not the time for this line of questioning. "You know how to prove if a kid is your DNA?"

The EMT seemed amazed that Jim Dandy was onto a new topic while this child was just found dead.

"No, I won't sign it," I announced. "She was my sister. She wasn't my child. I tried to keep her alive," I said to the EMT, allowing him think whatever he wanted by the vague yet powerful statement.

Jim Dandy should sign the death certificate. Maybe not directly, but negativity, neglect, meanness, smoke, and spit all added together and killed her. Her poor soul couldn't handle this dark house.

"Do you know about DNA?" Jim Dandy again asked the EMT.

"Not really," he said, shaking his head at the inane question.

"I don't even think she is my kid," he said.

"Oh," the EMT said. "Well, you need to sign this."

I watched as Jim Dandy struggled to form letters in his childish handwriting.

Mom would not come to, even after the EMT and a small female EMT had administered smelling salts. The EMTs decided to take Mom by ambulance as well, and Justin and I followed the ambulance in the Pinto. When I got to a hospital phone on the wall, I got in touch with Jimmy at Tom's house.

"That baby was never healthy, Delanie," Jimmy said over the phone. "Things happen for a reason."

A young, attractive Asian doctor appeared before Justin and me. "She has some symptoms of cardiomyopathy," he said, looking at his clipboard. "It is sometimes called broken heart syndrome. Does she ever experience unvented anger and stressors?"

Justin and I looked at each other. I looked at the doctor, blinked, and shook my head yes.

"We know the death of this baby is a shock," he asked, "but why the anger and stressors?"

"You don't know our father," Justin interjected.

"The attending EMT said it was a weird situation," the doctor said, then he scribbled something onto his clipboard and walked away.

We went in to see Mom in the ICU unit. "That baby was never meant to be."

She could barely speak. "It's okay, Mom. She wasn't healthy," I said, trying to make up an excuse.

"She was such a pitiful little soul. I knew from the start, she would struggle," Mom said, stating the obvious. The dark house was getting darker.

"Now she is in Heaven with Grandma Delanie," Justin finally said. "She is in a better place." People say those words all the time;

they were such a cliché, but they were so true. The times were getting tougher in the dark house; Jim Dandy was getting sicker, and really, we all just needed to get away. Jennifer was grounding us to that house like an anchor to the shore, and even though we loved her, and wanted her to live, sadly, we all knew deep down inside that it was for the best—and selfishly—for us. It was hardened thinking, even for the four stressed people who were so numbed by this bitter battle of a life with Jim Dandy.

"That son-of-a-bitch," Mom had gained enough strength to say, sitting up in bed, looking out the window. "I hope he rots in hell for this." I looked around to see if the doctor had heard this, but we were alone.

We didn't know what to say in response, because we all agreed. We didn't want to talk too much. We really didn't want to know if she knew something that we didn't.

We just wanted peace.

CHAPTER FIFTY-THREE

I would be receiving my college degree in two weeks. That long-awaited goal, dream, plan, whatever—it was within reach. My vision of the future was changing. I could see that Justin had changed; he would be a high school senior. With Jennifer's death, Mom had changed. When she got out of the hospital, she walked around the dark house in a stupor, sullen, no expression in her eyes. She would look out the kitchen window, stare at nothing really, make a cup of coffee, and leave it untouched on the countertop. Then she would walk to another window, watch a bird or a squirrel, make a comment about the animal, and then repeat the process. She hadn't returned to work and the bills were piling up. Jim Dandy didn't change or react. He kept watching and yelling at the television, eating the remaining food in the pantry, and didn't seem to worry one bit about the prospects for the future.

The quicksand had engulfed her.

Jennifer's death, although far more intimate and personal, ran concurrent with the death of rubber tire manufacturing in Akron. Only Goodyear was still standing—and for how long?

Mom inhabited a lifeless zombie body. The industrious factory workers, dedicated with sweat and blood, were now also limping, also like lifeless zombies, as they and the city tried to recover from the news that the giants would be leaving a huge vacuum in their once prosperous town. The upheaval of the thousands of jobs and the related industries would also suffer like dominoes tumbling upon the next one. Many of my friends from Eclipse Avenue—real people with children, house payments, and health issues, they would lose their jobs and insurance. They would have to find new livelihoods, retrain for lower-paying jobs in late middle age, and cut their living expenses. About once a week, the *Beacon Journal* reported that an ex tire worker had jumped off the All-American Bridge, taking his life and leaving only a note that he couldn't face the reality that his livelihood, his dedication, his heart and soul, for twenty or thirty years, had meant nothing. All of their old lives had packed up and moved overnight to Japan.

Mom continued to pace the floors, but she did eventually return to the gas station. She had no choice. Other than the food I brought home from King Arthur's Round Table, we had no food.

I kept my promise and repaid my loan to Mr. Camparti in ten to fifteen-dollar increments. While the unions were fighting to stay afloat in Akron and businesses were closing, I limped through final tuition payments, paid late fees, recovered from a bout of Strep throat, worked as much as possible, and passed with a D in a required math class, but I was getting a damned college degree unless hell had frozen over before I made it to campus to grab the parchment out of their grubby hands.

I drove my now old white Ford Pinto, with intact windows all around thanks to Hal and George, to E. J. Thomas Performing Arts Hall, the last place I had laid eyes on my beloved professor Dr. Phil Longworth, and an abusive asshole boyfriend Ray Cooper, sporting a sign in the back window that read: I'm Glad I'm a Grad!

Like an encore performance, I wore those same heels that Ray Cooper hated (which made me love them so much more), smiling to myself about my last performance where I left him sitting drunk and disorderly at *Cats*. I never told him I was leaving; I just left!

I walked confidently to the check-in desk and lined up for my name to be called to receive my leather-bound degree that read: "Delanie Jayne Dane, Bachelor of Arts in English" verified with signatures from the board of directors at The University of Akron that I had earned enough credit hours to be the first person in my family to receive a college degree.

I stood there alone on stage, not unlike that day of the National Honor Society induction ceremony back in high school, and waited to hear my name spoken. It was just a moment, but it seemed a millennium.

I was there.

I had made it.

It wasn't a dream. I was a college graduate.

Nothing could contain me, my boundless heart, my growing self-esteem, my open mind, my vivacious curves, or any other ounce of being that wasn't covered in that preceding list, to grab that degree with my own brand of vigor and hope and courage. I was determined that I would run, crawl, walk, or pull myself across that stage, extend my grubby paw like "a pair of ragged claws" as T.S. Eliot described in "The Love Song of J. Alfred Prufrock," and head off to the next chapter in my life, an educated woman with a bachelor's degree.

I was wearing Akron blue and gold cords around my neck in my black graduation gown, feeling hungry, teary-eyed, and on top of the world all at the same time. This was it. The end of the road: If I didn't trip, fall, break my neck, miss the deadline, fail the test, forget the payment, whatever: I had made it! It would be mine: the job, the life, the love, the freedom, the world.

I heard my name and it took me five whole years to walk across that stage. I was a whirl of color, in a sea of people, lifting each foot in those black pumps like it was weighted with a concrete block, placing it securely on the waxed floor. I looked out to that first row, and as clear as day, I saw Jane. It was her. She was smiling, clapping, looking up at me, in slow motion. We made eye contact for a brief second, and she winked at me, I swear.

I wanted to stop mid-acceptance, so I could get down there to see and touch her in person and thank her for everything she had done for me. I had only met her once in my life, but I felt that she was always with me. I couldn't seem to find her again physically, but she cared. Her words changed my life. She was real and true and good. So simple, so illuminating, for those two years since I had met her, with all the stuff piled high like a hoarder's basement, my eyes had looked for her everywhere and had made serious attempts to find her. I looked at the campus ministry, in the Chuckery, at McDonald's on campus, at Olin Hall. But finally, on this important day, she was right in that front row, cheering for me.

She had been with me all along.

I shook hands with the president and was handed the degree, leather-bound, like a greeting card to open. I hugged it to my chest and tears started pouring out of my eyes. I left the stage and tried to get to Jane, but the attendants would not let me leave the area until the other graduates were finished. Finally, about a decade later, the ceremony was over, and I was able to make a beeline for that first row of seats. I passed over people, excusing myself, trying not to step on toes and purses. She was the third person from the end, front row. "Was a lady named Jane sitting here during the ceremony?" I asked an older couple, obviously proud parents of a fellow graduate.

"Jane?" questioned the tall, dark-haired woman. "We have been sitting here the whole time and nobody has left."

"Well, there's a lady that I know, she is petite and has silver hair," I said. "She was sitting here when I went across the stage. I know it was her."

"I'm sorry," the man concurred. "But my wife is right. We have been there the whole time, and nobody has left this area."

"Okay," I said, discouraged, accepting their honest report.

Why would they lie? They had nothing to lose or gain either way. Apparently, I had hallucinated about seeing Jane. I turned to leave them, and I looked down at my feet. I piece of paper, confetti, made from shredded newspaper, about the size of a thick rubber band, was at my right foot. I almost left it there, but something compelled me to pick it up. It read, "with Jane's encouragement..."

"Is this yours?" I asked the dark-haired woman, who thought, by the look on her face, that it was a strange question that a shred of paper would be worth the asking.

"No. What is it?" she replied.

"It mentions 'Jane,'" I spoke quietly. "And Jane is the name of the lady that I thought I saw sitting near you."

"It is a penny from heaven," said the dark-haired woman.

In the late May heat and humidity, I felt a chill rush through my body, and goosebumps swept over my arms. After all those people mingled, hugged, and laughed in that huge hall, the noise and confusion dissipated. The parents of the grad, and the others around me, eventually left while I stood there holding that scrap of paper. It became clear to me that this degree, another piece of paper, wasn't the end of my journey; it was just the beginning of a long road that I must continue to travel. It wouldn't be easy, there would be problems, potholes, pivotal moments, but I really wasn't alone. I didn't need Jim Dandy and his troubles; I had paper, friends, and angels.

I walked to my Pinto, befuddled, still in my gown and carrying my mortar board; Justin was standing beside my car, holding a bouquet of hand-picked lilacs. "Congratulations!" he yelled, his hands cupped around his mouth. "Let's go have some lunch!"

"I'm so glad you're here," I said, hugging him.

"Del, we have to take care of Mom," he acknowledged. "She isn't getting over this thing."

I followed him in the Pinto to "this Italian place that one of my friends recommended." When we walked in, Mr. Camparti, his wife, and Hal were already at a table talking to Mr. Ignotti, the spaghetti supper volunteer from the student ministry building. "Hey, what are you doing here?" I asked Mr. Ignotti.

"Me? What are you doing here? I own the place!" he laughed loudly.

"My brother brought me here. I just graduated from college," I said proudly.

"Camparti called me up and told me about your big day," he recounted. "This is my place that I was telling you about. Small world, huh?"

"What a coincidence," I agreed. "Very Akron. Very small world."

"It's been a long road for my friend," Hal said. "Mr. Camparti and Justin planned all of this."

"There are no coincidences," Mr. Ignotti pronounced as two waitressed brought out lasagna, garlic bread, and salad. "Lunch is on me."

The jukebox was bragging about how Frank Sinatra did it his way. Seated here with a few of the greatest people in the world, I also did it my way. I saw a way out, a better way, a way to happiness, but life wasn't going to stand still while I celebrated. I still had bills to pay. I realized that I needed a new car; the Pinto had just about galloped to its last pasture. I needed to leave the darkness behind. Getting that coveted degree, had lurched me forward, but it also held me in the dark house for too long. It dawned on me again, that this degree was only the first step on the path to whatever the fabric of life would unroll.

Sometimes things in life must be earned to be understood. And there it was, clear as a bell.

I, Delanie Dane, headed back to the dark house to change into work clothes. Some small pitiful man named Jim Dandy was standing in the driveway, smoking yet another cigarette, throwing pebbles at an injured baby bird who couldn't fly away. "Well, here comes the Know-It-All," he smirked, blowing smoke my way. "What a waste of money that was. Where's the big-time job?"

"Time will tell," I said casually. "I just graduated not even three hours ago."

"Well, waste of money. Jimmy makes more money fixing cars than you do."

This pathetic shell of a man, I realized at that moment, was no longer an object in my way. He was a hollow shell. Like Reverend Hampton had explained, he was a person to be pitied, not hated. Jim Dandy, I discovered, was really very small, very unfortunate, very insignificant, and he was missing out on the textures, the velvets, patterns, and swirls of color, the light. "God, help poor Jim Dandy. God, please help Jim Dandy. I wanted him to be a dad, but he just couldn't, and for that, I was sad for him." I said as I got into the Pinto and manually cranked down the driver's side window. "Goodbye, Dark House," I said, and I sobbed. I didn't know why I sobbed, but I realized that I would never be able to explain the chasm of our relationship. He would never understand me, and that was the cold, hard truth of it.

I thought about that small but cosmically important piece of advice from Jane: I could only change myself. I thought about some of the people who mattered: the list too long to put down here. I thought about my future. I dreamed, in that glimpse of the passage of time, of a future: working, teaching, writing, traveling, meeting, talking, laughing. I imagined all the places I could see, all the people I could meet, all the meals I could savor, all the friendships I would enjoy, but I had to work hard. Ah, so much flavor, richness, texture, accomplishment. I thought about music, art, literature, and laughter piled high on an endless smorgasbord of experiences. The possibilities were infinitesimal. I dreamed of a new, bright life. I mustn't, I couldn't, give in. Jim Dandy's misery wouldn't consume Delanie Dane anymore.

I was free.

"Well," he urged, trying to lasso me back in as I released the clutch and inched the Pinto a few feet forward. "Where's it at? So, where's big job? Where's the big bucks? Miss College Graduate Bullshit!"

"It will still take a while," I said calmly, in control of my emotions. "Things don't happen overnight."

"Bullshit."

"Yes, it is bullshit," I repeated. "It is bullshit. I understand where you are coming from. I am young, and I have just started to live. I have a bright future, and I have hope. I have lots of friends behind and beside me. I can only go forward toward them and the light. You are to be pitied, Jim Dandy."

Another sentence, implied, was left unsaid. I waited for him to lash out and try to hit me in the face as I popped the clutch and moved the car forward.

"What the hell you talkin' about?" He dropped the flame of his cigarette, squished it back and forth with his dirt-crusted work boot, and he looked away, not knowing that he was gazing toward my Indian fountain in the woods. Shakespeare, Laura Ingalls Wilder, John Steinbeck, Mark Twain, Donna Summer, Elton John, dancers, painters, histories, articles, mountains, oceans, friendships, voices, smiles, and laughter of friends, and my own writing were all out there beckoning me forward like the droplets of water splashing from the source, from a fountain, from oceans far away. This pathetic soul in my presence needed forgiveness. This pathetic soul in my presence would never leave the darkness, and that was the sad truth.

I loved, loved, loved the life-changing momentum of the water surging forth from the Indian fountain. I cherished the memories of the people who encouraged me, laughed with me, helped me, here, at school, at work, and on Eclipse Avenue. I knew, as scary as it seemed, a degree wasn't a magical ticket. It was just the beginning. Some things were still tough. Life wasn't easy.

But I knew one thing for certain: I was leaving the dark house.

THE END

ABOUT THE AUTHOR

Renee Verite grew up in Akron, Ohio, when the city earned its name as the Rubber Capital of the World. She holds a BA in English from The University of Akron and an MA in journalism from Kent State University. Currently, she is a high school English and journalism teacher. Before teaching, she worked as a server, a sales person, and as a newspaper journalist. She lives with her husband, daughters, and her beloved pets in Ohio. In addition to reading and writing, she enjoys travel, history, gardening, exercise, research projects, word games, and spending time with family, friends as they enjoy good food!

This is her first novel.

Learn more about her and the book at www.reneeverite.com